"Arnie Grossman's brilliant talent for storytelling really shines in this wonderful comic fable of life and love in modern-day Los Angeles. This profoundly entertaining book fully engages the reader in Paul's continuing life quest through its lush and lavish style. A great read."

—Pat Schroeder, president and CEO of the Association of American Publishers and former congresswoman

"*Going Together* made me want to throw myself under a train—if only to be rescued by the characters in Arnold Grossman's delightful new novel about love, loss, and oddness in L.A."

—Betty Londergan, author of *I'm Too Sexy for My Volvo*

"This quirky, darkly funny novel about neurotic lovers in L.A. is to die for. Somebody, please make this into a movie. Steve Martin, are you listening?"

—Sandra Dallas, author of *Tallgrass* and *The Persian Pickle Club*

Going Together

a Novel

Going Together

Arnold Grossman

Fulcrum Publishing
Golden, Colorado

Library of Congress Cataloging-in-Publication Data

Grossman, Arnold.
  Going together / Arnold Grossman.
    p. cm.
  ISBN-13: 978-1-55591-606-0 (pbk. : alk. paper) 1. Advice
columnists--Fiction. 2. Beauty operators--Fiction. 3. Los Angeles
(Calif.)--Fiction. I. Title.
  PS3557.R6713G65 2007
  813'.54--dc22
                              2007019481

Printed in the United States of America by Malloy Incorporated
0 9 8 7 6 5 4 3 2 1

Editorial: Faith Marcovecchio, Katie Raymond
Cover and interior design: Jack Lenzo
Cover created from images © JupiterImages

Fulcrum Publishing
4690 Table Mountain Drive, Suite 100
Golden, Colorado 80403
(800) 992-2908 • (303) 277-1623
www.fulcrumbooks.com

For my grandchildren:

Michaela, Leah, Adin, Nina, and Zoey

Chapter 1

You can't always get what you wa-ant.
—The Rolling Stones
But you can always end what you do-on't.
—Paul Malouf

In the middle of a Los Angeles summer afternoon, within the cool damp of the Metro Center subway station, Paul Malouf stood close to the edge of the platform, well beyond the yellow caution line. Looking down at his feet, he noticed there were no spit stains on the orange tile flooring, fitting for Southern California, the land of cleanliness and spitlessness.

This was his first visit to the L.A. subway system, principally because it was known for not going anywhere in particular. In Paul's view, it was a less-than-grand experiment designed to get people out of their automobiles, a hopeless exercise for a city in which people have a symbiotic relationship with their cars and are therefore unwilling to trade the security of their steel-and-plastic wombs for silver tubes loaded with alien hordes. The idea of careening underground, packed together with perspiring sausages of humanity, might work in New York, where people disdain cars and tolerate subways, but never in the City of Angels, where sweating or smelling in public is a felonious assault on the senses.

Paul had lived most of his life in Los Angeles. When he was seven years old, his parents migrated to California from New Brunswick, New Jersey, where his father had been teaching screenwriting at Rutgers University. A warm climate and the offer of a prestigious job at the University of Southern California had been the deal clincher. But neither the climate nor the job improvement could head off the massive heart attack that struck Paul Sr. when Paul Jr. was a sophomore at Pacific Palisades High School. His mother, who had once been a reporter for a New Jersey newspaper, went back to work on the copydesk of the *Los Angeles Times* and eventually convinced her only son to pursue a career in journalism. A supervising editor at the *Times* (who, it seemed, could never stop staring at the widow Malouf's breasts) took an interest in Paul—most likely to get a closer look at things. The interest led to a recommendation for a scholarship to study journalism at UCLA. Not knowing what else to do with his life, Paul took the scholarship and did rather well in his studies, graduating with a Phi Beta Kappa key. He gave it to the first woman he had carnal relations with, only to lose both the woman and the key that had unlocked her wonders for him. A fair trade, he almost convinced himself.

Twelve years after graduation, following jobs at Long Beach, San Diego, and Sacramento newspapers, he was hired by the *Times* to write lifestyle features. His career progressed unremarkably—until the night he became thoroughly drunk in hopes of easing the pain of yet another breakup. He had been sure he would love this woman for his remaining days, but she confessed to loving someone younger, better looking, and wealthier. In his despair, Paul sat down and wrote a lengthy and sympathetic letter to himself as though he were the author of a column for the lovelorn man.

The problem—which was to become a strange opportunity—was that he had written the letter at his desk at the *Times* at two in the morning and had neglected, in his sotted state, to erase or file it. The next morning, a curious editor looking for an overdue assignment logged onto Paul's computer and found the letter. He took it to be a sample of a column Paul wished to write. So impressed was the editor with Paul's letter that he asked him to write three more.

Rather than admit that he himself was the jilted addressee, Paul thanked the editor for the opportunity and set about writing three more letters to imagined men in search of counsel on relationship problems: one with a heart broken like his own, another with a crushing job loss as a radio announcer caused by a sudden onset of stuttering, and the third a man who contracted a sexually transmitted disease from his wife of two weeks.

The editor was delighted with the letters and immediately convinced his superior, the managing editor, to begin a thrice-weekly column called Man to Man, by Paul Malouf. All it took to convince the managing editor was the question "Do you have any idea how many twisted, unhappy men there are in the Los Angeles basin?"

The feature was an immediate success, and it launched Paul's accidental career. Little did any of his sizeable following know that one of Southern California's most popular lifestyle features, eventually to be syndicated in more than 300 markets, was conceived in drunken self-pity and born as a cynical joke on the world. Which tended to strike Paul as a metaphor for his life.

In the beginning, he actually enjoyed the work. It required no particular writing skills, but simply amounted to reading his mail and replying sympathetically to the more interesting letters, sometimes astutely, but more and more frequently with a certain amount of irony—which readers seemed to enjoy. The volume of mail increased to the point that the paper hired an assistant to cull the most likely candidates from a sea of mostly unprintable mail, ranging from psychotic ramblings on the human condition to offers of sexual delights from women and, on occasion, from men as well.

Paul eventually entered yet another relationship, this time with an attractive woman named Sam, which turned out not to be short for Samantha, or anything else. "It's what my parents named me," she had said, with no further elaboration. She was eight years Paul's junior, an avid tennis player, and an equally avid drinker—like both her parents, who spent most of their time at a country club that denied admission to blacks, Hispanics, Asians, and Jews but welcomed with open arms white Protestant drunks.

Paul had no idea why he fell so deeply in what seemed like love. He neither played tennis nor drank vodka. He constantly read books; she read nothing, save Neiman Marcus catalogues. Still, he believed from the moment he first saw her that there was common ground. Of course, that ground was beneath the putting green at the family's country club, to which Sam had led him two hours after they met. A colleague of Paul's had invited him to the club, to an evening of terrible music called "Pops on the Grass." The colleague introduced him to Sam, telling her Paul was an acknowledged expert in affairs of the heart, whereby she and her vodka replied, "Does that mean he knows how to fuck?"

In less than an hour, they were on the putting green, writhing and flailing on their own common ground.

"How do you like *those* pops on the green?" she asked following his first climax and her fourth.

Before the next season's evening of bad music, they were married. After twelve years marked by frequent, extended, and unexplained absences on Sam's part, the presumed love of Paul's life announced one morning while applying her underarm deodorant, "I'm leaving you."

"For what?" he asked.

"For the tennis pro at the club."

"But he's sixteen years old."

"Oh, please. You're just jealous. He's twenty."

"And you're thirty-seven. When you were graduating high school, he was suckling on his mother's breasts—not yours."

"Don't be so crude," she countered. "Be a man about it. By the way, did you use my razor again? You know how I hate when you do that."

Paul was intelligent enough to realize that the marriage had never even come close to meeting his needs for love and companionship. In fact, it had made a mockery of such notions, leaving him in a state of depression that neither therapy nor pills nor even other women could ease. Oh, he tried all three, sometimes consecutively, which made for a string of some of the worst encounters with women known to man.

One particularly bad experience resulted from a brief affair with a beautiful, slender fashion model, Erica, who left him after three months of nonstop sex. She announced she was off to Paris to further her career, with a French photographer "just along for the ride." *Some ride*, Paul thought, and did his best to forget her and the sex. But four months later, Erica returned to Los Angeles and announced she was with child. Paul's child.

Try as he could to make the math work, it simply did not, as she acknowledged she was in her third month of pregnancy. Still, he decided he must do the right thing and offered to marry Erica and become the child's father, in spite of its decidedly French parentage. But she insisted she had to abort the pregnancy, lest it put an end to her skinny body and, therefore, her career. It would cost a few thousand dollars, she told him, and he sadly agreed to fund what struck him as a reprehensible measure. When she asked for a check to cover the bill, he painfully wrote one for five thousand dollars.

But he became deeply concerned for her health and insisted on knowing the name of her ob-gyn, which she foolishly furnished him. When he called the doctor, he was told, "Look, you sound like a nice guy. How well do you know Erica?" When Paul asked why, the doctor said, "She's not pregnant, unless something immaculate has happened, which I find a tad unlikely."

"Are you sure?" Paul asked.

"Positive. Which her pregnancy test wasn't. You, my friend, are a victim of what's commonly called a shakedown."

When Paul confronted Erica with what he had learned, her response was a nonstop tirade during which she held a kitchen knife above her head, her eyes on fire, while she threatened to sue him for invasion of privacy.

The passage of time did nothing to help him out of the emotional black hole into which the divorce and close encounter of the worst kind with Erica had plunged him. In fact, time only made the pit deeper and him more hopeless.

And now, four years after he had left behind Sam, the home he foolishly quitclaimed to her, and the tennis pro, Paul was still writing his columns, living in an apartment on San Vicente Boulevard, and trying, on a daily basis, to answer the one burning question about his life:

Why?

Not why his life had taken the turns it had taken. Not why it had not been more fulfilling. Not even why it had brought him a marriage that never transcended tennis, vodka, and Neiman Marcus.

No, the question was why was he still in it, this life?

He searched his feet and the gleaming tiles of the subway platform for an answer. But, of course, there was none.

Then a feeling that he was no longer alone in the station descended upon him. He had not been aware of the sounds of approaching footsteps. But the air around him felt pierced by another presence. Knowing there was someone nearby, he slowly turned his gaze away from his feet and to his left, where he saw a woman, also standing curiously close to the platform's edge, also looking down at the space between her feet.

She must have felt his eyes on her. She raised hers and looked straight across the tracks to the far wall of the station. Paul made a quick assessment: nicely styled short auburn hair; pretty profile: long eyelashes framing dark eyes that made a slight, quick dart in his direction and then back again, high cheekbones, and rounded lips with only a trace of lipstick; black silk blouse over tapered beige slacks and black brogue shoes with a definite sense of humor. A handsome woman.

Handsome or not, she had intruded into his space. He felt proprietary about the subway station, even though he had never before been inside it.

He edged ever-so-slightly closer to the rim of the platform, the toes of his black loafers less than two inches from the five-foot drop-off to the tracks below. He cast a quick, stealthy glance at the woman and was certain she, too, had edged forward on the platform. Was she mocking him?

He felt a slight vibration in the balls of his feet and, at the same time, heard a soft rumbling sound. An inbound train was approaching the station. Both the vibration and the rumble grew stronger and were soon accompanied by the sound of steel meeting resistance on steel as the powerful brakes slowed the train for its station stop.

He took a deep breath, inhaling the dankness of the tunnel and the unexpected, subtle sweetness of gardenia, a sensory contrast that at once pleased and confused him. He did not need to turn his head to the left to see the front of the first car fly from the dark of the tunnel into the brightness of the station. The rumble reached its peak, and Paul closed his eyes, tensing the muscles in his legs. But as the lead car streaked toward him, Paul did nothing other than to remain where he was, bracing himself against the blast of onrushing air. The second, third, and fourth cars passed by, each slower than its predecessor, until the fifth car came to a stop in front of him. Its doors hissed open, but no one exited the nearly empty car. Nor did Paul enter it. He merely stood his ground and waited for the doors to close again and for the train to move out of the station.

He glanced to his left again and saw that the handsome woman had done precisely the same thing he had done. Her toes remained close to the platform's edge, and she, too, held her ground. The only difference he noticed were two strands of hair that stood straight up on the top her head forming a *V*, an apparent result of the broadside of rushing air.

Paul turned toward the escalator at the end of the platform and walked by the woman, passing within no more than a foot and breathing in the scent of gardenia. She darted a glance in his direction.

"Something you didn't like about that train?" he asked.

She half-turned toward him, expressionless. "Are you talking to me?"

A strange question, since there was no other living soul in the station.

"I was just curious; nothing more, nothing less."

"And what, pray tell, were you curious about?"

"Pray tell?" Quaint, he thought, *in an archaic way*. He focused on the two upright wisps of hair. She seemed to notice his glance and slipped a hand upward, taking a gentle swipe at the *V*, but to no avail. It sprang right back up, defiantly.

"How do you get your hair to stand up like that?"

Her pretty, round mouth opened, but no words came out. Only a puff of air.

"Actually, what I was really wondering was why you just stood there and didn't get on the train," he said.

"Well, now, you're one to be asking a question like that. You didn't get on either."

"I had my reasons," he said, realizing as the words left his lips that it was a really stupid thing to say. But what else could he offer? He settled for something even worse: "Have a nice day."

"'Have a nice day'? You must be a writer," she mocked.

His face felt hot and red. "If you're a jumper, you need to work on your commitment," he said, and quickened his pace toward the escalator.

Chapter 2

Waiting for the light at the crosswalk on Wilshire Boulevard to turn green, Paul tried to concentrate on something other than the unsettling encounter he had just had with the curious woman on the platform. He thought about the approaching deadline for his next column. Of the three letters worth replying to, he supposed he would try to answer the one from the merchant seaman whose ship had arrived in Long Beach two days early. He had decided to surprise his fiancée, an exotic dancer, and indeed he had. But the surprise was on him. She was not alone when he quietly opened the door to their bedroom at seven in the morning holding a new addition to the satin pillow collection he had built for her in his global travels—this one proclaiming in gold Hebraic-like letters, *Bali Chai!* Happily slumbering in bed beside her was another exotic dancer he recognized from Risqué Business, his fiancée's workplace. The two of them looked so content, both sleeping with smiles on their faces, clasping hands. The crushed sailor left the apartment as quietly as he had entered, satin pillow in hand, and immediately returned to his ship, where he sat down to write Paul.

It's not that I'm jealous. It wasn't a man she was sleeping with, but a woman. A beautiful woman, in fact. The more I thought about the two of them, the more I became aroused. Should I tell my fiancée what I saw? More important, should I tell her my honest feelings: that I'd kind of like to, well, join the two of them? Is that totally sick?

Adrift in San Pedro

Paul wrote the response on his mind's chalkboard as he walked the two blocks to his parked car.

Dear Adrift,

You just have a case of see-sickness, if you get my drift. You see something, and it makes you ill. Not because it disgusts you, but because you begin to wonder what you've been missing all these years on the bounding main. So, two women sleeping together at first troubles you, then it arouses you. Lighten up. Get rid of the ballast that's been holding you down. Experiment. Follow your urges. Ask her to let you crash the party. Three's only a crowd if one's an anchor dragging down the fun.

Paul

Something familiar touched his senses, interrupting his thoughts of the poor sailor. Gardenias again. He turned to see the woman from the subway directly behind him. She acted as though she had not noticed him. He nodded. She did not. Part of him urged an approach. Another part warned him not to. Approach or avoid—that was the question. Before he could decide, she spoke.

"Are you banging on me?"

"What on earth are you talking about?" He felt his sphincter muscle tighten a notch or so. "*Banging* on you? Could you possible mean *hitting* on you? You think I'm trying to pick you up, n'est-ce pas?"

He knew, of course, how foppish the French thing was. That's why he did it.

"Congratulations. You know two words of French."

"Four," he corrected. "It's a contraction. And what, besides an inflated ego, would make you think I'm hitting on you? "

"You looked at me in the station. Twice, at least."

"Yes, I confess to a glance or two. You were in my space."

No response. Just another rush of air through her attractive, full lips. A puff. Or huff.

"And," he continued, "the reason I looked was I thought you were going to—you know … " He traced an upward arc with his hand, then brought it down, simulating a plunge.

"Oh, now we're a reader of minds, are we?"

If only she knew how much he hated the use of the first

person plural in that way, even more than he hated dropping French words into a conversation.

"Why else would you be on a subway platform, standing dangerously close to the edge, and then not get on the train?" he said. "Wait, don't tell me, you're a train spotter."

"I might ask you the very same question."

"If I'm a train spotter?"

"If you, in fact, are the one who was planning to—" She now mimicked the arc he had drawn in the air and added a soft "whoop," which ended in an upward inflection, like a question.

He squelched a laugh and shook his head. "You know, you really should consider seeing someone, if you aren't already."

"My social life is not any of your business."

"I'm not talking about dating. I'm talking about getting shrunk. The couch. The Kleenex box."

She glared at him. If looks could maim, he would surely have been an instant paraplegic.

"You, sir, are rude and inappropriate, perhaps even worse. Calling people jumpers or telling them they need psychiatric care does not a decent person make."

"Forgive me, but when you speak, it sounds like you're reading from a book. Do you always do that?"

"I have no idea about what you are talking."

"That's funny," he said.

"It wasn't meant to be. Now that you have delved into the pathology of my speech, is there anything else you wish to comment on?"

"No, nothing else on which I wish to comment."

"You mock me."

"*Wuthering Heights*?"

She blew one last puff of air and turned abruptly to walk away. He shrugged and crossed the street, passing a couple who were smiling and looking at him as though they had listened to the strange conversation that had just played out.

"Genuine L.A., isn't she?" Paul said to the couple as he picked up his pace and continued on his way.

——

Four hours later, as he drove toward the beach and the setting sun, Paul's black cotton shirt was steam-pressed to his back by the black leather seat of his black Mazda convertible, the price paid for leaving the top down all afternoon in sunny Southern California. He shook his head as he reconstructed the encounter with the woman. Just another whack job running free in the streets. Yet something about her—her strange choice of words, her ability to be amusing without knowing it—almost, but not quite, made him wish he could see her again. However, there were enough troubling things in his life, thank you very much.

As he waited at a red light on Venice Boulevard, a billboard caught his eye: Music for Lovers Only, it proclaimed, KLUV, 1160 FM, above an image of a man and a woman embracing on a sunset-lit beach, like the picture on a condom package. He couldn't resist the urge to see just how bad the music might be and tuned to the station. He was not disappointed.

"This is Sunset for Lovers, on all-romance eleven-sixty," waxed the baritone voice in a poor imitation of the late Barry White. "As the golden sun prepares to drop into the Pacific, you're together, just the two of you, waiting for the stars that will soon take their place in the night sky, to set the stage for love."

He could not believe someone actually wrote those words. Worse, someone had the temerity to speak them, over the public airways.

The light turned green, but the car in front of Paul's didn't move. He could see why through the car's rear window: a couple was locked in an embrace. The young man's head was tilted down; the young woman's was stretched back, to allow them to do God knows what at a stoplight on Venice Boulevard. Paul's hand reflexively hit the horn, sending a blaring message to the couple, who must have been listening to KLUV, he was certain. The two lovers responded in unison, each with a raised middle finger. So much for love at sunset.

More and more lately, Paul found himself wanting to visit the beach at day's end. Not that he had a particular emotional connection to Los Angeles sunsets; he had witnessed thousands of them and had long since ceased to be awed by them, knowing full well that what created the brilliant-red light show was all the toxic pollution that hung in the air over the L.A. basin. One person's beauty was another's bad cough. Still, there was something about the ocean that drew him to it, its power, for one thing, like a fast-moving subway train. Its finality. He usually went there when something had become particularly troubling. Not that the sea buoyed his spirits. In fact, it pulled them down even further, something he could always look forward to.

At Pacific Avenue, a block short of Venice Beach, Paul turned right toward Santa Monica. The humid air carried the scent of the seacoast: a mix of dead fish, smoldering incense sticks, and grilling hot dogs. It was a short drive past high-priced condominiums, cheap souvenir shops, a crowded dog park, and finally into the city known by constipated conservatives as "the Socialist Republic of Santa Monica" for having had the audacity to enact rent controls as a means of keeping normal working people off the streets and in their apartments.

Paul parked his car on the broad avenue that stretched north along the palisades, dropped four quarters into the meter, and strolled through the narrow park back to the Santa Monica Pier, on which stood its famous carousel along with stalls selling everything a tourist would want to eat or take home to Munich and, always, a line of fishermen along the railing at the western end.

———

"Excuse me, lady, but you might want to put a couple quarters in the meter."

The woman from the subway was startled by the voice

that came from behind her as she began to walk away from the car she had just parked. She turned to see a scruffy-looking man of about thirty or thirty-five dressed in clothes that clearly had seen neither soap nor water in some time. His hair was red, wiry, and totally unkempt, as was his beard. Silhouetted against the red early-evening sky, he seemed color coordinated.

"I beg your pardon?" she said.

"No need to beg my pardon. Just a good idea to plug the meter. They ticket here all the time. Forty bucks. Which could buy someone a room and a shower for the night."

She nervously opened her purse and rummaged for change. She pulled out a nickel and three pennies, examined them, and read the cautionary sign on the meter: No Free Time. Operates 24 Hours.

"They won't work," said the red-fringed man. "Quarters only. I know, it's intransigent of them, but such are the ways of the power structure."

"I guess I'll just take my chances," she said, starting to walk off.

"Wait."

She hesitated and turned back to him. "What is it you want?"

"Your money," he said, smiling.

"Oh, God, no. A holdup. I have a gun," she said, her voice cracking like an adolescent's.

"Where, in that little purse of yours? Relax. This isn't a holdup. Just some ordinary, run-of-the-mill panhandling. I could use enough money for a meal. Could you possibly spare me some? I'll watch your car for you."

"Oh, I'm sure you will. And will you take my tires?"

"Lady, I don't need tires. I don't have a car to put them on. I just need a little sustenance."

"I actually don't have any money. Just this," she said, holding out the eight cents. "But if you're really hungry, I can write you a check." Without pause, she took a checkbook and pen from her purse, opened the book, and held the pen at the ready.

"To whom do I make it out?"

"Lady, please, look at me."

She did, wide eyed.

"Do you really think someone is going to cash a check for me? Do you suppose I can saunter up to the counter at McDonald's looking and smelling as I do and order a dollar-ninety-nine Happy Meal—with a check? May I ask where you've been the last decade or so? George W. Bush is president of the United States of America. Dick Cheney is second in command of the very same United States of America. And you think I can cash a check?"

She stared into his face. He stared back. Their eyes seemed to communicate something. Finally, she said, "I think I see your point."

"I'm pleased that you do," he said. "Very pleased."

She put the checkbook and pen back into her purse and shrugged. "I'm sorry. I wish I could help."

"No need to. In fact, here, let me do this." He reached

into the pocket of his grimy, once-khaki trousers and pulled out two quarters. "I think you need this more than I do."

She looked at the two shiny coins in his open hand and shook her head. He plopped the coins into the parking meter, causing the whir of a motor within.

"There," he said. "You've got half an hour. Have a nice time."

She opened her mouth to say something, but only a puff came out. He nodded, smiled slightly, and waved delicately with the fingers of one hand as she turned and quickly moved away.

———

By the time Paul reached the end of the pier, the sun was already touching the horizon and rapidly descending out of view. He found a vacant stretch along the rail, and, rather than watching the orange disk disappear, he stared down at the rippled surface of the water some forty feet below.

When he looked up from the water, only a few clouds colored orange and magenta from below remained of the sunset. An elderly Asian man swung a small, silvery fish over the railing and, silently and routinely, removed the hook from its mouth and dropped it into a bucket of water. None of the other fisherman acknowledged the man's catch. To Paul's right, at the pier's far corner, a young couple stared off in the direction of the departing sun, their heads touching. He was reminded of the lovers in the car in front of him who had flipped him their middle fingers. Where were they now? Holding up a convenience store?

The peaceful silence was broken by the rapid staccato of high heels on wood approaching from behind. He looked down at the surface of the bay again, which had turned from orange-dappled green to black. The more he stared at the tiny wavelets on the surface, the closer the water seemed, until he felt he could almost lean down and touch it. The sound of heels suddenly stopped. The scent of gardenia wafted on the salt air.

He turned his head slowly, certain he was mistaken about whom the scent belonged to, since it was doubtless the fragrance of scores of L.A. women. But mistaken he was not. There she was again, looking quite the same as she had just four hours earlier, with one difference: she had changed clothes. Now she wore a white cotton blouse above an ankle-length white wraparound skirt. He, in black, had not changed. It wouldn't have occurred to him, since he had no plans for the evening, at least none that would have called for a wardrobe shift.

"Missed it by just six minutes," he said, nodding at the darkening horizon.

She had not seen him standing at the rail, and her mouth flew open as her eyes fell on him. "Good grief, you *are* following me."

"And just how would I do that? I've been here. You just arrived. Which makes you the follower, I would say."

"That is absolutely absurd. Why on earth would I follow

you? And just what is it I missed by six minutes?"

"The sunset. I assume that's why you were clickety-clacking along so frantically," he said, looking down at her white shoes and noticing the slenderness of the heels. "Those things are hazardous. They could get caught between the boards."

"Now it's my shoes. At least it's not my mental health, for which I should be thankful, I suppose. In addition to being presumptuous, you're wrong. I did not come here for the sunset. If that had been my purpose, I would have been here by seven-forty-eight."

What kind of woman would memorize the time of sunset? Simple: The same kind of woman who talks like a Jane Austen novel. The same kind of woman who visits subway stations but doesn't ride subway trains.

"I guess it's not my business, but if it's not the sunset you came for, what was it?" he asked.

"Aha, the first thing you have said that rings of truth: it's not your business."

His sphincter muscle twinged again. "And here's another truth: I don't give a seagull's feathered rump what it is you're doing here. Enjoy the evening."

With that, he raised himself more erectly than was normal for him and stepped toward the land end of the pier, only to walk right into a silver metal pail, knocking it on its side and spilling its contents of seawater and three desperately flopping fish.

"Nice going, mister," said the Asian fisherman he had

been observing. He then dropped to his knees to recapture his quarry.

"I'm sorry, really sorry," said Paul, his face on fire, as he, too, dropped to his knees and grabbed one of the fish. It popped upward out of his clenched fist like toothpaste out of a tube.

"Don't squeeze hard!" shouted the fisherman, now holding one of the other escapees, which he placed in the righted bucket.

Paul lunged again for the fish as it danced toward the pier's edge. He reached around a foot in a white shoe, but did not have to look up to know whose foot it was.

"Enjoying the show?" he asked, still looking down at the foot, the shoe, and the fish directly behind it. He reached for it, and the fish jumped defensively, sliding under the white shoe. The woman lifted her foot, trying to step away. But when she put her foot down again, she drove the spiked heel directly through the body of the poor evasive fish.

She reacted with alarm, dancing and shaking her leg in what seemed to Paul a bizarre jig, but the impaled fish remained on the heel of her shoe. The Asian fisherman stared, expressionless. Paul wished he had a video camera.

"You've harpooned the great silver beast in the nick of time, before he devoured us all," he said.

"Get this thing off me," she pleaded, continuing her odd dance.

Paul tried to oblige her. He got down on one knee and grabbed her ankle.

"What are you doing?" she shrieked.

"Trying to free you. Or it. Hold still."

A small crowd began to gather. Paul grabbed the fish, which still managed bravely to wiggle. He pulled at the creature forcefully, and it broke free, landing on the wooden deck and resuming its dance, in spite of a pencil-sized hole piercing its body. The fisherman swooped down on it, picked it up, and returned it to the bucket.

Paul stood and faced the woman, whose *V*-shaped prong of hair was at full attention once more. He offered his hand. "Paul," he said.

She stared at the hand that had held the fish and made no attempt to grasp it. "That's your name?"

"It's not his," he said, nodding toward the bucket. "And you are?"

"Helen."

"Next time you go fishing, you might try more-conventional gear. I don't think shoe-spearing is allowed in California."

He thought he saw the beginning of a smile at the corners of her mouth. But she stopped it before it could get anywhere.

She grabbed the nearby railing with one hand and removed the shoe from her foot. She held it away from herself, as if it were somehow contaminated, and wrinkled her nose, as if it smelled as well.

Paul took the shoe. "Allow me," he said, and walked to a nearby concrete sink with a sign above it that proclaimed

For Fishermen Only. *Why not fisherwomen?* Paul wondered. He rinsed the heel of the shoe and dried it with a paper towel thoughtfully furnished by Los Angeles County. Paul then walked back to Helen and handed her the shoe.

"You're safe now. Not a trace of evidence to link your shoe to the crime."

She gingerly replaced the shoe on her foot and said, "I suppose I should thank you."

"No need. The whole thing was my fault. I kicked the bucket, so to speak. I'm still curious, though. If you didn't come for the sunset and you didn't follow me here, what was it that made you scamper out to the end of the Santa Monica Pier?"

"I don't know why that concerns you. It's a public place, in a free country, and if I choose to visit it, that's no one's concern except mine."

"Unless, of course, you planned to do bodily harm."

"To a fish?" she asked.

"To yourself." He traced an arc again with two fingers, upward and down. "Splash."

"Oh, I see. Now you think I'm planning to jump off the end of the pier. Well, we're quite the expert on human behavior, aren't we?" That third-person thing again. "While we're on the subject, I might ask you what you happened to be doing out here."

"I had a hankering for twice-caught fish. It's a popular Thai dish."

"This conversation is as absurd as the one we had earlier," said Helen.

"I know. So, where do we meet next? On a bridge? Are there any bridges in L.A.? I don't think so. I wonder why."

He thought he saw a change in her face, a softening, a relaxing of muscles. And then he noticed a change atop her head. The *V* of hair no longer stood erect. Was it something she was able to control?

"Why are you staring at me?" she asked.

"I'm sorry. You seem a little different."

She bit her lip and looked straight into his eyes for the first time. "Different? Do you mean I'm no longer a threat to myself?"

"I wouldn't go that far. I still think it's obvious why you came here."

"At the risk of disappointing you, I can assure you that I would not, under any circumstance, do what you think I intended to do here."

"Why not? It would probably do the job."

"Don't be ridiculous. Do you have any idea how filthy that water is?"

"But why would that matter?

"There's everything in that water. Hepatitis, mysterious rashes."

"So what you're saying is, if the water were clean enough, you'd be comfortable making the big leap?"

Then Helen did a strange thing. She folded her arms and walked in a small circle, looking down at her feet, deep in thought. She stopped long enough to look at him and say, "You're trying to get me to admit to something. But it's not going to work. Of that you can be certain." And she resumed the circular walk.

Helen suddenly stopped and said, "As long as we are on the subject, I might ask you why *you* are reluctant to admit what you might be planning, like a leap from a tall building."

"If you must know, I have a real fear of heights."

"I see. So should I not ask you what difference that would make if you were thinking of, you know … " She mimicked his little hand depiction of a jump. "Like my aversion to filthy water?"

"Okay, I'm sorry. No more accusations. Look, why don't we go somewhere and have a drink."

"Of what?"

"Wine is usually good."

"I don't drink alcohol."

"Coffee?"

"I don't drink coffee."

"Well, it's a figurative thing. It doesn't have to be coffee. It can be tea. Or a bottle of soda. Water, maybe. Clean water."

"And why would we do that?"

"I just think it would be interesting to get to know one another. After all, we seem to have *something* in common. I'm curious. We both went to the subway and the Santa Monica Pier in the same day. Don't you think there's at least a little coincidence there?"

She slowly nodded her head and looked down at her

shoe, turning it back and forth slowly.

"You have to admit, it was pretty funny, you dancing around with a flapping fish on your shoe."

"Poor creature," she said, as though she actually felt its pain.

"Maybe he was suicidal. Couldn't stand the filthy water he was living in."

She looked at her watch, a large round one with a yellow duck whose wings pointed to the time. "It's getting late. I should leave."

"Late? The little ducky says it's only ten after seven. No time for water?"

"Are you going to expect me to give you my phone number?"

"For a glass of water? I know you're not that easy."

She said nothing, but started walking briskly away from him. He watched her, smiling to himself.

After several steps, she stopped and turned to look at him. "Changed your mind?" she asked.

He shook his head. "No. I didn't know if you were accepting or going home or calling a cop. It's hard to tell."

She turned away and started walking again. He had to rush to catch up with her. As he did, he felt something unusual in his chest. The anvil that was usually there, pressing heavily downward, had become lighter. It felt freeing. He almost thought he had a bounce to his quickened step as he pursued her.

They walked the entire length of the pier without saying

a word to one another. Paul simply could not find an appropriate thing to say. Besides, their pace was so quick he was sure he would gasp for air if he tried to speak. He noticed that everyone around them strolled while the two of them looked as though they feared the pier was about to collapse into the bay. *Interesting idea*, he thought.

"How's that?" he asked, his voice wavering as he came to a stop on Ocean Avenue. He pointed to a coffee shop on the corner.

"How is what?" was her response.

"The coffee shop across the street."

"The Cultured Cup?" she said, reading the sign, shaking her head.

"Something wrong with it?"

"Just the name."

"Well, we can always ask them to change it. The Dew Drop Inn."

"Hava Java," she parried.

"Perk-n-Surf," he thrust. "What's your favorite bad business name?"

"Helen of Troy."

"What is it?" he asked.

"A salon."

"Hair?"

She nodded, then started clickety-clacking across the street as the Walk light came on.

"I don't think it's a contender," he said. "Too obtuse."

"Offering Hairstyles of Legend?"

"That helps. Pretty terrible after all."

She actually smiled. "I know."

They entered the coffee shop, which was peopled mostly by local types reading books, huddled in serious conversation, and writing on laptop computers, all sipping overpriced coffee. Paul and Helen chose a small, empty table and surveyed the scene.

"It never ceases to amaze me how people will come to a noisy place like this to work," he said, nodding toward a young man with a laptop computer, his brow furrowed and an eyebrow arched. "He looks very unhappy, either with all of us, with what he's written, or with the fact that he hasn't written a word."

"Isn't that what Hemingway did, in Paris?"

"Not with a laptop. A pencil," he said. "You like Hemingway?"

She rolled her eyes and stuck out her tongue. "He was sexist."

"Like laptops, sexism hadn't been invented yet," Paul pointed out.

"Humph!" she puffed.

"What writers *do* you like?" he asked.

"I enjoy Sylvia Plath's poetry. And Virginia Woolf."

"Is that a joke?"

"No. Why would it be?"

"Come on. They both, you know … " and he made that arcing gesture with his two fingers again, up over the table and down.

"So did your friend Hemingway. That has nothing to do with why I like their writing."

"I guess not," he said. "What about painters? Do you like van Gogh?"

"Yes, as a matter of fact I do."

"Frida Kahlo?"

"Of course. Who on earth doesn't?" she said.

"Mark Rothko?"

"Your point?"

"They all did it." Once again, the arced pantomime. "The curse of the creative class, I suppose. Actually, it could be it's not such a curse. Maybe they just know something the rest of us haven't figured out yet."

"Hah! And you think I should see somebody."

"I'm not talking about me."

"May I ask what you do for a living?" she said.

"I write," he said.

"I see," she said, softly, but a little triumphantly as well.

"I'm not that kind of writer. I do a column. For newspapers. It's a job."

"You write a column?"

He nodded.

"About what?"

"It's not important," he said, in honesty, not humility.

"Everything a person does is important, if only to himself." She fixed her eyes on him.

After what seemed like a long silence, he said sheepishly, "I give advice."

"To whom?"

"Men. Men with problems. Relationships, career, marriage."

"No women? Just men?"

"I had a high school English teacher who once told me to write only about things I know. That leaves women out. "

She nodded slowly, and they both fell into silence. It was soon interrupted.

"Hi, I'm Steve. How are you folks doing this evening?" The too-cheerful voice came from behind them. They both turned to see a young man with a shining, shaved head. He was dressed in a black T-shirt, black jeans, black shoes, even a black apron.

"We're a bit shaky," said Paul. "Just survived an attack by a fish, out on the pier."

"I knew it would happen one of these days," said the credulous waiter. "The way we encroach on the inhabitants of the sea, it's no wonder. They were here long before us," he added, shaking his head. "Did someone catch a shark?"

"We didn't stay long enough to identify the species," Paul replied. He glanced at Helen, who was biting her lower lip and looking down at her hands.

"Rachel, come here. You've got to hear this. A shark attack—on the pier!" called the waiter to a young woman nearby, also dressed in black on black. Heads turned and looked up, including the one belonging to the suffering laptop writer.

"Please," said Paul in a whisper, holding a finger to his

lips. "We really don't want any publicity. You know how it is in this town."

The waiter was puzzled. He strained to understand what he had just been told. Finally, he smiled as if a lightbulb suddenly went on in his head. "Don't worry, gotcha covered," he said with a wink. "Forget it," he said to the waitress, making a zipping motion across his lips with his fingers. "I'll tell you later."

The waiter turned back to Helen and Paul. "Well, after that ordeal, I imagine you could use some coffee."

Paul nodded and smiled gratuitously.

"What'll it be? Couple of lattes?"

Paul looked at Helen and back to the waiter, shaking his head.

"Cappuccino? We make it regular, decaf, and organic."

Another shake of the head.

"I know. You're espresso types."

"Actually, I'd just like a regular cup of coffee. Do you have that?" said Paul.

The waiter looked injured. "That's it? Plain coffee? Well, I suppose, if that's what you want."

"Yes, that's what I want. Is that a problem?"

"No, not a problem. It's just that, well, given who you are, it surprises me. But, hey, it's a free country."

"I hope it still is," said Paul.

"And you, ma'am?" he said turning to Helen. "I'm sure *you* won't settle for just a cup of coffee."

"You're right," she said. "I'd like water."

"Water? Okay. With gas or without gas? Pellegrino?"

"I was hoping for the kind that comes out of a faucet, without gas or Pellegrino, whatever that is, thank you."

The waiter flashed a dumbstruck look at Helen. Then he turned to Paul, who shrugged. Then back to Helen, who smiled politely. Finally, he walked off, mumbling something about water, coffee, and sharks.

"I think he likes us," said Paul. "So, where do we meet next?"

"What makes you think we'll meet again?

"Well, there are only so many places where people go to—"

She stopped him before he could do his two-fingered arc again. "I wish you wouldn't keep doing that."

"Sorry. But I'm just not comfortable using the *S* word with someone I don't know all that well. Never on the first date."

"Date?" She sat upright, pushing back in her chair. "This is a *date*?"

"No. It's a figure of speech. A joke. Relax," he said, putting his hand on her arm, his first encounter with her bare skin, which felt warm and soft.

She apparently did not find his hand warm or soft. She recoiled, quickly pulling her arm away, as if bitten or burned by something.

He tried to ignore her reaction, but found it difficult. It was not as though he had pulled her body to his, embracing her and kissing her hard on her mouth. It was a mere touch, an emphasis of a point, an attempt to establish trust. *Right*, he thought, *fat chance for any trust here*. He felt like a serial toucher.

"He's back," said Paul, eyeing the approaching, officious server.

"One *regular* coffee and one glass of tap water," said the waiter, eyebrows raised, placing the cup and glass on the table. "By the way, there's a minimum of six dollars after five P.M.," he continued. "I don't think you're going to make it. Would you like something else?"

"Do you have any sardines?" Paul asked.

"Sardines?"

"Sardines," said Paul.

"Sir, this is a coffeehouse. We don't serve sardines."

"You don't? Come on, when was the last time a sardine came in and asked for a cup of coffee?"

"That's very funny, sir. Hilarious. Now, if there's nothing else you wish to have, I'll get back to my other tables." And he sauntered off, shaking his head, muttering again.

"That was an awful joke," said Helen.

"It was meant to be. Seriously, I would like to get together again. We could try the water somewhere else, if you'd like."

"Why?"

"Don't you think we might just have something in common?"

"Such as?"

"You don't seem to suffer fools gladly. Look how uncomfortable you are with me."

"Are you fishing?"

"No, I leave that to you. You were good out there. Do you ever laugh?"

"I try not to. Whenever I do, it turns into a snort. It can be embarrassing in a theater. Someone behind me once said, 'Good God, I bought tickets to the orchestra, not the corral.'"

"That was rude."

"Yes, it was. I should learn to control myself."

"Why would you want to spoil things?" he said.

She did not answer, but merely looked down at the grain of the wood on the tabletop.

"I've told you what I do. Now it's your turn," said Paul.

"Hair."

"Any chance of elaborating?"

"You asked what I do. I do hair."

"Of course. You're a hairdresser."

"Stylist."

"Of course again. Do you work in a parlor?"

"A *parlor*?" Now *that* made her laugh. And, true to her word, it was equine, a snort that was somehow not unattractive in the least. In fact, he found it endearing. But she obviously did not. Her eyes widened, and she clamped a hand over her mouth. "Do you see?" she said. "You've made me do it."

"What did I say that was so funny?"

"Where did you pick up that word, *parlor*?"

"I don't know. I guess that's what it was called in my

home. My mother always went to the beauty parlor on Saturday, to get ready for church on Sunday. Good hair was probably one of the commandments where we went. Anyway, where are you a stylist?"

"In a salon."

"What's it called?"

"Helen of Troy."

"Wait a minute. You said you're Helen. You own Helen of Troy. Hairstyles of Legend."

"It's enough to make you sick, isn't it?"

"Then why did you name it that?"

"I didn't," she said. "The name came with it."

"Couldn't you change it?"

"Hardly. It had too big a following. It's a Beverly Hills institution."

"Must be a fascinating business," he said, not quite sure he meant it.

"I doubt you mean that."

"Do you actually get your hands wet, or do you just supervise?"

"Supervise? I handle clients from nine in the morning until closing. Sometimes after closing. And on Sunday. I take one day off a week, when the salon is closed, on Monday. That's what today is. Usually, I don't take the full day but stay on call for emergencies, like a doctor. Can you imagine, there are women who are convinced they'll go into cardiac arrest if I don't open up and do their hair?"

"In Beverly Hills? Yes, I can."

"I spend most of my waking hours listening to problems. Do you have any idea how many women in Los Angeles think that when there's something wrong in their lives, it can be fixed with new hair? Then, when they realize that two hours and three hundred dollars later they're still the same people with the same problems only with different hair, they blame me. I'm sure their therapists don't say, 'I've got it! Get new hair. You'll be a new person. Your problems will disappear.'"

"Don't be so sure. They get a patient who drives them far enough up the wall, who knows, they might prescribe a new look. At least it takes the heat off them for a week."

"That would be highly unethical," she said.

"Ethics? We *are* talking about therapists, aren't we?"

"Are you saying psychotherapists are charlatans?"

"That's one of those words that sound like something else. *Charlatan*, something with whipped cream and chocolate sauce. *Coup de grâce*, that's another one."

"Do you always avoid difficult questions by being funny?"

"Who says it's a difficult question? And who says I'm funny? As for your question, no, I don't think *all* therapists are pastries. But I'd venture to say some of them are ethically challenged. The ones who seduce their patients. Like my former wife. Actually, I may have that wrong. I think she seduced him, after the tennis instructor."

It was the fastest he'd ever seen a face turn red. She looked down at her hands, which were clasped on the table-top as if in prayer. Maybe she *was* in prayer. *Please, Lord, reach your hand down and pluck this idiot from his chair and drop him somewhere far away. In that dirty bay, perhaps.*

"I'm sorry. That was inappropriate. I embarrassed you. I embarrassed myself."

"I do think it's a bit more information than I'd like to have," she said. "But it's to be expected."

The hair on the back of Paul's neck rose, along with his defenses. "Expected? Could you elaborate?"

"No need to be defensive," she said.

"Defensive? Why do you say I'm defensive? And why are all these people talking about me?"

"Are you ever serious?"

"Only when I'm not being defensive," he said.

The waiter reapproached, asking facetiously if anyone would like any more tap water or regular coffee. Paul declined the gratuitous offer, paid the six-dollar minimum, and offered to see Helen to her car.

"It's really not necessary," Helen said as they left the coffee shop. "I'm sure I can find my way."

"I didn't mean you might get lost. I was merely offering to accompany you. Who knows what might happen along the way."

"I can take care of myself, I assure you. However, if you'd like to walk with me, that would be fine."

"Yes, it would be fine," said Paul. She looked at him, suspiciously. "No, I'm not being funny. It would be my pleasure."

Chapter 3

"It's in this block," said Helen as they walked north on the blacktop pathway that skirted the edge of the bluffs overlooking the bay.

"So is mine. What an interesting coincidence."

They continued another short distance and Paul stopped. "There's my car," he said, pointing to the black sports car.

"Which one?"

"The one with the top down and with three inflated tires," he said.

"Oh, that's too bad. You do have a flat tire."

"And I think I see who made it that way."

He fixed a stern glare on the scruffy man bending over the deflated front tire.

"I know him," said Helen.

"Really? An old friend?"

Paul studied the man with the bright-red, totally unkempt hair and beard.

She shook her head. "I met him when I parked my car, which is the one right behind yours."

It was a sensible sedan, a Japanese import, he thought.

But what struck him was how immaculate it was, how its silver paint glistened in the blue light cast down by the nearby streetlamp.

"That's a very clean car," he said.

"Thank you."

He approached the scruffy man. "Excuse me."

The man looked up from the tire and surveyed Paul. Then he noticed Helen standing behind Paul. "Hello again," said the homeless man.

Helen only nodded and smiled cautiously.

"You've got a flat tire," he said to Paul.

"That's very observant. Any idea how it got that way?"

The man shrugged. "Lost all its air."

Helen stepped alongside Paul, inspecting the tire, and then turned to the man. "He thinks you did it."

Paul took a step back, just in case the man was sufficiently angered by the accusation to do something physical. Sizing him up, Paul wondered if he could take him down, if it came to that.

"Why would I do a thing like that? That takes more mean-spiritedness than I possess, in spite of my current lot in life. It hurts my sensibilities that you'd think that of me. I may be living without shelter, but I am not without principles."

Paul could not tell if his head was being played with. But he did feel foolish, whether or not the man was serious.

"I'm sorry," he said. "It just looked suspicious."

"If he had a suit and tie on, you wouldn't find him suspicious," Helen chimed in.

"Okay, okay, you're both right. I was wrong to jump to conclusions. That's not at all what I'm about," said Paul, smarting from the accusation. What was he supposed to do, say that some of his best friends sleep in parks? "Right now, I've got a problem. It's on my car. And I can't drive it home until I fix that problem. So if you'll excuse me, that's what I'll do."

He went to the trunk of his car and opened the lid. He stared into the darkness and reached inside. He stopped, shook his head, and looked up at the sky. "No jack."

"You have no jack?" asked the homeless man.

"That's right," Paul replied, looking back into the trunk, taking inventory. "A spare tire, an earthquake survival kit, a tennis racket … " He stopped. "And I don't play tennis. A lawn chair, one, two, three, four umbrellas."

"Why so many umbrellas?" asked Helen.

Paul looked up, turned, and stared at Helen. "Because it never rains in sunny California," he said, slamming the trunk lid down. "But no jack."

"Is it possible *you* might have a jack?" the homeless man asked Helen.

Her eyes darted around the scene, from the curious red-haired and -bearded man to a frustrated Paul to the flat tire to her car and back again to the man.

"Yes" was all she said.

"Might our friend here use it?"

No answer.

"It's not a trick question," said Paul, which drew a smile

from Homeless.

"I suppose he can. I just don't know if it will work on his car."

"Lady, a jack is a jack is a jack."

Paul stepped to the rear of Helen's car, waiting for something to happen. Sensing the attention focused on her, Helen went to the trunk, pointed her remote control toward it, and pressed a button. The lid popped open. She stepped back and waited for Paul to peer inside. He found something made of black metal, but larger than he would imagine a jack to be. He wrestled it out of the trunk.

"Is this a jack?" he asked.

Helen shook her head. "It's a portable step climber. For exercise."

Homeless whistled and said, "You could kill yourself on one of those."

A wry grin appeared on Paul's face. He raised his eyebrows at Helen, but she merely turned away.

He put the heavy contraption back in the trunk and pulled out something much smaller. Also black. Also steel. He held it up, like a trophy fish. "I got one," he said.

"Congratulations," Homeless said.

Paul stepped over to his car and positioned the jack under the front bumper. He pumped the jack, slowly at first, then more deliberately as his black sports car began to rise. Just as the flattened tire was lifted above the pavement, a slight groaning came from somewhere beneath the car. Paul stepped back and watched the car sway and slowly move away from him. Then it unceremoniously slid all the way down to the ground again, the jack buckling under the car's weight. It all ended with a soft thud. Paul picked up the jack, which was now bent over on itself. He looked at Helen, who looked at the jack, then at Homeless, who looked to the sky.

"Maybe it was the wrong jack," Paul said meekly.

"Maybe it's not supposed to go under the bumper," added Homeless.

"Maybe it's a metaphor," said Helen.

Paul rolled his eyes.

"Well, folks," said Homeless, still gazing at the night sky, "I think we're running out of options here."

He looked at his wrist, which had nothing strapped to it. "It's getting late. Looks to me like you need triple-A."

"I'm not a member," Paul said.

"I'm afraid I let my membership lapse," said Homeless.

Helen, meanwhile, had seated herself on a nearby bench. Paul approached her with the oddly bent jack in hand.

"I'll get you a new one tomorrow. Give me your address."

She turned to face him, looking alarmed. "My address? I can't do that."

"It's safe, I can assure you. I haven't chopped anyone up in some time."

No response.

"I could leave it for you somewhere. On the pier? The subway?"

She opened her purse, which she had been clutching to

her bosom, and retrieved a checkbook.

"Oh, no, not another check," Homeless said.

She tore out a deposit slip and handed it to Paul, who read it and said, "You want me to leave it at Bank of America?"

"My address is on the slip."

"It's a post office box."

She nodded.

"You want me to leave it in a post office box?"

She shrugged.

"You want me to mail it? This doesn't even have a name on it."

She shrugged again. "I have to be careful."

"Of what? Men bearing jacks?"

"This is definitely a screenplay," said Homeless, looking back to the sky again.

"What is?" asked Helen.

The three of them fell silent.

Chapter 4

The previous evening's melodrama had finally ended when Paul flagged down a Santa Monica police cruiser and recounted his plight to the officer who, only after checking with the dispatcher to learn that lending an official police jack to a citizen was within department rules, agreed to help. "Guess that's what To Protect and Serve means," Paul had commented as he watched the officer work, drawing not so much as a smile.

Now, driving along Venice Boulevard, as Paul studied the bent jack lying beside him on the passenger seat he recalled one of his late father's favorite stories, a long metaphor about a man stranded in the desert. He could still repeat, word for word, the cautionary tale.

"You remind me of the jack story," his father had said when, as a young teenager with a dark view of the world and his possibilities within it, Paul had disclosed his apprehension over his very first date, a planned visit to the local roller rink with Skippy Huffington. He had arranged the date on a dare from two of his friends who accused him of being a total pussy for not having the courage to ask out the vivacious thirteen-year-old. Skippy had professed an interest in him to several of her friends.

What prompted Paul's father to relate the jack story was his son's confession that he was certain Skippy would humiliate him. She *had* to be a better skater than he was and, if that was the case, she would broadcast to the entire school that he was, indeed, a total jerk (Paul would never use the word *pussy* in his parents' presence) for choosing roller-skating for their first date.

"There was this man, a traveling salesman," said his father. "He was in the middle of the desert, on his way to some sales calls, when he got a flat tire. He opened the trunk of his car and discovered he had no jack. The nearest town was twenty miles ahead. He was really upset and knew he had no choice except to trudge the twenty miles in the searing heat.

"As he walked, he started thinking and talking to himself. 'Maybe there isn't even a gas station there.' This thought upset him, but he kept walking. And sweating. Then he said, 'Oh, there'll be a gas station all right, but with my luck, it'll be closed.' Another few miles, and he told himself, 'It'll probably be open, but maybe they won't have a jack I can use.' He kept going, working himself up, his clothes soaked with sweat. 'Oh, they'll have a jack all right, but they probably won't let me borrow it.' Another few miles, and he really got mad. 'Use it? They'll want to rent it to me.' The town was in sight, and he could see a gas station. 'Rent it? No, they'll want to sell it to me. They know the fix I'm in.' He got closer to the station. 'I'll bet they'll want a hundred dollars for a twenty-dollar jack! No, they'll know I have no choice. Two hundred dollars!'

"Finally, he was there. The station was open. A man was sitting on a bench, watching the salesman drag himself up to the station. The attendant looked at him and said, 'Can I help you?'

"And the salesman, barely able to walk, said, 'You can take your goddamn jack and shove it up your ass!'"

Taking another glance at the useless jack beside him, Paul thought, *I'll get her a new jack, and she'll probably tell me to stop bothering her. Maybe she'll call a cop. In which case she can take that goddamn jack and ...*

He reflected on the events of the previous evening, and he felt that familiar feeling again, somewhere between ambivalence and fear. Yes, she was an interesting woman. An appealing woman. An enigmatic woman. But something warned him to avoid any further approach. She obviously had an endgame of her own. But who was he to talk? *Ah, that was it: had he stumbled across someone like himself? Now that would take the proverbial cake, icing and all, wouldn't it? Two of a kind. Peas in a pod. Forget it, Malouf. Give her a new jack and move on. Fine. But where?*

He pulled up in front of a large auto-parts store in Culver City and surveyed the windows, which were filled with things made of chrome and posters of large-breasted women holding spark plugs and oil filters. Not the kind of place he generally frequented.

Holding the bent jack, Paul approached the counter. A

huge man, weighing at least 250 pounds, with long, bushy hair and a beard, was studying a black, oily piece of something or other that he held in his grimy fingers. Paul waited patiently to get his attention and studied his black, tight-fitting T-shirt with an American flag emblazoned on the front and the words Try Burning This One! Paul coughed involuntarily, which caused the clerk to lift his eyes and glare at him—actually, right through him. The flag on the black shirt moved as the man's chest muscles twitched.

"Yeah?" His voice was whiskey deep.

Paul held up the bent jack. "I'm looking for one of these."

The man glanced at the jack and back at the object in his hands. He shook his head. "You want one all bent like that?"

"Very funny," said Paul.

The big man looked up again, scowling. "Wasn't meant to be."

He dropped the oily thing and reached across the counter to grab the jack, which Paul thought he was about to be clubbed with. Instead, the man held it over his head as though it weighed no more than a number-two pencil and shouted, "Herman! We got any of those cheesy OEM jacks that get bent all the time?"

A voice came back from behind a bank of metal shelves filled with boxes. "Yeah, we got a couple."

"Bring me one," boomed the man. "And don't breathe on it and bend it all up."

"You gonna sell one to some poor joker?"

The clerk just shook his head and slid a stained order pad onto the counter in front of him. "Anything else?"

"That's it. Just one cheesy OEM jack, thank you," Paul said.

The man shrugged and wrote something unintelligible on the pad and a price, $32.49. He turned it around for Paul to see and said, "We don't take checks."

"I don't give them," Paul replied, and reached into his pocket for some bills. He put two twenties on the counter, and the man grabbed them with one of his greasy hands.

"Got anything smaller?"

"No, they're all the same size." He was surprised at his own foolhardiness; the man could easily lift him over the counter if he wished and toss him all the way back to Herman, who now appeared with a new, unbent jack in his hand.

The flag-loving clerk ignored the remark—or failed to understand it—and simply punched some keys on the cash register, put the bills in the drawer that popped open, and counted out the change, his lips moving all the time.

Herman, a slender man with bad skin and hair that seemed slicked down with 10W-40 motor oil, asked Paul, "This jack for you?"

"Yes, I'm the joker."

"Oh, hey, I didn't mean nothin' by that. Just kiddin', know what I mean?"

Paul took the new jack from Herman, who looked like he kept rats for pets, and then took the change from the man in the black shirt, whose expression had not changed once.

"You can keep that one," said Paul, nodding toward the bent jack lying like a twisted steel pretzel on the counter.

"We don't take trades," the man replied.

"Have a nice day," said Paul.

No response from either of the men.

Paul turned and walked out the door, hearing a metallic clang as Helen's jack thunked against the bottom of a trash can.

During the slow drive along Santa Monica Boulevard back to his Westwood apartment, Paul noticed he was approaching Ben's Burger Bar, a sidewalk stand specializing in the obvious. A large cutout of a glistening brown hamburger on a tan bun was perched atop the stand like an alien spacecraft that had missed its approach. He was not necessarily hungry, yet he had an urge to visit the place he had passed a thousand times without even thinking of stopping.

He parked, fed the meter, and approached Ben's, which consisted of a long counter under a red-and-white striped awning, eight chrome and red vinyl swivel stools, and a griddle on which two patties of meat sizzled under the watchful eye of a short, stocky woman. Two of the stools were occupied, both by men who had the slouch of drivers, either of trucks or taxis.

"What'll it be?" asked the woman, who flipped the two patties, slammed a bun on top of each, and turned to face Paul, who wondered who and where Ben was. His question was answered when he saw a framed picture of a smiling, round-faced man with the caption Our Founder, Ben Bronstein, 1939–1989. He studied the menu while the woman waited patiently. The offerings were listed in white letters painted on a blackboard. There was a Boulevard Burger for $1.99, a Grand Slam with cheese and tomato at $2.29, a Cecil B. DeBurger with green chile for $3.19, and a $3.99 Sunset Strip, featuring thick-sliced bacon and guacamole.

"What has the most fat?"

The woman, too young to be the widow of the revered founder and too old to have been his daughter, eyed Paul suspiciously. One of the drivers at the end of the counter looked up and cocked his head.

"Whad-a'-you, the fat police?" she asked.

"I like juicy, fatty burgers," said Paul. In truth, he could not recall the last time he had eaten a hamburger of any kind, unless veggie or turkey burgers counted, which clearly they did not at Ben's Burger Bar.

"If you're lookin' for one of those dried-out fat-free numbers that skinny models eat, you came to the wrong place," said the woman, turning to the two customers. "Right, guys?"

"No, that's why I'm here. Fat is good. The more the better. What do you recommend?"

She made a nodding gesture over her shoulder toward a sign on the end wall: "Beef-Eater's Special ... The Clogger ... ¾ Pound of Juicy Beef, 2 Slices Cheese, Fried Egg ... $4.99. The Killer of All Burgers."

A broad grin broke out on Paul's face. He nodded slowly.

"I'll have a Clogger. Rare."

The woman studied him further. "You up to it?"

"Definitely." He eyed a mound of French fries glossed with cooking fat, warming on the grill. "And fries."

One of the driver-customers turned to the other and grinned. The woman bent down to open a refrigerator door beneath the counter and came up with two large, fat-flecked patties that she tossed on the grill like a couple of cards in a poker game, triggering a cloud of smoke and a crackling chorus.

Now Paul did something so out of character that any friend, relative, or fellow health club member witnessing it would have been shocked into speechlessness. He pulled from his shirt pocket a pack of cigarettes he had bought earlier at a Ralph's Supermarket, tried twice to open it before succeeding, took one of the clean white cylinders from within, placed it in his mouth awkwardly, and fumbled with a disposable lighter.

"You're in the nonsmoking section," the woman behind the counter deadpanned.

Paul looked up and around, the flame flickering on the lighter. Before he could protest or inquire, she added with a nod of her head, "Smoking section's on the next stool."

He was too flummoxed to ask if he was being toyed with. He didn't have to. The two customers broke into laughter, as did the woman.

"It's okay. Just playin' with your head. It's a Ben's tradition," she said.

Paul knew his face was nearly as red as the vinyl on the stools and the stripes on the awning. He smiled politely and finally lit the cigarette that was still between his lips, his every movement followed by his audience of three.

"Those things'll kill ya," said the woman. "They did it to Ben," she added with a reverential glance at the picture on the wall.

"How long did it take?" asked Paul.

"He went fast, once they found out his lungs were shot."

Paul nodded and took a deep drag on his cigarette, which sent him into a fit of convulsive coughing accompanied by a spray of mist that fell on the counter in front of him, driving the shocked woman backward in retreat.

"Sorry," was the only word Paul could force out of his burning throat.

One puff was enough. Maybe he would try again with less of an audience. He looked around for an ashtray. None in sight. The sidewalk? Something prevented him from grinding a cigarette out on the concrete, even if he was in a smoking section. He walked back to his car, reached in, and opened the small sliding ashtray on the dashboard. Unaware that the two customers were watching him, he tamped out the cigarette and went back to his stool. Only then did he realize he still had an audience as the two men elbowed each other and smiled.

The killer of all burgers arrived, steaming hot and dripping grease onto the waxed paper underneath it. He slid the burger toward him and noticed a path of grease following it along the countertop before taking a large bite. He recalled once hearing from an intern at the newspaper that a truly good American hamburger will bleed grease right through waxed paper. Well, he had finally found one that qualified. He soon realized, though, that he had bitten off more than he could digest. A wave of discomfort in his esophagus told him he had introduced something far too foreign to his system. He tried a French fry, which nearly slipped from his grasp. Another message from the esophagus, and he knew he would have to ease into his new diet instead of gulping it down with such abandon. His body had far too long a history of things free of fat and frying for this sudden onslaught of tobacco smoke, lard, and red meat. Still, it must have worked for the late Ben.

———

It was something of a struggle for Paul to make it from his car in the garage to the front door of his two-story apartment carrying six overstuffed plastic bags from Ralph's Supermarket. He tried wedging half the bags between his raised knee and the door while he struggled to get the key into the lock. It worked, until the door flew open and he and the bags of groceries fell into the vestibule. Boxes of frozen foods scattered across the oak parquet floor. He landed atop a large box of Dove ice-cream bars and a carton of Jimmy Dean precooked sausages.

He got up and turned on the living room lights. The apartment was spacious, one-fourth of what had originally been a sprawling Spanish Mission–style tile-roofed home. The rental agent had boasted that the home had once belonged to Charlie Chaplin. But Paul knew full well the apocryphal stories real-estate people liked to tell about famous former residents. If Chaplin had lived in all the homes with which he had been credited, the poor man would never have had time to unpack.

Greeting Paul in the step-down living room was a prized photographic acquisition: a large framed blowup of Dr. Jack Kevorkian looking intently across the spacious room. Not everyone who visited Paul's home realized who the subject of the overpowering photo was. More than one guest thought it was Jack Kerouac. Paul, who was not comfortable lying, had simply said, "That's ol' Jack," which indeed it was. Others had guessed Eugene O'Neill, Jean-Paul Sartre, Charles Lindbergh, and even Charlie Chaplin himself. Paul had always been amused that no one asked who the glaring subject was, most likely for fear of admitting to not knowing someone famous, which is a sin in the L.A. culture.

The room was furnished sparsely, with mostly black leather, glass, and chrome. The only clutter consisted of piles of books and magazines, some on tables, some on the floor next to an Eames chair in which Paul enjoyed reading and listening to music. There was no television set in sight. In fact, the only one he owned was a miniature battery-powered portable on which he watched Dodger and Raider games in his bedroom or on the patio. There had been a large-screen set behind cabinet doors, but he gave it to a charity for the blind after watching a reality show in which people had worms stuffed into their mouths. It was around this time that he acquired the Kevorkian blowup, which was not coincidental.

Stopping in the bathroom, he checked himself in the mirror, as if he might see some indication of a change, having eaten a large part of the Killer of All Burgers and a few slippery French fries as well as having sucked one drag of cigarette smoke into his lungs. Reason told him it was a little too soon for any change, yet he was curious. No change in skin color. What had he expected? Jaundice? Bulging, bloodshot eyes? He did feel he looked somewhat unpleasant, but that was his usual reaction to his own image. He surveyed his black hair with its dusting of silver. "Salt and pepper," it was called. But it was well on its way to just salt, he was convinced, even though he had not yet celebrated his fiftieth birthday. A young woman in the adjoining cubicle at the *Times*, a restaurant reviewer, had recently told him his graying hair made him look well seasoned. He thanked her but reminded her that he was not a plate of linguini. He wore his seasoned hair short, not because it was the trend, but because when he let it grow longer it curled wildly to the point that it appeared a poodle was sitting on his head. And he truly hated poodles. His complexion was on the dark side, as were his eyes and the brows above them. His face had been described as handsome in a rugged way by people he never believed. He found it unpleasant to look at, which is why he shaved with the bathroom light turned off, adding an element of danger to his morning routine. "It's a good thing you weren't born a girl," his mother once told him. "You'd be homely with that face. But it works for a boy." He had also been concerned that he might appear two-faced, ever since his former wife had asked him if he ever noticed that some men have faces that are out of balance; the left side can be quite different from the right. As a result, he sometimes would turn the bathroom light back on after shaving and cover first one side of his face, then the other with a towel. He eventually came to believe he did, indeed, possess two opposing facial halves, with one looking more sinister than the other. He feared it might be a warning sign of a dual personality, but then realized that he had mistaken the mole on his right cheek for a mark of menace.

Paul returned to the vestibule, where he gathered the grocery bags and their spilled contents and went to the kitchen, large and well equipped for someone who rarely cooked a meal but instead relied on a microwave oven to defrost many. He took a large black plastic trash bag from the pantry and opened the door to the freezer half of the refrigerator. Filling the shelves like so many books was a collection of enough frozen dinners to last several weeks, neatly arranged on end, every one of them in the same green box with the same company logo: Healthy Way. The individual titles running down the sides with both the calorie and fat count below were the only difference: Lite 'n' lively Lasagna, 180 calories, 6 grams fat; Slimmin' Shrimp Scampi, 220 calories, 4 grams fat; Power Pasta Primavera, 200 calories, 6 grams fat; and on down the list of dinner names that displayed a moronic obsession with alliteration.

He ceremoniously took the boxes, first one at a time, then two and even three in one grasp, and dumped them into the trash bag. By the time he finished, the freezer shelves were bare and the bag was bulging. The next step took a good deal longer, for the new items from Ralph's were not uniform in color, shape, and size the way the Healthy Way boxes were. He did the best he could to achieve some semblance of order by arranging the many boxes and bags by meal.

First came the breakfast items: precooked eggs Benedict sandwiches, several boxes of grilled sausages, waffles made with real butter, scrambled eggs with bacon strips and fried ham, steak with eggs, fried chicken strips with eggs, chicken livers with eggs—a cholesterol cornucopia.

Next came lunch items, including deep-dish pizzas, double cheeseburger patties, and deep-fried pocket sandwiches with ingredients such as steak slices and cream cheese to tempt the heartiest and most dangerous of appetites. Following them were the dinner items, which ran the gamut from Man-Sized Fried Chicken, Potatoes, and Gravy Feast to Diner-Style Chicken-Fried Steak with Butter-Mashed Potatoes and Gravy—for Old-Fashioned Appetites.

Finally, the dessert section of the freezer would now offer Mom's Banana Cream Pie Supreme, the irrepressible Dove Bars, in four king-sized packages of four, Wolfschmidt's Bistro-Style Black-Bottom Pie, and the tempting oxymoron Frozen Baked Alaska.

And so the process went until the freezer was jammed with more calories and fat grams, cholesterol, and sodium than Paul normally consumed in a year, which he would now easily go through in a couple of weeks. He reveled in the portent of it all.

Now all that remained was the disposal of all things healthy before they defrosted into a soggy heap in the trash bag. Throwing them in the Dumpster in the alley would be easy enough, but it would not sit well with his conscience. The unfortunates who rummaged through the receptacles would certainly not have access to a microwave. So he made a few phone calls to shelters he found listed in the phone directory. It was not until he tried the fifth one that he found a manager willing to consider a gift of a few dozen soon-to-be-no-longer-frozen healthy dinners. With a little persuading on the benefits of low-fat meals to homeless people who could use a healthier diet now and then, the manager agreed to take the collection. Which is why Paul drove so quickly along Westwood and Little Santa Monica boulevards in a race with the defrosting sunshine.

Satisfied with himself, or what he perceived as his new self, Paul thought, "All's well that bodes ill" as he raced along his way.

Chapter 5

Because it was Friday, the scene at Helen of Troy was at its chaotic peak. It seemed as though every woman in Beverly Hills needed special attention before some special event over the weekend. There was a constant cacophonous buzz within. The whir of hair dryers laid a base for the frantic chatter of clients, the indulgent laughter of stylists, and the rush of water in shampoo sinks. Every one of the twenty-eight black leather and chrome styling chairs was occupied, along with all seven manicure stations. In the waiting room at the rear of the large salon sat a dozen or so impatient women snapping pages of magazines with rhythmic annoyance. A fenced-off area was a waiting room for pets, and within it were a few exotic, small, and yipping dogs, coiffed as fastidiously as their owners soon would be.

Helen, who had already finished her fourth client of the morning, looked exhausted as she entered the salon's small employee lounge. She took an empty plastic Evian bottle, went to the sink and filled it, then plopped herself into a chair and began sipping.

"So, has he called?" asked a stylish man in his late thirties,

Harvey Stone, Helen's partner in the salon. Everything on his body was customary black. He was slender yet moderately muscular, as his tight T-shirt revealed. His manner of speech was flamboyant, as was his heavily pomaded hair, an array of varied-length spikes. To anyone with a tendency toward generalization, he was the consummate gay hairdresser. To those who knew him and knew better, he was merely being realistic. He was, in fact, "straight but not narrow," a phrase he liked to use to describe himself. Helen's favorite taunt was asking him when he was planning to come out of the closet and reveal the repressed straight man inside, to which his standard answer was "Get serious. I'd lose most of my customers. What self-respecting client of ours would entrust her precious hair to the hands of a straight man?" He of course had a point, Helen had to admit, in a city built on illusion where reality was to be avoided at all costs.

"You know, we *can* afford real Evian, sweetie," he said.

"It's a waste of good money," she answered.

Her water ruse had nothing to do with pretentiousness. It was, like Harvey's game, something that needed to be played. She shuddered to think what might happen if word got out that she drank water straight from the tap.

"And no, he hasn't called."

"Isn't that just like them," said Harvey.

"Like who?" She took another sip.

"Who do you think? Men, for God's sake. They don't call. It's in their genes. Hey, did you see that little plum I was doing?"

"I guess." She seemed sadder than usual.

"She smelled as good as she looked. The most gorgeous set of real tits I've seen in a long time."

"You're such a sexist pig," she said.

"I may be, honey, but I'd definitely like to lure her to my sty. So tell me, are you hung up on this strange guy with the shoe fetish?"

"There was a fish on my shoe." She made it sound logical.

"You're disappointed he hasn't called?"

She shrugged in the affirmative.

"I can't believe you gave him your number."

"I didn't."

A pause. An eye roll. Then, "And you're disappointed he hasn't called. Works for me."

"He knows about the shop. He could certainly find it."

"Oh, sure, a guy who sounds as neurotic as you are, he's going to walk into this hive of hedonism and ask for Helen of Troy. Don't hold your breath. Why didn't you at least tell him how to get in touch with you?"

"I wasn't sure I wanted him to."

"But you are now?"

Another shrug.

"Look, sweetie, I love you like nothing else, you know that. But you've got to get yourself out of this pit of ambivalence. You're a woman who could stand to be with a man. It's the way it goes. Well, at least for a lot of people. You should be taking a little risk. What are you afraid of? He's dangerous?

He's a mass murderer?"

She smiled. He shook his head.

Their conversation was interrupted when the door to the room opened and a striking young woman with jet-black hair, Rosa, stepped in. In one hand she held a broom, in the other a dustpan filled with wisps of highlighted blond hair. She was one of several young immigrants Helen had brought to the salon as trainees, intent on giving them careers as stylists rather than the fate they would otherwise face cleaning houses—or worse—in a system that only wished to underpay and overwork them. Rosa had already shown great promise with hairstyles that bespoke a Latin sensuality; a few clients had even returned to dark hair from dyed blond in an attempt to capture her magic.

"'*Scusa*, Miss Helen," she said in a strong Spanish accent. "A man he is here an' he hab a beeg theeng." She gestured with the hand holding the dustpan, sending a cascade of hair to the floor. "Sorree," she said, stooping to pick up the hair.

"A big thing?" asked Harvey, rolling his eyes.

"*Si*, yes … a black theeng … "

"Interesting," said Harvey.

"What do you mean, Rosa?" asked Helen.

"A man, he ask to see you. He wan' to geev thing … made of … how you say … " she tapped the metal dustpan.

"Metal," said Helen. "Black metal. Wait … a jack?"

"I dunno. He do not to tell me his name."

"What does he look like?"

Rosa shrugged. "Like he worry much."

"That's him," said Helen, turning to Harvey, who was smirking, enjoying the dialogue.

"The guy with the jack? Well, I guess he has enough brains to find out where we are. It's a start."

"Thank you, Rosa," said Helen, going to a mirror and rapidly running her fingers through her hair.

Rosa shrugged, smiled weakly, and left, saying, "*De nada*."

"I can see your indifference," said Harvey.

Helen ignored him and quickly put on some lipstick

"Yes, you obviously could care less about this guy." He went to her and grabbed her cheeks with the thumb and index finger of each hand. "There, a little hint of blush always helps. Okay, go get him."

"He's only replacing my jack." She checked herself again in the mirror. "Is my hair sticking up in the way back?"

"Here." He spat into his hand and plastered the back of her hair down. "There, now it's perfectly flat."

"And covered with spit. Thank you."

"You'd better get out there before he gets nervous and leaves his big black thing with the receptionist. And I'd better get out for my next appointment."

"You don't have one for another half hour. You just want to watch."

"I can't help it. I'm naturally prurient."

She went to the door, took a deep breath like someone about to go off the high dive and not sure if there was water in the pool, put her chin down, opened the door, and went through it.

Helen felt something, call it a tingle, when she saw Paul standing at the reception desk looking uncomfortably at the surroundings. She also felt the familiar urge to take a large step back, possibly all the way to the door through which she had just passed, like a red ball that gets smacked away by a paddle and pulled back on a rubber band for more. But she took a deep breath and approached Paul. She couldn't tell whether he had become more attractive in forty-eight hours or if she had become less indifferent. Truth was, she thought he was a good-looking man. The mole on his cheek added a point of interest to his face. She liked the fact that his hair showed no signs of styling nor any attempt to color the advancing gray mixed with the black. It was cut simply to a length that discouraged tricks or trends. His discomfort, which she hoped was only brought on by the alien environment of the salon, gave her a feeling of empathy if not outright interest, which commingled with the tingling.

"Good morning," said Paul.

"Hello. I see you found me." *Isn't that a little obvious?*

"I brought you a new jack." He held it up like a bouquet of flowers, she thought wistfully. And he actually smiled, which was something he had not done in their two previous encounters. She liked what it did for his face, but it disappeared as quickly as it had come.

"Thank you. I hope it wasn't too much trouble," she said. *Stop trying to play Audrey Hepburn, will you please? You'd like somebody to go to some trouble for a change.*

"No trouble," he lied.

He seemed not to know exactly what to do with what he held in his hand.

"So *that's* the big black thing I've been hearing about."

Paul was startled by Harvey's remark, which made him turn abruptly to see where it came from and, in the process, brought the jack in clanging contact with the stainless-steel facing of the reception desk.

"I'm her partner, Harvey. You must be the man from the pier."

Paul took Harvey's hand. "Yes, I'm Paul. I didn't know Helen had a partner."

"Call it a silent one, I guess. After all, who would go to a salon called Helen and Harvey of Troy? Are you about to be a client, or is it just the jack thing?"

Paul unconsciously ran his free hand over his hair. "No, just the jack."

"Well, anytime you need to work on the look, feel free to come in. We'll take good care of you."

"You do men?" Paul asked.

"Every chance I get," said Harvey.

Helen looked toward the ceiling and shook her head, as if asking for a way out. Harvey seemed to be satisfied that he had done enough damage and sauntered off, calling out to a woman under a dryer, "Julia, you look breathtaking." The woman, her face clownishly covered by round medicinal patches, smiled gratuitously and blew him a kiss.

"Your partner, he's interesting," said Paul.

"A bit over the top. But a dear friend."

"You're fortunate. I think he's also a good actor, the way he can play a gay man." She was startled. *How did he do that?*

"Well, you've got a jack again. And I suppose I should be on my way. It's lunchtime, though."

Was he or wasn't he going to ask?

"I imagine you already have lunch plans," he finally said.

"As I matter of fact, I don't. I usually just have some water."

"Don't you ever eat?"

"Of course I do. But it's not according to a plan. If I'm hungry, I eat something."

"But you seem to like water."

"It's essential," she said. "Eight glasses a day, at least."

"Why?"

"It's mostly what we're made of. Sixty percent of our bodies are water. But I'm sure you know that."

"I seem to remember it from a biology class. But it always struck me as odd. You'd think we'd be more fluid than we are, if that's the case. In any event, would you like to go for another glass of water somewhere?"

Helen was hard pressed to determine which of the two of them was being more obtuse. "We could take a walk, if you'd like. There's a fountain in the park."

"A walk might be nice," he said. "Not exactly my idea of a lunch date, but that's all right."

"Were you planning to invite me on one?"

He tilted his head.

"On a date?"

"In truth, yes. Does that trouble you?" he asked.

"It puzzles me. Why would you want to go to lunch with someone you think is looking for some cleaner water than is found in Santa Monica Bay?"

"Are you?"

"Am I what?"

"A jumper."

She remained silent for a few seconds, looking down at the floor, which gave him a chance to see her *V* of hair rise again.

"You really think I was about to do that, don't you?" she finally asked.

"It's all right if you were. Sometimes people feel pressed beyond their ability to deal with their world. And it's perfectly logical to entertain thoughts of doing something that has, well, a finality to it."

"You told me I needed help," she said, looking up.

"That was in the subway. I didn't say anything like that on the pier."

"Lucky me. You only watched me make a spectacle of myself there."

"It was charming, in its own way. You showed you're merely human," he said.

"How many humans do you know who dance with fish on their feet?"

Helen noticed that the receptionist, who had been

speaking on the telephone, had since hung up and was listening raptly to the conversation. She felt herself turning red at the realization and moved away, toward the front entrance. Paul followed her.

"Shall we, then?" he asked.

"Do we have to take that with us?" said Helen.

He acted as though he had forgotten what he was holding. He went to the receptionist and held the jack out to her. "May I leave this here?"

The receptionist looked down at it, then up at him. "What is it?"

"Ask that man over there," he said, pointing to Harvey.

He placed the jack on the floor next to the desk and followed Helen out the door. On the way out, he heard Harvey's now-familiar voice calling after them: "Don't do anything that would embarrass any of us, you two."

Paul winced. Helen blushed. And they both pretended not to have heard Harvey.

"Did you ever hear the story of the man and the jack?" Paul asked as they stepped into the sunlight on Beverly Drive.

"I don't think so."

"This salesman is driving in the desert, and he gets a flat tire miles from the nearest town. He opens his trunk and discovers … ," Paul said.

"That there's no jack," Helen interjected.

"You've heard the story."

"No, I haven't."

They walked north for two blocks until they reached the long, narrow park that lies sandwiched between Santa Monica Boulevard and the beginning of the hills section of Beverly Hills. There, residents look down on the less fortunate who live in the flats, the mere sound of which was undesirable, Paul thought. Traffic was crawling at its usual lunch-hour pace. The fumes mingled with the sweet fragrance of jacaranda trees and rose blooms in the city's conflicted love affair with the car and the flower. Paul stopped at a polished steel drinking fountain, waiting for a sweat-soaked runner to finish his long drink. When the man stepped away to resume his lumbering along the brown gravel path, Paul bowed slightly to Helen and held out his hand, looking like a maître d'.

"No, thank you. I'm not thirsty."

"Had your eight glasses already?" asked Paul.

She shook her head and noticed, with some approval, that the cruel sun shining on Paul did not expose any telltale scars of cosmetic surgery, which, together with the absence of hair coloring, made for an anomaly of sorts: a middle-aged Los Angeles man who was naturally comfortable with an unaltered self.

"Do you live here?" was his next question as they walked slowly along the path.

"No, not right here," she said, and immediately realized how dumb her answer must have sounded.

"I didn't mean the park. I meant this part of the city."

"I live close to Olympic."

"Ah, down there," he said. "With the people. It's still 90210, I imagine."

Now he was trying to get her address, she was sure.

"I'm not trying to pry your address from you," he said, reading her mind. "I just think it's funny, how we live by the numbers here. If you're three-one-o area code and nine-o-two-one-o zip, you're doing well, as long as you don't live too close to the ten or the four-o-five."

"Do you find everything in life comedic?"

"No. Only the tragic parts."

"I see," she said, but she really did not. She tried to imagine how he would treat life's happy parts. But maybe there were none for him. How sad. Or funny, for him. She could hear the voice of her most recent therapist: "Helen, most people experience highs and lows as they go through life, sometimes even to extremes. But they find their balance by existing, most of the time, in a middle ground between the two. You, on the other hand, never settle into that in-between zone. You're either way up there (with a sweeping flourish of his hand) or all the way down there (arcing his hand down very low and smacking it painfully on an end table)." So she asked him, was he diagnosing her as manic-depressive? "No, simply someone unable to find the comfort of balance. It must be difficult, not to mention exhausting, for you." *Ah, so I'm unbalanced, is that it? Emotionally lopsided.* And the tears flowed as she wondered where, tilted as it was, her life was headed. Not that piers or subways were the answer if all she did was visit them.

She shook herself out of her brief reverie. Paul seemed to notice the sudden head movement.

"Everything all right?" he asked.

"Nothing serious enough to make you laugh."

"You think I'm macabre, don't you?" he asked.

She shrugged, with the hint of a smile that never fully materialized.

"It's okay. What's good for the goose is good for the gander. What *is* a gander, anyway?"

"A male goose, I'm told. It's also a verb, meaning to walk aimlessly."

"Along a path in Beverly Hills, with someone who's trying to get you to go out with him?"

"But why do you want to do that—go out with a jumper?" she asked, too self-conscious to look anywhere but down at the tiny round stones on the brown earthen path.

"I tried to explain that. Kindred spirits, I'm guessing."

"Do you have an agenda?" she asked.

"Nothing global. Just something basic. Man meets woman … "

"Whom he accuses of being unstable, in need of therapy, which she is already getting and has been for several years, thank you very much," she interjected.

"And who likes to finish other people's sentences for them, you're welcome."

"You're being hostile again," she said.

"*I'm* being hostile? We come here for a walk. For a drink of water, which you don't want anyway. Next you ask me about an agenda."

He stopped walking and faced her. "Do you have some kind of phobia that every man who finds you attractive is intent on taking something from you—your innocence?"

"Hah!"

"'Hah!' what?"

"Hah, innocence. That went out with the last Jane Austen book."

"Do you think all this is about sex? Is that it?" he said.

"Isn't it always?"

"No, it isn't always. Can't I be attracted to you without wanting to lure you off to someplace dark, where the music and the light are both soft, where I wait expectantly while you decide whether to approach and then put down your glass of wine, look deep into my eyes, and begin to undo the buttons on my shirt, while you let me place my hands on your shoulders and draw you close, until our breaths commingle and … "

"Stop!" She said it so forcefully that an old man on a nearby bench dropped his newspaper and looked up at them in alarm.

"Well, do you think that's what's on my mind?"

He waited for a response, which did not come, and he appeared ready to stay there, his eyes on hers, until she answered. It was a question of who would break first. She lost, first biting her lower lip, which was no help, and finally letting her laughter force its way out. He smiled in return while the poor old man on the bench seemed uncertain of whether to call 911 on his cell phone or go back to his newspaper. He did neither, but simply got up and walked away, shaking his head.

"Well, this has been an interesting, uh, walk in the park," Paul said as they resumed walking. "But you didn't take any water. Is it something I said?"

"I do have to get back. An appointment." She looked at her wrist, but there was no watch on it.

"Could we possibly do this again? Actually, I don't mean this walk, in this park. You don't have lunch. How about breakfast? Do you have that?"

"Yes, of course. It's the day's most important meal."

"Along with plenty of water. Tomorrow?"

She stopped walking again and studied him. He smiled, waiting. She felt herself start to smile but managed to hold part of it back. *No need to go off the deep end*, she thought, enjoying the irony of the metaphor. He looked earnest for someone who tried to turn everything into a joke. She wondered how he acted at funerals.

"I could meet you somewhere." She wasn't about to invite a strange man—and he certainly did seem strange— to her home, even in broad daylight.

"Farmers' Market?"

She thought about it for a moment or two. It happened to be a favorite spot. She felt comfortable and unthreatened there, since mealtime visitors were largely television-industry people who were too engrossed in their career insecurities to notice, let alone bother, a woman by herself. She also liked the array of fresh produce casting a fragrance that, if she closed her eyes in the cradling sunlight, could transport her to a more tropical, less chaotic place.

"What time?" she finally asked.

"Nine?"

"Could we perhaps make it earlier?" said Helen.

"Sure. Pick a time."

"Seven."

"I'll meet you halfway. Eight. Would that be all right?"

"That's fine." Life, after all, was about compromise.

"At the rusty tables," Paul said.

"With the aggressive little birds that try to make off with your food."

"But I don't think they'd go for your water."

She ignored the wisecrack, and they continued walking until they arrived at the intersection of Santa Monica Boulevard and Beverly Drive.

"I'll say good-bye here," said Paul. "My car's in the city garage."

"I don't think you're over two hours. It's not free after that, you know."

"Yes, I've heard."

After an awkward pause, she looked at her bare wrist again. "It's time for my next appointment."

"As I said, I find you interesting. Tomorrow, eight?"

She nodded and smiled politely, then stepped off the curb.

"It'd be safer to wait for the Walk light."

She stepped back up. "You're concerned with safety?"

"Only for other people."

She found that almost touching, but not quite.

"Look, it's what I was saying about numbers," he said, pointing to a sign over a storefront. "90210 Post Office Boxes, Month-to-Month," he read. "A person could live in his car and have a Beverly Hills address. Who says this isn't the land of opportunity?"

She watched the green Walk sign come on and started out again. She wondered if Paul was watching her as she walked. She straightened her posture a bit and kept her feet closer together, placing one in front of the other. Her effort was not wasted, even though she could only guess that he was watching her every movement.

———

"Girl, where have you been? Your one o'clock is here, and she's on the ceiling" was her greeting from Harvey as she entered the salon.

She looked at the clock on the wall. "Six minutes late and she's on the ceiling? It's only hair."

"But it happens to be *my* hair."

The voice came from behind Helen. She did not have to turn to know it was Beverly Scheer, wife of Hollywood's notorious superagent Mel Scheer. If Helen was pressed for reasons why she would even think of visiting subways and piers, Beverly Scheer would be close to, if not at the top, of the list. Yes, Helen was all of six minutes late for Mrs. Scheer.

But the truth was, this was the first time in memory that the woman was not at least fifteen minutes late herself. A few weeks earlier, she had arrived forty minutes late for her one o'clock appointment.

"I want highlights today too," said Mrs. Scheer.

"But that would take an extra hour," said Helen.

"So? I've got time."

"But I don't. I have a two o'clock."

"It won't kill her to wait. I've got a very important cocktail thing tomorrow, and I want some color. Tell her to read a magazine, whoever she is."

The problem was, the two o'clock was within earshot.

"'Whoever I am' is someone you wouldn't know," said the woman. "I'm with the L.A. County Museum of Art, which I'm sure you don't frequent."

"Well, excuse me. I was there for a cocktail party just last week, and I don't recall seeing you."

"A cocktail party. I should have known."

"And what's that supposed to mean?" said an increasingly agitated Mrs. Scheer.

"Nothing, really. You can take my appointment, since I wouldn't want to deny you whatever it is you need for the *cocktail thing*," said the woman, picking up her things. "I'll find a salon that can keep its schedule."

"You might want to try that franchise place, the Upper Cut or whatever it's called. It might suit you better."

At that point, the woman approached Mrs. Scheer. Her smile dripped with animus as she said, "It's been so nice chatting with you, whoever *you* are. Here's my card. If you'd like to visit the museum sometime for something other than a party, I'd be happy to show you what hangs on our walls."

Mrs. Scheer held the card at arm's length, squinting down at it, and, turning to Helen, said, "Holy shit. She said she's *with* the museum. She's the damn president." She turned back to the woman. "Why didn't you say something?" she demanded.

"I almost did. Something like 'Go fuck yourself, you selfish bitch,' but I decided against it. Instead, I'll wish you a nice day."

Helen tried in vain to appease the museum president. "Please, don't go. I'll get my partner to take you. I'm so sorry."

"Don't bother. I like the sound of Upper Cut. And I think I'd like the clientele as well," she said, glaring at Mrs. Scheer, who, for possibly the first time in her adult life, was speechless. But not for long. She promptly launched into a nonstop tirade of four-letter words that echoed throughout the salon as the museum director quietly left.

Harvey led Helen out of the reception area and back to her station, where she crumpled to the floor in the corner, held a brown paper bag to her mouth, and breathed into it. Her eyes bulged with the labored effort.

"Easy, sweetie, easy. It's only a maniacal bitch blowing up," he said.

Helen removed the bag from her mouth long enough to say, "The whole world is blowing up." She then continued breathing into the bag.

"Are you sure it isn't something else that's gotten to you?"

She shook her head and sucked in deeply enough to collapse the paper bag, which fell in on itself with a whooshing sound.

"Or some*one* else? Like the man with the jack?"

"Whaffootawkinabowd?" she exhaled.

"You know very well. I saw that look. Whenever you get the tingle, your eyes shine like Christmas balls."

She removed the bag from her face. "You come up with the lamest similes."

A face peered in through an opening in the curtain. It was Rosa. "Mees Helen, dat lady dat makes dee screaming, she want to know where you go?"

"You didn't tell her, did you?" asked Helen, her eyes widening but definitely not shining.

"No, I di na know."

"Thank you, Rosa. Tell her I've been getting ready for her and she can come back now."

Rosa smiled and left.

Harvey looked at Helen sympathetically. "You going to be all right?" he asked.

"Oh, sure, just fine," she said, her voice a full octave higher than usual.

"My God, girl, what's in that bag, helium?"

Helen held her hands out in front of her as though to block something about to charge her. "Don't worry, everything's going to be fine. Just fine," she said, her voice back down from the falsetto. "I'll do Mrs. Scheer, I'll listen to her problems the way I do every week, I'll smile and nod when she asks me if I understand, I'll tell her she looks wonderful, she'll leave, and I'll get swallowed down into hell, right through the floor, for lying so egregiously. Just fine."

"Have you considered getting laid?" Harvey asked.

"Leave, Harvey," she replied, pointing at the curtain.

And he did, after puckering his lips and blowing two brief Los Angeles air kisses her way.

As soon as she sat down, Mrs. Scheer was ready to pounce. "Can you believe that bitch? I mean, can you believe her?" she asked Helen's image in the mirror. "All I did was make a simple request. And what does she do? She gives me attitude. Acts like she's better than me."

"I," said Helen.

"What?"

"Nothing," said Helen to her client. Then to herself, *The woman from the museum had a point. Of course she's better than someone who doesn't know her pronouns, among other deficiencies.*

"What do I need?" asked Mrs. Scheer, tugging at the ends of her hair and curling her lip in distaste at what she saw.

"How did you like what we did last week?" asked Helen.

"I didn't. It was too shiny. My husband told me I looked like a car."

"I'm sure he was just kidding." *I'm beginning to like the man.*

"One thing he doesn't do is kid. Trust me, he never learned how. I want to try something different. Maybe red. I definitely need a change. A new me."

"That might be interesting." *You're a terrible blond. For two hundred and fifty dollars, I can change you into a terrible redhead.*

"No, wait, that's a bad idea. That young assistant he's been screwing, she's a redhead. I don't want to give him the satisfaction of being reminded of her. But I guess it doesn't make that much of a difference. He hasn't wanted to screw me in God knows how long. Come on, Helen, help me here. Make me the woman he wants to screw."

"Have you thought of black?"

"All the time, honey. The guy who's doing our floors, he's black."

"Interesting." *Have you ever once in your life had a thought or uttered a word that was not completely disgusting? People are hungry, dying of incurable diseases, shooting one another in the streets, electing morons, and you can only think of your precious hair.*

"So, what do you think?" asked Mrs. Scheer.

"I'm not sure." *You are a very bad person, and I'm worse for taking your money and holding back what, in fact, I do think.*

"Something that will bring out the real me."

As Helen studied her client in the mirror, Mrs. Scheer's hair underwent a terrifying change: right before Helen's incredulous eyes, it morphed from a helmet of lacquered yellow into a mass of writhing snakes, dozens of them, their mouths open in menace, their slithering tongues darting in and out. Helen gasped and shut her eyes. When she opened them, the snakes were still there, writhing, slithering. The hairbrush fell from Helen's hand to the floor and her jaw dropped. She slowly backed away until she was outside the station, took one last horrified look, and walked—no, it was more like ran—through the salon and out the door, leaned against the plate-glass window, and slowly slid to the sidewalk.

Harvey must have seen Helen from his station. It took only seconds for him to reach her. "My God, baby, are you all right?"

She could only shake her head slowly.

"You look like you saw a ghost."

She shook her head again. "Medusa," she whispered.

"With the snakes?"

Her head moved again, this time up and down. She touched her face and looked at her hands.

"Am I stone yet?"

Chapter 6

A knot in the chest, the pain sometimes radiating down his left arm, was once a cause for alarm. But it was no longer troubling to Paul, since he had finally been convinced that it was merely the sign of excess stomach acid. It also helped that he had come to view a fatal heart attack in a different light, so long as the pain would not be too severe nor the duration too protracted.

The knot tightened as he rode the elevator to the twenty-second floor of the downtown skyscraper where he was to meet with his editor, Milton Glass, who had called earlier asking him to come in to discuss "something that concerns me." Although he considered Milton a friend, Paul knew "something that concerned him" meant he was furious about something. And that made for chest knots. After the phone call, Paul took two Prilosec tablets, which, if they didn't always untie the knot, frequently loosened it a bit.

The office of Western Syndications was like Paul's apartment, minimally furnished in black and chrome. The only color was in the graphic boasts of the company's writers, in the form of award plaques and promotional posters. Paul always winced at the wide horizontal poster that had appeared on buses throughout Los Angeles: Men Have Problems Too. Paul Solves Them, Man to Man, In the *Times*. The close-up photo reminded him again that his face was asymmetrical. He couldn't resist closing one eye again to be sure.

"Good morning, Paul. Something in your eye?" The British-accented voice of Pamela, the efficient, tastefully dressed receptionist, interrupted his reverie. She represented the most sought-after requirements for front-desk jobs in L.A. firms that had anything to do with entertainment or the arts. The accent was presumed to project intelligence and taste in a city where both were elusive.

"Hello, Pamela." (She didn't like being called Pam; it contradicted the accent.) "No, I was just testing something. Is my face lopsided?"

She was taken aback by the question. But she retained her cool. "In the photograph, or in reality?"

"Either."

She studied him briefly, then the poster, smiled professionally, and shook her head. "No, I think everything's quite balanced."

"Thank you. Is Milton in?"

"Oh, yes. He's expecting you."

"I know. Is he pissed?"

A flush appeared on her pale cheeks. "At ten-thirty in the morning? Really, Paul."

"Sorry. I didn't mean drunk. Angry."

She smiled patronizingly. "No more than the usual, I would suspect. Today is a major deadline day. I'll let him know you're here."

She pressed a button on the phone console. He liked the way her nails were done, in understated translucence. He also appreciated her floral scent, most likely of an English garden, although he had never smelled one. He had once asked Milton about her, indicating an interest, to which Milton had replied with a wag of the finger, "No fishing off the company pier." Paul accepted it as sound, if crass, advice.

"Paul is here," she said into the delicate microphone suspended beneath her chin. She looked up at Paul and said, "No, I don't think so. I will."

"Did he ask if I was pissed?"

She nodded. "You can go in."

He walked down the corridor toward Milton's office, thinking about Pamela. He was struck by a vision of her translucent nails digging into the flesh of his back. She pulled back and said, "I had no idea you had such a crop of hair on your back." To which he replied, "Are you pissed?" And she answered, "No, but let's get that way."

He was still grinning at his mind play when he greeted Milton, who was standing behind his desk and looked up from something to squint at Paul. He was a large, well-conditioned man in his fifties with broad shoulders, a narrow waist for his age, and brown, thinning hair that looked suspiciously like it had been professionally tinted. A man's man, many would describe him.

"Glad you're smiling," Milton said. "You can see I'm not."

"Good morning to you too. How are you?"

"How am I?" He jerked his head toward a chair in front of his desk, which Paul took to be a command to be seated. "How should I be after reading your latest piece?"

"Something wrong with it?"

Milton dropped himself into his black leather chair and picked up the white pages he had been looking at.

"Wrong? What could be wrong? 'Lighten up. Get rid of the ballast that's been holding you down. Experiment. Follow your urges. Ask her to let you crash the party. Three's only a crowd if one's an anchor dragging down the fun.'"

Milton dropped the pages back on the desk and looked over the narrow reading glasses perched on his nose. "Why should I find anything wrong with telling some poor sailor to invite himself to cut in on two lesbians making love? After all, isn't that the kind of thing American families are talking about over their apple pie? 'Hey, kids, want to watch Mommy get it on with the cleaning lady?'"

He tapped the pages on his desk for emphasis. "You write for the newspaper some kid on a bike throws on the front porch and a little dog brings in the house. Not for a magazine that comes from Larry Flynt in a plain brown wrapper, for Christ's sake."

"I guess you didn't find it funny."

Milton glared at him. "Funny? You call this funny? I call it sick. Telling a man to watch his wife fucking another woman."

"Why not?"

"It's deviant."

"What is? Them doing it or him watching?"

"Mary, mother of God," he said, looking up to the ceiling as if expecting to see her there. "He doesn't know why it's deviant."

"Have you ever seen two women making love to one another?" said Paul.

"Maybe in a video. By accident. In a hotel room."

Paul noticed the red build upward from Milton's wide neck.

"It's not natural."

"They use their imaginations. They're very gentle with one another. And respectful. They take their time, no rushing to finish. They explore, caress. And make use of other parts of their bodies."

Milton said nothing, waiting for more, deep in thought. Then, "What else?"

Paul smiled. "You obviously don't want to hear any more. It's too deviant."

"Forget the whole thing," growled an uncomfortable Milton.

"Good. You'll run the column?"

"No, I won't. Do you have any idea the mail we'd get? Not to mention how many papers would pull it."

"I was just trying to inject a little humor."

"Do me a favor. Leave the humor to the guys who do the funnies. That's why they call them funnies. You write a column. You give advice. That's why they call it an advice column. This thing you wrote is more like a career suicide note."

Milton did not see the smile, nor the raised eyebrows, on Paul's face.

"When can you get me another column? A normal one."

Paul reached inside his black blazer and took out several pages folded in thirds. He slid it across the desk. "Is that fast enough?"

Milton eyed him suspiciously and picked up the pages. He began reading, then slowly nodding, then skimming over to the second and third pages while Paul waited silently, watching a pigeon strut back and forth across the window ledge, aimlessly turning and walking, turning and walking, getting nowhere. He empathized.

Milton dropped the pages on top of the others, narrowed his eyes, and looked at Paul for a couple of moments. "You knew I wouldn't run that column, didn't you?"

Paul shrugged.

"Of course you did. And you had this backup, which is what I expect you to be writing, ready to give me, but only after I got sufficiently pissed."

"You don't drink in the morning."

"What?"

"Ask Pamela. It's a British thing."

"Whatever. I'm glad you have the time to write columns you know I won't run."

"Milton, Milton. You need to learn to relax. You're

always wound tight. It's not good for your health. That thing on your forehead starts twitching."

Milton put his hand to his forehead. "What thing? What the hell are you talking about?"

"A little to the right. There. Looks like a squiggly worm. Feel it?"

He put his hand down in disgust. "No, I don't feel any goddamn worm. And my health is fine, no thanks to you."

"Do you drink enough water? You know your body's sixty percent liquid? You need eight glasses a day, minimum."

"That's fascinating. What would my life hold for me if I didn't know about my water content?" He looked at Paul, concerned. "Are you all right?"

"As all right as I ever get. Why?"

"You seem a little off-kilter. I mean this column, I don't know where that came from."

"A sailor in San Pedro."

"But you get loony letters like that all the time. The difference is, you normally toss them. You know you can count on thirty, forty percent of your mail coming from fruitcakes. Now you actually answer one. And you know I'm not going to run it. Do you have too much time on your hands?"

"No. I have plenty to keep me busy."

"You're sure you're all right?"

"My blood pressure's boringly normal. So is my cholesterol. I'm the picture of health." *But just wait until some of that new stuff in the freezer kicks in.*

"I don't mean that kind of all right. I mean all right all right. Know what I'm saying?"

"You mean my emotional health?"

"I mean, are you getting to do the things a man needs to be doing?"

"Like going to Dodger games? They're not doing so well."

"Like getting laid."

"I guess that'd be better than a Dodger game. But no, I haven't lately."

"There's your problem. And why haven't you?"

"Well, for one thing, no one has come up to me lately and said, 'Hello there. You look like someone who hasn't had sex in a while. Want to try some with me?'"

"Ever think of working the problem a little more than that?"

He opened a desk drawer and retrieved a small maroon book. "I've got a few numbers here that I'd be more than happy to share with you."

"It's not black. Your little book."

Milton ignored him. "These are sure things. No complications. They're all certified in good health."

"Sounds like puppies."

"They're working girls. Classy ones. You make a date, meet them in a nice place, have a drink or two, they go back to your place. And you know the best part? You don't have to worry about how to get them to go home. They only stay if you ask them to, then negotiate the overtime charges."

"Sounds romantic," said Paul.

"I assume you're not looking for love. You've told me how well that's gone for you in the past. This could be the answer."

"To what question?"

"How you satisfy man's most basic need without wanting to jump off a bridge over it."

"But what about the artist who stabbed himself in the heart with a paintbrush when a prostitute rejected him?"

"Come on, how often does that happen?" said Milton. He didn't ask who the painter was or how he could do that.

"I appreciate your concern, Milton. But I'm fine, promise."

"Have you been going out with anyone—to dinner, a show?"

"I had a glass of water with someone."

"Oh, that sounds steamy. What's next, carrots?"

"We're going to breakfast tomorrow."

"What's wrong with dinner?"

"I don't think she's ready to see me after the sun sets."

"Sure, that's when you grow fangs and pointed ears. What's her name?"

"Helen."

"Sounds nice and normal. Helen what?"

"She hasn't told me yet."

"Why rush into intimacy? Where do you meet people like that?"

"On subway platforms, piers."

"And on which one did you meet this Helen?"

"Both."

"Both," Milton repeated. "I think I'm missing something here."

"In one day. What are the odds that I'd run into the same woman twice in one day, in a city this size?"

"Long. And you had a glass of water with her, plus she won't tell you her last name. I've heard of matches made in heaven."

"Serendipitous, isn't it?"

"That's not the word I was thinking of. But, hey, if it makes you happy, don't let me stop you. And while you're at it, don't let me stop you from finishing three more columns. The old-fashioned kind."

"I guess that means answering the woman whose husband has three testicles is out the question," said Paul, straight-faced.

"Good-bye, Paul. Have a nice day. Enjoy your breakfast tomorrow. And write me some fucking columns."

"You said you don't want that kind."

"Good-bye, Paul."

As he was leaving, Milton stopped him. "I forgot to tell you. The station wants you start on the thirtieth."

Paul had not given much thought to the radio show Milton had secured for him on Los Angeles's top-rated AM talk station. The radio version of Man to Man was scheduled for a thirteen-week trial three nights a week, from eight to ten, alternating with *Betty-Talk*, a women's call-in show with pop psychologist Betty Mendelsohn. As the start of the new endeavor loomed closer, Paul had been wondering why he had agreed to do the show. "Talk radio is a bunch of right-wing lunatics ranting to people with guns who live in trailers," he had said to a frustrated Milton, to which Milton had replied, "It's great promotion for the column, and the pay is like taking candy from babies." Paul replied, "I don't want to take candy from babies. It's not nice."

Nonetheless, Paul, tired of resisting Milton, had agreed to the thirteen weeks. At least it gave him something to do three evenings a week. But, of course, that was before he had met someone who might eventually agree to do something with him at night.

Standing in the doorway, he asked, "Would afternoons work instead of evenings?"

"No, afternoons wouldn't work instead of evenings," Milton mocked. "Women listen to radio in the afternoons; men listen at night."

"That's sexist," said Paul.

"It's demographics," said Milton.

Paul waved and took his leave, hoping to get one more glance at Pamela's fingernails on the way out. But in her place sat an overweight young man in a tight-fitting black T-shirt promoting the band KISS with a pair of lips and long red tongue. He was engrossed in a magazine and did not even look up or nod when Paul said, "Say good-bye to Pamela for me."

Chapter 7

Paul arrived at the Farmers' Market a good ten minutes early, which gave him time to pursue an urge to buy some flowers for Helen. In the span of thirty minutes, while driving up Pico Boulevard and passing the legion of flower shops nearly equal in number to convenience stores, he had decided and undecided on flowers at least a dozen times. Arguing with himself, he cited presumptuousness, outdatedness, nerdishness, nebbishness, and loserness in the case against them. The pro side of the argument favored appropriateness, traditionalness, solidness, and unpredictableness. By the time he parked his car, No Flowers led Flowers five to four. Walking through the parking lot, he thought of friendliness, which tied the score, so he flipped a quarter, which he dropped and chased as it rolled on edge across the blacktop, a scene a delivery driver found amusing. The driver stepped on the coin for Paul, looked down at it, and declared, "It's heads."

"Thank you," Paul said sheepishly to the man. *Flowers it is*, he said to himself.

He had time to stop at a stall overflowing with fresh flowers, which sent out an aromatic counterpoint to the smells of iced seafood, pungent cheeses, and brewing coffee. The market was a bazaar of outdoor stalls interspersed by a few enclosed shops, one of which offered an enormous array of meats and poultry served up by a cadre of white-coated experts on the legs, shanks, ribs, loins, breasts, and organs of everything formerly on hoof or wing.

Paul felt self-conscious about the bunch of long-stemmed red roses, so vivid was their crimson color as to suggest they might, in fact, be artificial. Even though the bouquet had been wrapped in white paper, the tops peered out to announce to the world that a man was bringing flowers to someone. To be less conspicuous, he carried them down at his side, trying to keep them upright and walk at the same time, which made him even more conspicuous and thoroughly awkward. He tried carrying the flowers behind his back, but that made him feel like a roller skater, so he simply held them in front of him, wishing the quarter had landed tails up.

He arrived at the courtyard with the rusting tables and, yes, with the aggressive little birds, which did not have much in the way of breakfast pickings yet. He was saddened not to find Helen there. He checked his watch. It was three minutes past eight. Maybe she thought better of the idea and chose not to come. Maybe she was just three minutes late.

"Hello?"

It was more a question than a greeting that came from behind him in a voice that was more diminutive than he had remembered.

He turned to see Helen standing there, her ankles touching, her hands holding, of all things, a bouquet of flowers, which seemed to mock Paul and his flowers.

"Nice flowers," he said.

"Thank you. Yours are pretty too."

Good God, he thought. *What a vision the two of us must be.*

It looked like they were prepared to duel with the bouquets. How unusual for a woman to bring a man flowers. But how presumptuous to think that she had. Maybe she had a relative in the hospital.

"I thought they'd look nice in the salon," she said.

"Actually, these aren't for me," he said. "They're for you."

"Really?"

He nodded and held them out to her.

"That's very nice. Thank you. But I don't understand. Why would you do something like that?"

"Because I think every woman should have a bouquet in each hand. Balanced. Truth is, flowers won the coin toss."

He couldn't believe he had said that. But something about the way she looked at him made him feel as flustered as a hormone-possessed teenager on prom night. And something also must have made her wonder what his problem was.

"Shall we get some breakfast?" he asked. "I've reserved a table."

She surveyed all the empty tables. "That's funny."

"Yes, it's how I deal with the tragedy of all those birds and no crumbs for them yet. You can have your choice of omelets over there," he said, pointing to EggsCetera. "Or, waffles," nodding to the sign over another booth, Waffleteria. "And then, there's a large selection of pastries," acknowledging Le Pan Handle, the most precious name of all.

"I wonder if I might find half a grapefruit and some yogurt."

At least she was breaking out of the water-only mode.

Paul approached a smiling woman at the EggsCetera counter. "Pardon me, but would it be possible to get a half grapefruit and some yogurt?"

Keeping her smile, the woman pointed to the sign above her. "Eggs. Thassall. Eggs."

He looked at the other choices and realized it would be fruitless, so to speak, to try the waffle or pastry stands. He led Helen to a table and asked, "What flavor yogurt do you like?"

"None. Plain is what I prefer. But you don't have to find it. I'll go."

"No, you can stay and watch our flowers. The birds have been eyeing them."

It didn't take him long to find a shop offering natural foods, including plain yogurt. He also found an accommodating fruit vendor who happily sliced a grapefruit in half and gave him a paper plate and a plastic spoon and fork.

"You ordered the yogurt and grapefruit?" he said, coming up behind Helen.

Her eyes widened. "Oh, very nice."

"Yes, they are," he agreed, placing his finds before her.

"No, I mean you. It's very nice that you did that. Thank you."

"I'm sure you'd like water to go with your breakfast?" he said.

"I have it." She reached into a leather drawstring purse at her feet and took out a bottle of Evian. She also took out a straw and placed it in the bottle.

Quaint, he thought. *Strange, but quaint.*

He left her again to get breakfast for himself, a sausage omelet with three eggs fried in an artery-clogging pool of butter. Jimmy Dean had nothing on him. When he returned to the table, Helen stared at his breakfast choice but, of course, said nothing. Nor did he explain his new diet regimen. But his stomach had not yet been conditioned to the alien food he was introducing to it, so he was not able to finish his meal. After all, it was only the previous day when he had sent down a bowl of oatmeal with nonfat milk and a cup of coffee.

"May I get you anything else?" he asked Helen.

"No, thank you." She looked at the remains of his omelet. "Wasn't it to your liking?"

"It was fine. A little generous for me."

"What do you normally have for breakfast?" she asked.

"It shows?"

"Yes," she said.

He changed the subject. "It's a nice morning for a walk. Would you join me?"

She agreed to the walk, which made him think that perhaps things were progressing. She might even throw caution to the wind and reveal her full name, but he knew there was no sense in rushing things. They cut through the market and walked toward the park that stretched between the Los Angeles County Museum of Art and the La Brea Tar Pits.

Feeling the first warmth of day, he invited her to rest on a bench. Each held a single flower bouquet, having found nothing else to do with them, and together they presented a curious tableau, an American primitive of sorts.

"See that couple over there?" said Paul, indicating an elderly man and woman on a bench. The couple, easily in their eighties, seemed both frail and resigned to something, to some destination. They sat close together, yet seemed unconnected. The man looked straight ahead. The woman looked down at the ground. And they neither spoke nor acknowledged each other.

"They look very sad," said Helen.

"I'm not so sure. They're waiting for something."

She studied the couple. "I see your point. What do you think it is they're waiting for?"

"For something to happen. Maybe for their children, who probably don't come by. Maybe for friends, but it could be they're all gone. Maybe for closure, hoping they can be together for it."

"You make it sound so hopeless," she said.

"It probably is. The waiting is the worst part, not the closure."

"What sort of closure do you want when you're their age?"

He looked around at the almost pastoral aura created by the soft, hazy morning sun and brilliant green slopes. Then he turned to look into Helen's eyes, with the barest hint of a smile. "But that's just it. I don't want to get where they are. They're not in control of the course their lives are taking. It's not really fair when you don't have that, when you settle for the waiting. There needs to be a remote you can hold, with a pause button, fast forward. And stop."

"That's an interesting metaphor, but it's not going to happen. There *is* no remote."

"Oh yes there is."

She thought about that, then turned away and looked straight ahead. "You mean a subway platform."

"Or a pier."

Now they both looked straight ahead in silence. An observer might have thought them quarreling lovers.

"Let's walk," Paul finally said.

She nodded and he stood. He held out his hand. She looked at it, then shook her head in a negative response.

"The flowers," he clarified. "Would you like me to carry yours?"

"I have an idea," she said, rising and picking up her bouquet. She started toward the elderly couple on the bench. He followed her, holding his bouquet.

"Good morning," Helen said to the couple as she approached them from behind. They turned in unison, unsmiling but not unfriendly, simply curious. Helen held out the bouquet and walked around to face them. Slowly turning their heads, their eyes followed her.

"We have an extra. I thought you might like these." She held the flowers out to them.

The man turned to the woman, waiting for a response. She shrugged, and he then did the same.

"That's very nice of you. But I can't imagine why you wouldn't want such a lovely bouquet of flowers," the woman finally said while the man nodded in agreement. Their hair was the same white color. Even the lines on their faces seemed to be the same, along with the whiteness of their front teeth, obviously not their own.

"Oh, it's not that I don't want them. I just don't know what I'd do with so many flowers. He brought me those," Helen answered, nodding toward Paul, who smiled gratuitously, again feeling self-conscious holding the bouquet in front of him.

"That's really very sweet. Flowers *would* be nice in the apartment, wouldn't they?" the woman asked of the man beside her.

"Yes, they certainly would. She means I don't bring her flowers anymore," said the man.

"Now that's not what I meant at all," the woman scolded, but with some warmth.

"Been married fifty-six years, but she's still entitled to flowers. Guess I tend to forget."

His wife put her hand on his shoulder. "You just have other things on your mind," she said to him.

"What things?" he asked.

Helen held the flowers out and the woman accepted them, hesitantly. She breathed in their perfume scent, which brought a broad smile to her face.

"They smell so wonderful. Like Mexico, when the bougainvillea are in bloom, don't you think?" she said to her husband.

He leaned toward the flowers, sniffed, and nodded. "They do. Definitely. Thank you very much, young lady."

"I hope you have a very nice day," Helen said, her eyes glistening.

"Oh, we will, now. Most certainly," said the woman.

"Yes, indeed," agreed her husband.

Helen and Paul continued on their way across the soft turf in silence until Paul finally spoke.

"That was a nice thing you did," Paul said.

"I did it to lighten my load."

"No you didn't."

Neither of them seemed to want the stroll to end. They continued in a southerly direction until they were at the iron fence surrounding the La Brea Tar Pits, where life-sized bronze statuary of long-gone mammoths stood mired in pools of black ooze.

"They were just trying to survive, and they got sucked into bottomless pits of sludge," said Paul. "Interesting metaphor."

"They could have walked around them. Maybe they walked in with a purpose."

"No, I doubt they did it intentionally. That's a concept,

not an instinct."

"Isn't it a human conceit to think we're the only ones who can do it? What about lemmings?" said Helen.

"That one *is* a function of instinct, not intellect. I'm sure a bunch of lemmings don't sit around and discuss how miserable life has become until the top lemming says, 'Hey, I've got an idea. Why don't we check out of this place? I know a cliff that's perfect. Just follow me.'"

He stopped and turned to her. "I know this might sound strange, when we're talking about what lemmings and mammoths might do, but I'm enjoying myself. A lot, in fact. I'm especially enjoying the company. And I keep wondering when we might see each other again."

"Why?"

He smiled and looked away, toward the mammoths. "Most women would either agree it would be a good idea, seeing each other again, or that it probably wouldn't be such a good idea for any number of reasons, like their husbands might not understand or they're too busy with their screenplay. But you just ask why."

"I don't have a husband. Or a screenplay."

"That amazes me. Not that you don't have a husband. But that you live in Los Angeles and aren't working on a screenplay."

"I'm not a writer."

"That doesn't stop anyone. Did you hear about the survey a disc jockey did recently?"

She shook her head.

"He stood on Sunset at noon, randomly stopped a hundred people, and asked one question: 'How's the screenplay coming?' Eighty-four claimed to be writing or had written one. Another twelve said they'd been planning to start theirs. The other four, who must have been tourists, asked what a screenplay was."

"How is your screenplay coming?" she asked.

"There is none. Never has been one. Never will be one."

"You don't like movies?"

"I don't like what it takes to make them. Not that I've tried. But I know people who have. From what they tell me, they feel like those mammoths. Instead of tar, they get sucked into something called development. And there's no way out. They just sink deeper and deeper, saying things like, 'Wait, I can put some car chases and wild sex into my story about the blind nun who helps the crippled child. Would that work?'"

"So you're content to write your newspaper columns?"

"Who said anything about content? It's what I do. A job."

"But you help people, don't you?" she asked.

"It would be nice if I believed I could. But I'm afraid I'm paid to entertain people. It's mostly voyeurism. At first I had this notion that readers could better understand their own problems by empathizing with other people's. Perhaps with a little catharsis thrown in. But I eventually realized that most people who read my columns get some kind of satisfaction out of someone else's misery. It's like watching those television shows where people are publicly abused and humiliated.

Once in a while I try to offer some honest advice that might help, but my editor doesn't buy it." He chose not to tell her about the jilted mariner.

"Why do you do it?" she asked.

"Why do you do what you do? I imagine because you know how, and it pays you. I didn't prepare for my job. I actually got it because I was drunk one night. But that's a story for another time. How did you get into the hair business?"

"I inherited the salon. From my late husband."

"You seem too young to be a widow."

"And my husband was too young to die. At thirty-four."

"How terrible for you."

"It was cancer. It came quickly and took him just as quickly. And if losing him wasn't catastrophic enough, I had to endure the whispers that began circulating. A man in his early thirties dying of cancer? A salon owner? What really took his life?"

"It can be such a nice town, can't it?" said Paul.

"He was one of Hollywood's leading studio stylists by the time he was twenty-four. He bought the salon for me because of the unpredictability of the movie business. He said, 'If anything should happen to me, you'll have a business.' It was absurd. What could happen to a healthy young man like him?"

She stopped and dabbed at a tear running down her cheek, took a deep breath, and continued.

"I'm sorry. I'm sure I've told you more than you wanted

to know. And I'm afraid I've ruined this pleasant day for you."

Paul felt helplessly awkward. His wanted to reach out and draw her close to him. But he could not. "I'm so very sorry" was all he could say.

"Excuse me," Helen said, and she walked away from him, turning her back. He knew enough not to follow or watch her. He waited in silence until, after what seemed a long time, she walked back to him.

"Are you okay?" he asked.

"Hardly," she answered.

"What about your family?"

"Both my parents have been gone for several years. My only sibling, a brother, died last year in a motorcycle accident." She tried shifting into lighter gear. "I've become a frequent burier at Forest Lawn. I might be close to a free trip."

It seemed out of character to Paul, her attempt at dark humor, matching his. He liked it nonetheless. Maybe they had more in common than he had suspected.

"You'd actually bury yourself in the ground?" he asked.

"How could one possibly do that?"

"You know what I mean. Why be placed in an over-priced box under an equally overpriced piece of turf? Why not ashes in an urn? Or a scattering at sea?"

He waited for a response. None came.

"I forgot, the water's dirty."

"You're mocking me again."

"Have you heard what Eskimos used to do, when it was their turn?"

"To do what?"

"You know." He did the little walking finger routine again. "It's interesting how they determined when it actually was time. It was when their teeth were worn down so much that they couldn't chew things anymore. That made them a burden. So when they reached that point, they'd find a little iceberg and set out to sea on it, with no provisions. After enough exposure to the cold, they'd just get into a sleepy state, so they wouldn't actually feel pain as the elements shut down their bodies. Eventually, they became part of the food chain. Polar bears, I guess. It's natural, and painless, from what I understand. Too bad you can't do that off the coast of Southern California. My luck, I'd just drift over to Catalina and be pulled out of the water by tourists and have to deal with a miserable sunburn."

Helen seemed to come out of her palpable sadness. "I should be getting back," she said, looking at her wrist.

"Have you lost your watch?" Paul asked.

"No. I rarely wear one."

"But you look at your wrist."

"People scratch their heads when they don't itch."

As they walked back toward the Farmers' Market, Paul felt a sadness that they would soon part and go their separate ways. He would return home and try to write at least one "normal" column for Milton, although he would much rather find a reason for Helen to stay with him a bit longer. He tried the first thing that came to mind.

"Since the salon is closed, maybe you'd be interested in

a movie."

"At ten o'clock in the morning?" she asked.

"Right. It might be a bit early," he said, convinced she thought either he could not tell time, even *with* a watch on his wrist, or that his mind was on something other than movies. "The art museum is open."

"Not until noon today," she said.

"The truth is, I'm searching for a reason to keep you."

"You're *what?*"

"Here we go again. I don't mean literally to keep you. I mean—"

"I know. I'm sorry. I was merely trying to be funny. But I don't think it works for me the way that it does for you."

They walked for a few moments in silence. Then she said, "I'm curious about something. You were moved by what I told you back there. I have the feeling you understand the pain of loss."

"Yes. Lost a wife."

"I'm sorry."

"But I'm not a widower. Just divorced. My father has been gone for years. I still have a mother. I see her twice a week. But she has no idea who I am. Another scourge. Alzheimer's. Absolutely no quality of life. She lives in an assisted-living facility, which is a euphemism for lockdown. She also has a full-time caregiver who treats her lovingly, like she's a child. Does her hair and makeup every morning. If you saw my mother, you'd assume she's a vital elderly woman. Until she asked you if you're her daughter. She had one, but insists she has six. She thinks they're some of the nurses who work there. Sometimes she's sure I'm my father. Other times, she thinks I'm a lover she had years ago, something my father never knew, or at least didn't let on to knowing, if he did."

"Brothers?"

"No. Just my older sister. But she did something I can never forgive her for."

Helen waited for the rest.

"She died, two weeks after her fortieth birthday. She was three months pregnant with what would have been my nephew. She was having her morning coffee with her husband. He asked her what she was planning to do on such a nice, sunny day. She rolled her eyes upward, dropped the coffee cup on the floor, and, without a word or a whimper, fell facedown on the table. A fatal stroke. Her only warning had been a series of annoying headaches. It happened so unceremoniously. Over a cup of morning coffee. It made death too easy. I sometimes wonder if my mother's dementia was a gift. It at least numbed the pain of outliving her child. She also gets to meet new people all the time. I'm many of them."

"I really should be on my way," said Helen.

"I'm sorry."

"For what?" she asked.

"I'm depressing you."

"No. The subject matter is. This talk of death."

"Death isn't depressing. It's what it does to those left behind. Fortunately, I don't have to worry about that. Like a tree that falls silently in an empty forest. I know what you're thinking: self-pity. It's an unattractive quality. But I'm just saving someone else the effort."

Helen stopped abruptly next to an empty bench. She plopped herself down on it and let loose the tears she had been damming up. They flowed freely down her cheeks. Paul approached and sat next to her. He watched her cry and felt an urge to join her, but something either male or self-protective prohibited it.

"Now I've made you cry," he said.

"You are not that omnipotent," she said, punctuating her observation by blowing her nose.

"You rarely use contractions, do you?"

"I beg your pardon?" Another blow into a tissue.

"I've noticed that. You don't say *you're* or *I'm* or *isn't*. That is not a criticism. It is something that I have been observing, that is all."

"If it isn't criticism, why did you bring it up?" she parried.

"Because I hoped it might divert you from crying. Looks like it did. And you used a contraction."

"You do know you are utterly frustrating, don't you? There, that's two."

"I think what we have here is the beginning of an interesting relationship, at least conversationally. It's one long non sequitur."

"I don't follow you."

"That's funny," he said.

"Thank you."

"And endearing."

She slid away from him on the bench, looking straight ahead. "You used the word *relationship*."

"Is that a felony?"

"How can you think of a relationship?"

"Very easily. I get this picture in my head of a man and an attractive woman."

"Whom he met at a subway station."

"And on a pier, yes."

"And accused of mental instability."

"No, he did not. Emotional illness is not an offense," he countered.

"He called the kettle black."

"He never denied his own instability."

"She made a spectacle of herself."

"She endeared herself."

She stopped. "She did? I did?"

He smiled and nodded slowly. She stood up from the bench and nervously brushed out wrinkles that were not on her blouse or pants. He stood too, still holding the bouquet of flowers. She walked off with a shake of the head and a shrug of the shoulders.

As they reached the top of the slope, the elderly couple on the bench came into view. They continued looking off into the distance. The man still held the bouquet, like a suitor. Paul called out, "Have a nice day." The man turned and squinted at him and Helen with no recognition. Paul held up the bouquet he still held and waved it, like a signal flag. The man smiled and nodded, then held up his bouquet and waved back with it. But his wife didn't turn away from whatever she was focused on.

"May I call you?" Paul asked, standing next to her car in the Farmers' Market parking lot. Before she could answer, he added, "And please don't ask why."

"Yes, you may call me."

"Good. The next question: Would you give me your phone number?"

She thought about that one for a bit, her mouth twisted to one side.

"Okay. Here's an easier one. May I give you my number?"

"I couldn't take that," she said.

"No, please, I insist. I'm not even on the no-call list. I accept telemarketing calls. It's someone to talk to at dinnertime. Here, my card."

He reached in his pocket for a business card, on which was printed only the name Paul Malouf—no company, no e-mail address or fax, just a phone number and street address.

She turned the card over, looking for more information, but saw none.

"Simple, isn't it? A calling card. Like the kind men in Victorian novels put on silver plates when they visit ladies in bodices. You'd look good in a bodice. I could bring you one next time, instead of a jack."

She blushed and turned away, pretending to look at something in the distance.

"It's the classicist in me."

She shook her head.

"Okay, maybe it's the lecher in me. I shouldn't be talking about clothes on your body. At least not until I know your name. What is it, by the way, your name? Or do you want to withhold it until after we're married?"

"What!" The word came out with a sucking in of air. He wondered how she did that.

"Just wanted to see if you were paying attention. Yes, I said married. No, I wasn't serious. But watch out, if I ever see you in a bodice, I might throw caution to the birds."

"To the wind."

"No, I don't like clichés."

"It's Fair."

"What is?"

"My name. I'm Helen Fair."

"Wow."

"And what is that supposed to mean, 'Wow'?"

"It's just, well, I guess, fitting. It goes with Forster and bodices. But I can see why you wouldn't put it on a card. All the bad jokes. Be fair with me, or my fair Helen, and all that kind of thing. It's a very pretty name. I mean that."

She nodded and smiled for the second time since he had met her, a smile he liked even more than the first.

"So, then, Ms. Fair, are going to call me?"

"Most likely, no."

"Is it my bad jokes? My appearance? My boring conversation?"

"I'm simply not comfortable calling a man, at least for social reasons."

"That's fair. Oops, sorry. It's going to be hard avoiding those things. But don't call me socially. Make it a business call of some sort. Ask me to demonstrate how your new jack works."

"Like my old one, I'm sure."

"Maybe you have a dripping faucet."

"And you can repair it?"

"Probably not. But I'd get someone who can, Darrel."

"Who is he?"

"I have no idea. But it's a good name for a plumber."

"You're resorting to humor again."

"And you're using contractions. We're getting somewhere."

"Do you have a pen?"

"Actually, I do." He reached into a pocket of his jacket and held out a pen. "You never know when you might need one."

She took the pen and wrote something on a corner of the white paper holding the flowers, tore it off, and handed it to him. He took the card and read what was on the back side: Helen. 310-573-9190.

He grinned and nodded his head slowly. "Nice card." He hoped he didn't look too much like a cat with feathers in its mouth.

"Home number?" he asked.

She nodded.

"I'm honored. And I shall cherish it. I'll even call it, actually. Thank you."

"You're welcome. I would expect you to."

"So, you'll go out with me again?"

"I suppose yes, I would go out somewhere with you, if you were to ask me."

"Helen Fair, you've made a good choice. If you have any doubts about my character, I'll be happy to offer references. My mother would be a perfect place to start. Talk about a tabula rasa."

"Do you have something in particular in mind as to where we would be going?"

"I hadn't gone that far with it yet. But how would dinner be?"

"Maybe not the best idea. But it's kind of you to offer," she said.

"Lunch?"

"I never understood eating food as a social activity. I realize that places me in a very small minority. But if you think about it, eating is not a particularly attractive thing to watch."

"Especially when you're unaware of the glob of something awful on your teeth and you keep smiling."

"And you wrestle with whether or not to tell the person about it," she added.

Which led Paul to wonder if he had finally met someone as twisted as he was. Of course, that was highly unlikely. In time, she might get there, but parity was too much to hope for at this early point.

"Movies are a problem too," he continued. "It's something better done alone, I think. Why sit in the dark for two hours with someone you can't talk to? And then, what do you do afterward?"

"Go somewhere to eat."

"There you are. No meals. No movies. It's a challenge. But I feel up to it. I'll call you with something specific."

"That would be fine."

"I want you to know, I'm not one of those men who don't call."

"I'm sorry. What does that mean?"

"You're serious. You don't know."

She made a charming gesture that indicated she was serious. And didn't know.

"It's the most common complaint of single women: the man who says, 'I'll call you' and doesn't. Never plans to. But he just doesn't know how to be honest with something like, 'I really can't think of any reason to continue this any further. It was a pleasant enough evening, but I have a deep fear of commitment, so I'll be trying someone else and I probably won't call her again, either. Good night.'"

"I can't say I've had that problem," she said.

"Men *do* call you."

"No. I don't give out my number. As a general rule," she added.

"If I were a normal person, I'd feel pretty good about myself. You broke your rule for me. But as disturbed as I am,

I can convince myself you gave me the number of a Chinese restaurant."

"And now I suppose you'll have to find out for yourself."

"I will, hoping fervently someone doesn't ask, 'Pickup or deliver?'"

"I do have a question. If you still think I have a sinister plan for myself," she said, mimicking his two-fingered arcing jump, "why do you want to see me again?"

"If I do still think that, I'm not really sure whether I want to stop you or join you."

"If I had not been in the subway station, what would you have done when the train approached?"

"You didn't say you had two questions."

"Shall I read something in your evasiveness?"

"That's up to you. The point is, I'm here, and so are you. Beyond that, who knows what might have been, which sounds to me like lyrics to a bad song."

"It's been an interesting morning," she said.

"I disagree. It's been an enjoyable morning. Every minute of it, from old people waiting to mammoths sinking. Gerontology and paleontology, all in one stroll."

"Thank you for breakfast, Paul."

"Thank you for your number, Helen."

He thoroughly liked the sound of his name coming from her lips, and her name from his. He also liked the almost child-like way she waved at him, moving her hand across a plane, as she turned to leave. He handed her the bouquet of flowers.

"And thank you for the flowers. They're quite beautiful."

He wanted to tell her they complemented her beauty, but caution prevailed. "Hope you enjoy them" was sufficient.

He watched her attentively, enjoying the way she unlocked the car door, slid into the seat, and closed the door. He waited while she started the motor, fastened her seat belt, checked the side mirror, and pulled away. He hoped she might look back and offer one more wave, which she did not. But that was all right.

Chapter 8

On the trip back to her home, near the northern edge of Hancock Park, known for its Tudor architecture, the smile on Helen's face could have misled anyone into thinking that there went a happy woman. Helen herself was not aware of her smile until she happened to look into the rearview mirror and reacted as though meeting a stranger. She retracted the smile, but it soon reappeared, beyond her control.

Pulling her white Honda into the driveway and waiting for the garage door to open, she surveyed her tidy home, a small white stucco bungalow with a black tile roof. (It was the black roof that had convinced her to buy the house, the only one she had found that was not topped by Los Angeles red tile.) Her home had inexplicably become more attractive than it had been when she left it just a few hours earlier. In truth, it *was* explicable, but she was not one to acknowledge what had enhanced her view of the world. Even if she were willing, she could quickly convince herself that whatever it was, it would soon fade like the brilliant color of the flowers beside her.

The garage now stood open, but she did not immediately drive into its dark interior. She wanted to stay longer in the bright sunlight, which cast a soft dappling pattern from a large jacaranda tree onto the gleaming front wall. There was a comfort to the outdoors she was reluctant to leave. And there was a familiar sadness to the foreboding, colorless interior of the garage. Something welled up below her sternum and advanced through her chest and into her throat, where it remained, a reminder of the emptiness that lay beyond the deceptive brightness and warmth of the outdoors. She swallowed hard, trying to drive the foreboding back down lest she burst into tears, and drove into the garage. Once inside, having pulled forward until a yellow tennis ball suspended on a string touched her windshield, she stopped the car but did not immediately turn off the ignition. She instead let the car idle, looking through the rearview mirror at a branch of the jacaranda tree, alive with purple-tinged buds that would soon burst into violently colorful bloom. And the something rose again to her throat. This time, she let the tears come forth. She pressed the remote control unit on the sun visor and watched the garage door descend with finality on the proscenium behind her. The only light in the garage came from a bare bulb on the ceiling, like the solitary lamp on a darkened stage from which all signs of fantasy had been stripped. She knew better than to let the motor continue running in the closed garage. Yet she hesitated for a few moments before turning the ignition key to the left. She felt and heard the final rumblings of the motor. The lightbulb turned itself off. And she now sat in silence and darkness, neither of which brought her comfort, but both of which welcomed her with familiarity.

She entered the kitchen through the door at the rear of the garage and stepped into light again, now streaming in through the leaded-glass windows that faced the rear yard and gardens. But it was a light she could only see, not feel the way she had felt it in the marketplace, in the park, near the elderly couple, at the fence enclosing the perplexing statuary, and, at all times, next to Paul, with his odd sense of humor and his obvious, if not awkward, attempts to please her.

The house looked as though it had just been professionally and thoroughly cleaned. The truth was, though, that it looked that way on any given day, even though Helen's cleaning woman only came once every two weeks. On those days, there was barely enough to keep the woman busy for the full four hours.

Helen stood at the black granite countertop looking wistfully out at her garden, which was kept as neat as the interior of her home with the help of an elderly Hispanic man named Manuel, who visited more frequently than the cleaning woman—once a week. She looked down at a single banana, a rich yellow with no specks of brown and only a tinge of green at the top. Something troubled her. She placed her hand on the banana and moved it two inches to the left, slightly rotating it. It seemed better placed to her now.

She went through the dining room, in which stood a heavy dark-walnut table whose top shone as though it had been polished daily. Six matching chairs stood at attention, each spaced perfectly from the next. The floors were dark, wide boards of oak, polished well enough to compete with the table. The living room was a step down, through a wide archway. The walls were stark white throughout the entire house, setting off the bright colors of several large contemporary paintings, mostly nonobjective, a few with abstract subject matter, like the one hanging over the stucco fireplace. The subject was a severely angular rendering of a woman, mouth open painfully wide, hair standing wildly on end, screaming out at the world. It could have passed for an angry Modigliani, conceived in a nightmare.

She noticed that the red light on the answering machine, which sat atop a Mission-period desk, was blinking. She quickly stepped over to it and pressed the Play button.

"Good morning, Mees Helen, thees ees Manuel, your gardener."

He had been tending her garden for more than four years, yet he still felt compelled to remind her of his identity whenever he spoke with her.

"I thin Iris bulbs today an' make loose the soil aroun' rose bushes. Hope you like. Bye-bye."

Of course she was always pleased to hear from Manuel. She was fond of him and his gentle manner and appreciative of his devotion to his work and to her. He frequently left brown paper bags of fresh produce from his own garden on her doorstep. When she once tried to pay him for some beautiful, large tomatoes, he refused, seeming injured that she would think he would charge for his gifts.

"End of messages," the wavering electronic voice intoned. She really hadn't expected a call so soon from Paul.

He most likely was not even home yet. And if he was, why on earth would he phone her so soon?

She went back to the kitchen, where she had left the flowers Paul had given her. She methodically made a diagonal cut one inch from the bottom of each stem, even though they had already been trimmed precisely that way. As she ran warm water into a pewter vase, the phone rang. Rather than allow water to drip from her wet hands onto the polished floor, she let the phone ring three times before the answering machine clicked on.

"Hi. This is Paul Malouf."

She smiled to herself, but made no effort to go to the living room and pick up the phone.

"I suppose you're not home yet, wherever that is. But I just wanted to verify that I had the right number. Not that I'm implying you could have written your own phone number wrong. I may have dialed it wrong. But I obviously didn't. And now it's verified. Had I been thinking, I would have hung up as soon as I heard your message, but then, if you're like me, you hate hang-ups. And I really wish I could somehow erase this message, because it's beginning to sound pretty stupid. I'll try you again, and I hope I'll have something more intelligent to say. Have a nice—no, never mind. Good-bye."

He certainly wasted no time in calling, she told herself. But isn't that what she was hoping for? Then she reminded herself of something: getting involved with a man, one who had as dark a view of the world as she had, was probably not the wisest thing to do. That said (to herself), she looked at Paul's card, which was wrinkled and a bit damp from being held in her hand since he gave it to her. She studied the number and wondered if returning his call would be a bad idea. Of course she knew it would be. But that did not stop her from wondering. Why not throw caution to the birds, as he had malaproped, and make the call? Because it would run counter to everything she had agreed with herself to avoid. She picked up the phone, listened to the dial tone, bit her lower lip, poised her finger over the "three" button, and abruptly hung up.

She went back to the kitchen and looked again at the flowers on the counter, checking the lone banana along the way, deciding it would now look better closer to the vase. She recalled the dueling bouquet byplay at the Farmers' Market and the flower-waving between Paul and the old man on the bench. It all brought forth another smile, which, as the fifth of the day, put her far above a full week's quota. And it was barely noon.

The harsh ringing of the doorbell interrupted her reflection. She went to the front door and peered out through the security peephole to be greeted by a tilted, contorted face, eyes bugged wide and tongue hanging out. She had seen it countless times before: her partner Harvey's usual pose.

"Where you been, girl?" he asked as Helen swung the door open.

He stopped to kiss her on the lips and led her into her living room.

"You smell good enough to eat. You have a date? In the morning, for God's sake?"

"It wasn't a date."

"A tryst? An all-nighter? You go."

"I had breakfast," she said. "At the Farmers' Market."

"Congratulations. But the question is, with whom and what kind of night did you have that left you with an empty stomach?"

He glanced over his shoulder into the kitchen and smirked.

"At least the guy had enough class to leave you flowers. Which is more than that jack guy did."

"I had breakfast with him."

"Oh. Then I'm sure that's all it was. A guy like that wouldn't have a clue about getting a woman into bed, unless it was for a nap."

"He was nice to me. Thoughtful."

"Clumsy is my guess."

"He's unsure of himself."

"Great. The insecure leading the unavailable. Did he do anything interesting, like invite you away for a weekend?"

No response.

"Dinner at his apartment?"

A shake of her head.

"No, I imagine he didn't even try to engage your lovely lips. Shook hands, probably."

A nod.

"This is getting too steamy."

He preceded her through the dining room to the kitchen to examine the flowers, stopping to move the banana back where it had been.

"At least they're not half dead. So tell me about breakfast at Le Cirque. Oh, I'm sorry, Farmers' Market, with the birds. Have something special, like grapefruit and yogurt?"

"He doesn't eat healthy."

"There's one point in his favor. Men who eat bran have their heads up their butts. Regularity. How boring is that?"

"What are you doing today?" was her attempt to get him off the subject.

"I'm thinking of taking the boat out. The wind looks like it'll be strong by two. Want to come?"

She always enjoyed going aboard Harvey's sailboat, as long as it remained in the slip.

"I don't think so. But thank you."

"I got this new gadget that's supposed to work better than the wristbands and the patches. It's a hat with some kind of little electronic thing inside that blocks whatever makes you want to throw up. Balance or something."

She looked at him skeptically.

"I'm serious. Hey, if it doesn't work, maybe it'll at least keep aliens from landing on your head."

"I have things I need to do around the house."

He looked around with raised eyebrows. "I can see. You probably haven't polished the floors since before breakfast. I don't have to sail. Want to go to a movie? There's a new Italian picture at the Royal."

"I don't think so. Sorry if I'm a bore."

He approached her and took on a more serious air. "Hey,

it's okay. I just don't want you to stay holed up in this house on your day off. Tuesday mornings are the worst. Most of us come in rested enough to somehow make it through another five days of the mad women of Chaillot. But you always come in with that mask of doom, like you've beaten yourself up emotionally for a straight twenty-four hours. And I know it only happens when you're here. It's bound to. The place doesn't shine because it needs it. It's because you need it. But you can't polish away the demons. I'd give anything if they'd build a freeway ramp here and force you out."

"This is my home."

"It's also your dungeon, as beautiful as it is."

She began to sniffle. And her breathing became more rapid. Harvey knew where to reach, in the drawer beneath the counter, which contained neat stacks of brown paper bags. He pulled one out, opened it up, and handed it to Helen. She took it, nodding her head in thanks, placed it over her mouth and nose, and breathed deeply—a familiar routine for both of them.

He stepped behind her and wrapped his arms around her waist.

"It's okay. Easy, slow breaths."

She complied.

"You know why I do this to you, don't you?"

She nodded, without breaking her rhythm.

"Because I love you."

Another nod.

"Of course, it's a Tristan-Isolde kind of love, you have

to realize." And he squeezed her a little tighter.

"Hah!" was her muffled response into the bag.

"You know you've always wanted me, but you're afraid the sex would be so good, you'd lose your mind." He bumped his groin against her backside playfully, and she pulled away, not so playfully.

She turned around and took a few more slow breaths before removing the bag from her face.

"Better?" he asked.

"Better. But I really do want to stay home. I may go up to Melrose later. Would you like to join me?"

"I can think of better things to do. It's L.A. Culture all over the place. There's a tractor pull in Anaheim."

"What's a tractor pull?"

"You're such a goddamn elitist. But you have a good time on Melrose. Make sure it's a long time, okay? Stay out late. Just don't hang around here too long."

"I'll be fine. Really."

The phone rang again. This time she headed straight for it, nearly losing her balance on the slick flooring as she tap-tapped back through the dining room. She caught the phone before the fourth ring.

"Hello?"

"Am I speaking to Mr. Fair?" It was the voice of a woman who clearly would rather be doing something else for eight dollars an hour.

"Do I sound like a Mister Fair?"

"Sorry, ma'am. You must be Mrs. Fair."

"I am not."

"Are you the lady of the house?"

"I am not a lady. I was, until you interrupted my privacy. But I have two suggestions for you: One, kindly remove my name from the list of people whose homes you are wont to invade."

"I don't *want* to invade your home. I just want to tell you about a wonderful opportunity."

"And that brings me to my second suggestion. Remove your headset."

"Why?" the puzzled woman asked.

"Please. I have no wish to hurt you."

She could imagine the look of disbelief on the woman's face, in some windowless room filled with other home invaders and a sea of computer screens.

"I've taken it off. Now what?" the woman asked warily.

With that, Helen picked up an aerosol can with a plastic horn attached to the top and the words Nautical Air Blaster on the front. She held the horn to the phone and pressed a button on top of the can, which triggered a piercing blast that could be heard, according to the label, from a distance of one mile.

"Jesus Christ, that's loud," said Harvey.

"You promised me it would be," said Helen, who had noticed the device on Harvey's boat and asked where she could buy one.

She put the phone to her ear and heard only the dial tone.

"I may be crazy, but wouldn't it be easier to just hang up on those calls?" asked Harvey.

"I feel a need to send a message."

"You know what Sam Goldwyn told a screenwriter, don't you? 'You wanna send a message, go to Western Union. You wanna have some peace, hang up the friggin' phone.' But I just had a thought. The way you ice-skated to the phone, maybe you're waiting for a phone call from someone other than the aluminum-siding people."

"I don't know what you're talking about."

"Yes you do."

"Well, maybe I do."

"And I'm assuming from that funny little flush of red on your cheeks it's gotten your body heated up a little. Or he has. It's obviously the guy who gave you the cheap flowers." He tilted his head. "Well?"

"Don't attach more importance to a bunch of flowers than they deserve," she said.

"I can assure you I won't. But the question is, how much importance are you placing on them? What do you know about this guy?"

"Not much. He's persistent. A little out of the ordinary."

He looked toward the flowers again. "You'd never know it."

"He's had sadness in his life."

"Now that's out of the ordinary, isn't it? Sweetheart, if you became attracted to all the men who've had sadness in their lives, there'd be a line out front that extended to Bakersfield. Four abreast."

"I can relate to what he's been through."

She was surprised at her need to justify him.

"Let me guess. He's divorced. Maybe more than once. He's not happy with his job. And he spends a lot of time alone. Not exactly a suicide case."

She shot him a look of alarm.

"Wait just a minute. Have I hit on something here? Has he told you he thinks about putting a gun to his head?"

She said nothing, looking like a guilty child.

"He did, didn't he? That line's getting as old as 'My wife never understood me.' Haven't you heard? People who say they're leaping off a tall building are only talking the talk. They don't jump the jump. They want someone to say, 'Oh, please don't do that. Let me help you back from there. My bed or yours?'"

"He's not jumping off a building."

"That's what I'm saying. They don't."

"He's afraid of heights," she said, as though it was perfectly logical.

"Give me a break. I suppose he won't go off a pier because the water's polluted."

Much too close for comfort.

"May we please change the subject?"

"What does this Lochinvar do for a living?"

"He writes."

"A screenwriter? Please say he's not."

"He's not. He happens to write a column for news-papers."

"On what? Where to get bargains on flowers?"

"Advice. To men."

"Wait a minute. In the *L.A. Times*?"

She nodded.

"Syndicated?"

Another nod.

"I know who he is. Man to Man, right? I don't believe it. The guy who writes that column is the same one who brought you a jack? And flowers?" He rolled his eyes.

"How do you know him? You read his column?"

"No, I don't read it."

She smiled a smile of doubt.

"Not on a regular basis."

A smile again.

"I've glanced at it a time or two. Maybe three, that's all."

Helen had a way of knowing when Harvey was stretch-ing the truth or avoiding it altogether. He would usually cross his arms, as he was now doing, or walk to a window and look out, which he did next, pretending that something had caught his attention.

"Did you write to him for advice?" she asked.

"The jacaranda tree is going to bloom pretty soon," he said, looking out the window and acting like he had not heard her.

"You did, didn't you?" she said, approaching him. She

tapped him on the shoulder. "You can't even see the tree from that window. It's all right. There's nothing wrong with seeking advice when something's troubling you."

"You really think I'd do something like that? Join the losers of the world who are on display for the world to see?"

"I don't think they use their names, do they? As I recall, they sign their letters with things like 'Sad in Santa Monica.'"

"Straight in the Closet," he said, looking at the sky now.

She punched him hard on the shoulder. "You did it! You wrote in!"

He winced and rubbed his shoulder. "I figure you'd eventually get it out of me. Okay, now you know."

"It's nothing to be ashamed of. So you write letters to someone who might be able to help."

"*One* letter. A year ago."

"I'm fascinated," she said. "Did he print your letter?"

"Oh, yes, he definitely did."

"And he had some advice for you?"

"In a slightly twisted way. He said I should be concerned that the woman I was dating would show up at my workplace. How was I going to explain my behavior to her? And he turned out to be prescient."

"My God, that's right. What was her name? Roberta?"

He nodded.

"What were the chances that she would walk in, without an appointment, out of all the salons in Los Angeles?"

"They were good enough. She walked right in. And right out again, when she saw me gushing over Mrs. Frankenthauler's new cut."

"You never heard from her?"

"Just once. She called and said she had a good shrink who has helped people with sexual-identity problems. And she hung up on me when I told her I'd like to come over there and show her my true identity. Actually, she hung up when I explained how I'd do that. I said I'd be happy to drive her to the edge of insanity by penetrating every orifice into her body. All six of them."

Helen was puzzled. She silently counted to five on her fingers and stopped.

"The navel. But it's a stretch, I know."

"Oh," she whispered, with a flush.

"Well," he said, his arms folded again.

"Well." She had no idea whatsoever about where to take the conversation, except to end it as abruptly as possible.

"You're not serious about, what is it, a tractor thing in Anaheim, are you?" she asked.

"A pull. No, I think I'll just take the boat out. Last chance."

"Thank you. But I really do want to catch up on things."

"Fair enough. I hope he calls so you can get out of here. If he doesn't, you can always write him a letter signed 'Waiting in West L.A.'"

"Have a nice day, Harvey."

"Screw you, too, sweetheart." He gave her a friendship kiss on the lips and left.

———

Paul sat in his black leather recliner, staring at Doctor Kevorkian. He held the wireless phone in his hand, his finger poised over the "on" button. What had he been thinking? Had he been thinking at all? He was making sure he had the right number? That's what directory assistance is for. No, he was acting like a moonstruck adolescent. He could have simply hung up when he heard her confirming voice. But she most likely had caller-ID or last-call return. And she would know exactly who had called: a forty-four-year-old with seventeen-year-old hormones and a four-year-old brain. He put the phone down and said to the stern-looking doctor on the wall, "We never learn."

The phone rang, sending a jolt of anticipation through his chest. He waited until the fourth ring, to send a message of indifference.

"Hello?"

The indifference was wasted.

"I hope you're writing." The voice was Milton's.

"Just getting ready to."

"You mean your hands were on the keyboard?"

"You're sounding more and more like a truant officer, Milton."

"And you're acting more and more like you've got something on your mind other than your nationally syndicated column and your radio debut. Whatever it is, I hope it's worth it."

"I was trying to get the answer to a question. Do you happen to know how long the suicide clause is in effect in an insurance policy?"

"I didn't even know there was one. You're getting the strangest damn mail lately."

"It's true, there is a clause," said Paul, evasively. He never lied, preferring to instead step around the truth. "I thought it was for one year. If you bought a new policy, you couldn't collect any money if you ended it all within the first twelve months."

"Of course you couldn't. You'd be dead."

"Very funny. You know what I mean."

"Why don't you just toss the letter and focus on something people care about reading? Who wants to hear from some poor sap who's stupid enough to take his own life?"

"Your compassion for the human condition is admirable, Milton."

"We're not in the compassion business. We lighten people's day. They read how bad off some other poor sap is, and they think maybe they're not in such deep shit themselves. You end up giving them a big laugh."

"So I'm a sit-down comic."

"Why do you think millions of people read their horoscope every day? To find hope for everyone else who was born the same month? It's self-interest. 'Maybe I shouldn't tell the boss to shove the job today, because my horoscope tells me I'm about to be recognized for my good work.' There's your help. Some guy who writes that crap saved a foreman a punch in the face."

"That's my point. Maybe I can save somebody's family a couple hundred thousand dollars if he waits a few months before he does himself in."

There was a long pause on the other end. Then, "Wait a minute. So you're not going to try to talk the guy out of offing himself? You're going to tell him to just take a rain check until he can hit the big insurance payoff? That's sick."

"It's entertainment. Isn't that what you want?"

"Just tear up the letter, will you please? Put him in the thank-you-for-your-letter-we-cannot-answer-or-print-every-one-we-receive pile. And write about something people care about."

"And I'll nominate you for the humanitarian-of-the-year award."

"'See Paul write. Count Paul's money that he makes doing it. And now hear Paul on radio, where he'll make even more money.' That's as humanitarian as it gets. Now, when do I get the radio show memo you owe me?"

"As soon as I finish today's barrel of laughs. Did I tell you about the letter from the guy who likes to bowl with dwarfs?"

"Is it a club?"

"No, Milton, he doesn't join them for bowling. He uses them. As bowling balls."

"Now that's funny, in a sick way, but funny," said Milton.

"It's disgusting," said Paul.

"Use it."

"I can't."

"And why not?"

"Because I made it up."

A long sigh. Then, "Write, Paul, write."

"Hang up, Milton, hang up."

And he finally did.

Paul proceeded to busy himself as best as he could, given the distraction that had entered his world in the form of Helen of Troy. He chose a few letters that he knew would meet with Milton's approval. One was from a woman, an anomaly of sorts, since the column was generally perceived as off-limits to females. Paul regretted this perception and frequently tried to change it with invitations to women to write to him.

> *Dear Paul,*
>
> *I realize your column is like a men's club, yet I feel compelled to write you about a problem my husband is having, one he is reluctant to speak even privately about, let alone in a newspaper for all the world to see. It's a sexual problem. Until recently, we enjoyed frequent and satisfying intimacy. But then a strange problem appeared. Whenever my husband would near*

climax, he would be seized by uncontrollable sneezing. Needless to say, there is nothing I can think of that's more distracting than a man moaning ecstatically along with his partner and then suddenly sneezing so violently that I have, more than once, landed on the floor. He is too humiliated to discuss the problem with a doctor or an allergist. My hope is that if you publish this letter and my husband sees it, he will assume another couple somewhere in America has the same problem, which might lower his resistance to seeking help. And, of course, if you can shed any light on the matter, that would be deeply appreciated.

Floored

He highlighted in yellow key sentences and crafted his response:

Dear Floored,

My guess is that the problem is triggered by an emotional response to lovemaking rather than an allergy. It's difficult to imagine your husband has suddenly become allergic to you or to sex, unless you've recently repainted the bedroom or acquired new sheets or drapes. But I can't imagine that if he's allergic to them, the response would only come …

He stopped and deleted the last word.

> *the response would* arise *only at the point of cli-*
> *max. My suggestion is to consult a psychothera-*
> *pist. Maybe you should first do it …*

He stopped again and deleted the last two words.

> *you should first* visit *the therapist alone. He*
> *might very well have a comfortable way in which*
> *your husband can lay … can* place *his problem*
> *in front of someone who can help.*

There you go, Milton. Carefully edited for question-able Freudian entendres. Cleansed enough to earn an *M* for mature audiences. That's entertainment.

Chapter 9

It was time for Paul's weekly visit with his mother. It pained him deeply to accept that he would never again enjoy the intelligent conversations that had created a strong bond between mother and son. She was his only remaining family member, but, in fact, little of her remained other than her vacated physical shell. Behind the blank gaze lay a mass of scrambled, atrophied circuits that would permit her nothing more cognitive than a smile at some childish gift he would bring her—a bag of candy corn or licorice nibs (she shunned Godiva, which she once gushed over with delight). He would look into her still-beautiful, pale-blue eyes for a hint of recognition. But all she seemed to see was some other man from her past, real or imagined. Or, sometimes she would see a boy child of two years, whom he assumed might have once been he.

Cheap candy in hand, he got into his car in the Rite Aid parking lot and continued his journey to the assisted-living center that looked so inviting from the outside but was so depressing within. As he was accustomed to doing each week, he found himself sinking into a dark pit. Unlike the mammoths of La Brea, he knew what he was sinking into and where it would lead him. Yet he could not—or chose not to—step around or back away from it, like the boy in his recurrent dreams, frozen in delicious fear on railroad tracks that carried a rushing locomotive toward him.

He tried his usual ploy to override his depression: whistling as he drove. But it had no effect on his dark mood. He only fooled nearby motorists who happened to glance his way. They could not have known that he was whistling a dirge.

On this particular day, he decided on a detour before visiting his mother. He had recently read that people with dementia frequently respond better to animals than to humans. Now that had intrigued him, since he had long since concluded that his greatest problem had to do with the humans he interacted with. His was not a problem of memory loss, which he sometimes found unfortunate, but he wondered if both he and his mother might find some comfort in the company of an animal, a domestic one. Cats were out of the question, since he found them far too judgmental for his liking. Dogs, on the other hand, seemed far more accepting, and both he and his mother had a good deal that needed accepting. There was no way, of course, that his mother could have a dog living in her room. It was forbidden, along with most other comforts, such as stereos, TVs, and DVD players, which posed dangers of electrocution. He had assured the manager of guest services (i.e., camp commandant), a woman with a permanent disingenuous smile, that his mother would not take her TV into the bathtub, but to no avail. Rules were for the safety of guests (i.e., inmates), she said. Bull crap, they were for making life easier for the caregivers (i.e., the screws).

Further discussions with the commandant revealed that pets were allowed to visit as long as they were on leashes, would be kept out of common areas, and stood no higher than twenty-four inches. When he asked why tall dogs were the objects of discrimination, the ever-smiling overseer acted as though she had not heard the question and wished Paul a nice day.

So Paul was venturing into new territory today, to a place located just off La Cienega Boulevard under the Santa Monica Freeway. It was the Los Angeles Pet Adoption League, whose acronym, LAPAL, sounded like a dog food. Or a dog.

The exterior of the large one-story building, unlike his mother's assisted-living center, was not particularly welcoming. There was too much chain-link fencing, and a tall, ominous smokestack that rose at least another story into the sky. Paul felt a twinge of foreboding at the sight of the stack, the same kind of foreboding he felt whenever he saw the commandant's grimacing smile.

The interior of the building was far more inviting. A pleasant, matronly woman wearing a badge that identified her as a volunteer smiled at Paul and said cheerfully, "Good morning, sir. I hope you're here to visit our available friends."

"As a matter of fact, I am."

He forgave the woman her exuberance and her use of

the word *friends*.

"We have quite a few special ones. Are you looking for a puppy or an adult?"

"An adult would probably be best," he said, as he pictured little puppies wagging their tails and urinating everywhere, including on the lobby carpet at the center. "And no taller than twenty-four inches." He thought how absurd he must have sounded. "It's not my requirement. A rule at the place he'd be visiting."

"You said *he*. That narrows it down further. A male dog, no taller than twenty-four inches."

"But about the height: they didn't specify whether the measurement had to be taken standing or sitting or lying. So a dog with twenty-four-inch legs and a twenty-four-inch body would pass lying down, wouldn't you think?"

"I'm not quite sure I follow you," she said.

"Do you have any lying-down twenty-fours I could meet?"

"I'm sure we do. If you'll just let me see your driver's license, we can get started."

He wondered why his driver's license was needed. Were there pet-adoption impersonators out there?

The woman made a few notations on a log sheet, checked his license, and looked up at him. "The picture doesn't do you justice," she said. "You look so sad in it, like someone who could use the company of a new friend."

He smiled patiently, though he wished the woman would simply let him get on with his visit before he changed his mind about pet adoption.

"There," she finally said. "Just pin this badge on and go through the door over there."

She pointed to a heavy steel door with a small glass window, similar to most of the doors at his mother's current residence.

"Just follow the red paw prints to the available dogs. And enjoy your search for a new friend."

He clipped on the acetate-covered badge that proclaimed he was a Visiting Friend, proceeded through the heavy door, and followed the red paws painted along the gray walls. His approach triggered a chorus of canine voices, from the most diminutive squeaking yelps to the most intimidating deep-throated barks and snarls. He passed a beagle with moping eyes, his chest sagging almost to the concrete floor of his kennel, drool dripping from his jowls. Next was a German shepherd who paced back and forth and then lunged, teeth bared, at the glass that stood protectively between him and Paul. A pair of pathetic-looking black mongrels that resembled Romulus and Remus stood silently observing Paul as he walked by. Then he was stopped by what looked like an interesting prospect, albeit a very large one. His coat was a shaggy gray and white. The card on the kennel described the dog as Clyde, an Irish wolfhound mix. It looked as though he would barely meet the twenty-four-inch limit lying down. Clyde slowly got to his feet on legs that were easily another two feet high. He eyed Paul and wagged a long tail that, in itself, was at least another twenty-four inches.

As Paul studied the animal, a worker holding a leash approached. "Interested in Clyde?" the young, smiling man asked. Dressed in a denim work shirt and jeans, he wore a badge that identified him as Friend Attendant.

"I think so," Paul replied. "What can you tell me about him?"

"A great dog."

"Housebroken?" Paul asked.

"Yes, he is," said the attendant.

As if on cue, Clyde seemed to smile as he drew his rear legs forward under his body, arched his back, and proceeded to drop a few large pieces of excrement onto the concrete floor, which prompted Paul to turn to the attendant inquisitively.

"They don't consider their kennels houses," said the attendant. "Would you like to meet him?"

"How do I do that?"

"You can take him out to the bonding yard and have some time with him."

"I guess the bonding yard it is," Paul said.

He could not believe he was going to a something called a bonding yard to meet a dog that was housebroken, except in his own house.

The yard was round with a concrete floor and enclosed by a six-foot-high chain-link fence. Paul wondered if the circular construction was intended to keep dogs from cornering visitors rather than bonding with them. The volunteer led the big panting dog through the gate into the yard and had to struggle to keep him from going right back out.

"Come on in," said the volunteer, grunting at trying to restrain Clyde. "Hurry."

Paul entered the yard, feeling foolish. The feeling quickly gave way to apprehension when the volunteer squeezed himself out of the gate, which he shut in Clyde's face.

"Be a good boy, Clyde," the volunteer said. "This is your chance to go home with somebody."

Now the two of them, Clyde and Paul, were alone in what felt very much like a cage. The dog ignored Paul and wandered to the far side of the yard. He arched his back again and dropped yet another load of feces.

"Come on, boy," Paul said in the friendliest voice he could muster.

Clyde ignored him and instead barked at the sky.

"Clyde, here, come on fella."

He clapped his hands and then bent to place them on his knees.

The dog looked up at him and, as if realizing for the first time that someone was enclosed with him, galloped across the yard barking and lunged at Paul, planting his two large paws on his shoulders and shoving him back against the fence. Reflexively, Paul held up his left hand. That turned out to be a painful mistake, as Clyde apparently mistook Paul's arm for a tree limb and grabbed it with his enormous mouth. The second mistake Paul made was to pull his arm out of Clyde's mouth, because the dog's teeth were closed down on it. He felt the pain of Clyde's teeth dragging across the flesh of his arm, digging several long gashes along the way.

"Down, boy, down," Paul said, watching the parallel rivers of blood rise to the surface of his forearm. Somehow he got Clyde to back off and, fearful someone might be watching from within the building, he patted the dog's enormous head and said, "Good boy, good boy," thinking to himself, *Stupid goddamn oaf, can't tell an arm from a stick.*

"How are you two getting along?" It was the hopeful voice of the returned volunteer standing outside the gate to the yard.

"Fine, just fine," said Paul.

"Doesn't look so fine," said the volunteer. "What happened to your arm?"

"Just scratched it."

"You're bleeding."

Paul looked at his arm. The crimson rivers were overflowing, sending crimson droplets down onto the gray concrete. "Yes, it looks like I am."

"Did he attack you?"

"No, that's not it. I called him, and he came to me. My arm found its way into his mouth. When I tried to take it out, I guess he didn't realize it was still closed, his mouth."

The volunteer looked increasingly troubled as he gingerly opened the gate and slid inside. "That wasn't a very friendly thing to do," he scolded from his safe distance across the yard. He warily eyed Clyde, who looked back and forth between Paul and the volunteer, wagging his tail and drooling onto the concrete. Paul wondered if the dog liked the taste of his arm and was considering going back for seconds.

"We'd better get you inside and treat your wounds," the volunteer said.

Paul wanted to simply leave the bonding yard and the entire premises of the Los Angeles Pet Adoption League far behind. But the volunteer explained that there were strict rules about reporting and treating any injuries to visitors. It had to do with liability and safeguards against rabies. *Wonderful*, thought Paul. *Now I'm going to foam at the mouth and bay at the moon.*

As he followed the volunteer along the narrow hallway of the shelter, droplets of Paul's blood littered the floor, complementing the red paw prints on the wall. It was a perfect color match and told a graphic story: follow the red paws to the dogs, follow the red drops back out.

"Oh my goodness, what do we have here?" asked the friendly woman at the reception desk.

"What we have here is a misunderstanding between man and beast," said Paul.

"Clyde did it," added the volunteer.

"One of our little friends?" she asked.

"No, one of your big friends," said Paul. "But it wasn't what it appears to be. He didn't actually attack me."

"Whatever it was, you'll have to speak with the director and, I imagine, our resident nurse."

"You have a nurse?" asked Paul. "Does this happen often?"

"Goodness no," she said through her smile. "It's a state law. Whenever you have a mix of animals and people under the same roof, you must have a medical professional on hand. You know how things are in California."

Paul assumed the woman was referring to all the laws and regulations protecting people and animals against virtually every possible threat. He once covered for the newspaper the filming of a political commercial in which a chicken was the star performer. Paul was fascinated by the required presence of a registered chicken wrangler and two state humane officers. When he asked one of the officers what dangers he was protecting the chicken against, the man told him with a straight face, "He could be overworked and get too fatigued." To which the other officer added, "Tired chickens make a lousy supper." The wrangler also explained that the chicken is the dumbest animal in the world, with a pea-sized brain. "These film people got to act fast on every take. A trained chicken can only remember what it's supposed to do for about two minutes. Then it gets erased from that pea brain of his, and you got to train it all over again."

Recalling the chicken, Paul wondered how much room Clyde's brain took up in that enormous head of his. Mistaking his kennel for a toilet or Paul's arm for a tree limb offered clues.

"Oh, that doesn't look too bad," said the nurse, studying Paul's bleeding arm. "It could have been worse."

What a comfort, Paul thought, looking around the small office. A fortyish woman dressed in blue scrubs and wearing a stethoscope around her neck, the nurse looked overqualified for her role of checking occasional dog bites.

"Do you only see people?" he asked.

"I'm sorry?"

"Just curious. Do you take care of the animals too?"

"I'm a registered nurse, not a veterinarian," she said, obviously taking offense.

"Of course. I wondered if there was some doubling up, like a doctor who also has a law degree, that sort of thing."

She shook her head. "You need a tetanus shot, unless you've had one in the past three years."

"I don't know if I've ever had one," he said. "What about rabies?"

"There hasn't been a documented case of rabies in California in fifteen years."

He wondered about the undocumented ones, but he also knew rabies is generally caused by bites from bats and squirrels, neither of which he had considered adopting to keep his mother company.

"Shall we?" asked the nurse, who had already picked up a syringe and squirted a drop into the air.

"Right now?"

"It's as good a time as any. In fact, it's the best time, before any infection can set in."

"What kind of infection?"

"Lockjaw."

Which prompted a curious vision for Paul of being unable to open his mouth and trying to speak through clenched teeth.

"Just what is lockjaw, other than what the name says it

is?" he asked.

"Very unpleasant is what it is. The clamped jaw is just the most familiar part of it. You go into spasms, and your head is forced back." She illustrated by forcing her own head back, teeth clenched. "Then comes paralysis. Your lungs can stop functioning. Then it's fatal."

"Fatal? If I don't get the shot?"

"It could well be," she said, unclenching her teeth.

"Interesting," said Paul, wondering if his misfortune might lead to a fortunate alternative to subways and piers.

"Is it painful?" he asked, looking at the needle she held in the air.

"You'll hardly feel it. Just a little stick in the arm."

"No, I mean the lockjaw business. The lungs and all that."

"Oh, I imagine it must be. It's suffocation. A terrible way to go."

So much for that alternative.

"Okay, I'll take the little stick in the arm."

The nurse seemed to relish the moment, as though she did not have much of an opportunity to save people from painful death in her role at LAPAL's headquarters.

"Do you have a preference of an arm?" she asked.

"Would it work better in the arm Clyde wanted?"

"Only if that would make you feel better," she condescended. "It just needs to get into your system. It could work as well in your rear end."

Paul chose not to drop his pants, which would merely

aggravate his humiliation, and offered his right upper arm, just for the balance of things. The nurse had been right; he barely felt the needle go in and out.

"You do nice work," he said to the nurse, who ignored the compliment.

Instead, she tossed the syringe in a red plastic bin with various warnings on the lid and placed an adhesive strip on the spot on his upper arm.

"You may get a sore arm, but nothing more than that," she said. "Now let's clean up those wounds."

She studied the evenly spaced slashes, which still seeped blood, and announced, "You could get them stitched, but I don't think it's necessary. The only reason you might is to avoid scarring. But with all that hair on your arm, I doubt they'd be that noticeable. It's your call."

Paul opted to go stitchless. A few scars beneath the hair could serve as useful reminders that introducing a dog into his life was not at all a good idea. The nurse then proceeded to cleanse the wounds with something that stung. She methodically wrapped about ten inches of his forearm in gauze, which, by the time she finished, was stained by several bright-red spots as blood seeped through.

"There," she finally said, and handed him a prescription. "This is for penicillin. Take two a day for five days. Be sure to finish it all. It will prevent an infection in the wound. Change the bandage once a day until there's no more seepage. Then you can take it off altogether. Any questions?"

"What about the dog?"

"He doesn't need a shot. He'll be fine."

He wondered if she was trying to be funny, but humor didn't seem to be her forte.

"I meant, what will happen to him?"

"He'll be kept in isolation for ten days and monitored for rabies. They'll also want to see if he displays any more aggressive behavior."

"If he does?"

"Well, that's for management of the league to decide."

"They won't do anything drastic to him, will they?"

"Only if it's necessary," she said.

Paul felt a sadness at imagining the big, clumsy dog's life being terminated for what was merely a minor offense against humanity.

"Is something bothering you?" the nurse asked.

"I don't believe in capital punishment," he answered. "Unless of course it's self-inflicted."

She stared at him as if he were some sort of specimen in nursing school. "We don't think of it quite that way. And what exactly do you mean, 'self-inflicted'?"

"It's not important. Thank you for the shot and this very nice bandage."

"Are you talking about suicide?"

No response.

"I think you are. You know, there's help available for that."

"That's what I understand. The Hemlock Society, for one."

"Good heavens, no. That's not what I meant," she said. "There are suicide-prevention groups. In fact, I volunteer for one, Jump to Jesus."

"That's a catchy name. Instead of jumping in front of a train, you tell people to jump over to Jesus, right?"

"Yes, to choose life with him rather than death without him," she said.

"What about Muslims, Jews, and maybe atheists? Where do they jump?"

She thought about that one. Then, "We welcome everyone. If they're prepared to accept Christ, of course."

"Of course. It's totally equal opportunity. Like, 'Don't jump to the wrong conclusion.' What do you think?"

"You may enjoy ridiculing us, but in the end you'll see who has the last laugh."

"You'll laugh at people who hit the pavement instead of Jesus?"

"Good day, Mr. Malouf. I really have to get back to my work."

He worried what that work might be and took his leave.

———

As he parked his car in the assisted-living center lot, Paul realized his bandaged arm would likely cause curiosity or concern, but then realized his mother would not think anything of it, given the state of her mind. But, on the other hand, the smiling commandant might notice.

And, of course, she did. "Mr. Malouf, have you been in an accident?" she asked, momentarily looking up from the computer screen on which she was focused, still wearing the programmed smile.

"Nothing serious. Just an animal attack."

"Not on our grounds, I hope." She click-clacked something on her keyboard.

"Just a tiger that was hiding in a tree. He pounced on me, but I managed to fight him off."

"That's nice," she said, still smiling, still focusing on the computer screen in front of her, confirming that she never heard what anyone in the facility, patient or visitor, said. "Don't forget to sign in," she reminded him automatically.

Paul obliged, signing the guest register, the logic of which, if it were a requirement for security reasons, escaped him. Who would want to sneak into such a place? Or, who would want to sneak someone out of it?

"Hi, Mom," he said as cheerfully as he could, opening the door to his mother's compact living space, about the size of a small hotel room. It was called a suite, but that was a stretch. He had crammed too many of his mother's possessions into the limited space in an attempt to give her the comfort of familiarity: her collection of dolls, a profusion of family photos, and the many knickknacks collected over the years. But the attempt was to little avail, since she was barely aware of her surroundings and frequently asked who the people in the pictures were, including him, her late husband,

and her deceased parents.

"Randall?" she asked, surveying Paul. "How did you get here? My husband will be home any minute."

He had no idea who Randall was, although he has was reasonably certain who his mother thought he had been: one of many imagined lovers, including Peter, Oscar, Hugh, and Max, along with the other figments of her dementia. She'd mistaken Paul for each of them during various visits. The irony was, of course, that she had never had an affair in all the years she was married to Paul's father. But she had once written a never-published novella about a woman who had an endless series of clandestine lovers—twenty-six, to be exact—each named for a letter of the alphabet, from Adam to Zebulon.

"Mom, it's me, Paul." He somehow could not bring himself to stop trying to jog his mother's memory enough to remind her she had a son. He was willing to assume whatever identity she preferred, which did not threaten his own sense of self. But he continued to hold out false hope that her condition could somehow improve.

"Oh, you must be Xavier. I'm sorry. There were so many."

Startling images came flying at Paul, visions of his mother in the fiction she had written, in bars, in cars, or, perish the thought, even in hotel rooms. He also saw his late father sitting in his recliner, engrossed in the *New Republic*, acting as though no one, at least in his universe, could possibly be in cars, bars, or beds with people other than those to whom they were married.

"I'm not Xavier, Mom."

"Who's Xavier?" she asked. Then, "Did you bring candy?"

"Yes, Mom, here."

He held out the bag of candy, lighting up his mother's eyes and bringing a smile to her face. But the smile disappeared when she saw the bandage on his arm.

"What happened to you? I told you riding that bike is dangerous. I don't know why your father bought it for you. You're not ready."

Paul felt a surge of hope, although he was conditioned to accept it as fleeting. Something could trigger in his mother a flash of memory, but it could disappear just as quickly as it arrived.

"I know, Mom. I should listen to you. Bikes are dangerous. But it was a dog."

"What dog?"

"I don't know. A dog I met, and it bit me. It was an accident."

He should have realized his explanation was too complex.

"You can't bring a dog into the house. I told you. We have a cat and a parakeet. That's enough. But what happened to your arm, Max? Did you cut yourself?"

Now he was Max, from the middle of the imagined alphabet soup of suitors.

"Would you like to have a dog visit you?" Paul asked.

His mother lowered her head and seemed to be trying to understand his question. Then, "Paul had a dog once. But it bit him on the arm. And he was always falling off his bike. Do you know Paul?"

He fought back tears along with anger. This was once a vital, inquiring woman, a writer, a lover of books. Yet now she could not read the menu in the dining room. She could only write the simplest of words on a greeting card, in the scrawl of a young child, mostly unintelligible. How eminently unjust to rob a woman of a mind that she was capable of putting to good use. Although he realized the selfishness of his fears, he could not resist projecting her fate onto himself. Is this what the future held for him? If the heart attack that took his father did not strike him down, would he be assigned to this landfill of humanity, looking forward only to a bag of cheap candy?

The rest of his visit consisted of very little that resembled conversation. If he asked how she was feeling, the answer was always the same: "As good as can be expected." If he inquired of the food, again, the answer never varied: "Terrible." What had she had for dinner? "Who knows. It's all the same." Did she need anything? "Candy." He knew better than to ask her if she had been trying to read or had returned to her knitting. Her days were spent in the resident lounge in front of the large-screen television set, although she mostly slept there, unaware of what was broadcast. Her nights, thankfully, brought a full eight hours or more of sleep. Did she dream of pleasant memories she could not process in her wakeful mind? There was no way to tell, since, if she did, she would not recall it.

He concluded every visit with the same heavy pain, which he tried to mask with a smile and with his standard farewell. "Got to go, Mom. I love you."

Her only response was a nod and a puzzled look.

One of his mother's doctors, discussing his mother's condition, had once said to him, "There are worse things that could have happened to your mother than this." To which he angrily replied, "Name one." The doctor could not. Nor could Paul, who stood up and said, "Why aren't you people finding a cure for this cursed end stage of life?"

"We're working on it."

"Not hard enough," said Paul.

To which the doctor could only come up with a sigh and a shake of his head in reply.

Chapter 10

"Hello, Helen. This is Paul."

"This is a surprise."

"Why is that?" he asked. "You weren't expecting to hear from me?"

"Not this soon."

"Oh, I'm sorry. I completely forgot about the waiting period. I'll try you next month."

"No, please don't do that," she said.

"So I'm not being premature or presumptuous or any of the other *pres*?"

"No. Just surprising."

"I always call."

"Who?"

He wondered if she was playing with his head. "I meant, I'm not one of those men women complain about, the ones who never call."

"I have no such complaints."

"All right then, moving along, how are you?" he asked.

"I'm well. Thank you for asking."

"You're welcome. I'm well too. Actually, not completely

well."

"You're ill?"

"No," he answered. "Just slightly wounded. By a dog."

"How terrible. A dog attacked you?"

"Not really. He was trying to play with me. A game of keep-away. With my arm."

"Are you in the hospital?"

"No, I got away with a few ugly slashes is all."

"I have a dog," she said.

"This was a really big dog. Irish wolfhound."

"Mine is a Great Dane."

"Which makes yours bigger than mine. Does he like to play with people's arms?"

"No. But he *is* attracted to genitalia. Only in men, though, even though he's a male dog."

"Never goes for women?"

"Not really."

"I certainly have no problem with that. You're born what you are."

"Who is?"

"You know. Orientation."

"It's a dog," she said.

Paul could not believe where the conversation was going. More important, he was concerned about where it was not going. He had called for the express purpose of asking Helen to go out with him again. But he worried that he might not get to that point.

He decided on directness, away from talk of big dogs.

"I had a reason for calling, if you can imagine."

"Yes?"

"I'd like to see you again."

If only she knew how conflicted that wish made him feel, which, to his own surprise, had nothing to do with his sexuality. Here he was, with neither a plan nor a hope for anything specifically involving the future. Yet he was driven by a genuine desire to begin something with this woman, who had the most charming way of speaking in circles that he longed to enter.

"When, actually, would you like to see me again?" she asked.

At least she didn't ask why this time.

"I had in mind tomorrow evening."

"Tomorrow evening." It wasn't a question.

"Yes. Are you busy then?"

"No. I'm rarely busy in the evening."

"Which means what, exactly?"

"Only that I have no plans."

"Well, that's a start. Now, the next question is, since you're not going to be busy, would you like to spend the evening doing something with me?"

"What would that be?"

"Since you don't like eating in public, I've come up with a different idea. Sightseeing."

There was a pause that told Paul she was either having difficulty grasping the notion or she was trying to find a way to ask him not to call again.

Finally, she said, "Do you mean buying one of those maps to the stars' homes?"

Did she really think he would do something as tacky as ogling homes of the famous? "I mean seeing Los Angeles from above."

"How would one do that?"

"In a helicopter."

"You have one?"

"No," he said. "But I can rent one. With a pilot. It's an amazing way to view the city at night."

"Is it dangerous?"

"I certainly hope so," he said, and then winced at what her reaction might be. Interestingly, there was none.

"I must say, that's an intriguing invitation. I've never ridden in a helicopter. It's generous of you."

"And?" he asked.

"And what?"

"And would you like to go?"

"Yes, I would, if you don't think I'd get in the way of things."

He had no idea what she meant by that. How does someone get in the way of something that had been planned for her? Better not to ask.

"Good. I can arrange for the pilot to meet us at Santa Monica Airport a little before sunset. Which means I should probably pick you up at seven."

"At my house?" There was a hint of concern in her voice.

"That would seem to make sense, unless you're planning to be somewhere else."

"No, I'll be home, thank you."

"Would you now like to take the next big step and give me your address?"

Another pause. Then, "I suppose I should do that."

"Do you have a pencil?" she asked.

"No. But is a pen all right?"

She proceeded to tell him where she lived, and then followed with a detailed explanation of the best route to her door, including a description of a lawn display of statues of Snow White and all seven dwarfs, which, much to his relief, were not in her yard, but in one directly across the street.

"I'll see you at seven, then," he finally said.

"Is there anything I should bring?"

"Just a valid passport."

"What? Where are we going?"

"Relax. It's just a joke. If you have binoculars, you might want to bring them."

"Will opera glasses do?"

"Of course," he said, picturing her in an elegant evening dress, seated in a box at a grand opera hall, peering through bejeweled glasses. It aroused something warm within him.

"Good night, Helen."

"Yes, thank you. Good night."

———

"He's taking you *where*?" Harvey's eyes bulged in disbelief.

"On a helicopter tour of the city. Why do you find that so strange?" said Helen, trying to compete with the whir of hair dryers without raising her voice.

"Oh, nothing's strange about that at all, sweetheart. It's just an everyday kind of date. What happened to old-fashioned ideas like dinner or movies or Rollerblading, for God's sake? Helicopters are dangerous."

"Life is dangerous," said Helen.

"All the more reason not to push the ever-lovin' envelope any further. Does he have a license to fly one of those things?"

"No."

"Oh, that's great. Just great."

Helen put her hands on his shoulders. "Listen to me, Harvey. He doesn't need a license. He's hiring a pilot and renting the helicopter."

"I liked this guy better when he bought you cheap flowers and an even cheaper breakfast. What's next? Skydiving?"

"Of course not. He can't stand heights," said Helen.

"So he takes people out in helicopters. That makes a hell of a lot of sense."

"Harvey! When you're done chatting, would you pleeeeeze take this damn oven off my head, before I catch on fire?" bellowed a nearby smoky-voiced woman draped in a black salon cape, her head covered by a plastic dryer.

Harvey turned to the woman, smiled sweetly, and said,

"I want to leave it on long enough to make a fricassee out of your pea brain."

She nodded and smiled, having not heard a word he said over the din.

"You'd better take care of her," Helen said.

"You'd better take care of you. This guy obviously isn't planning to."

"He wants to see more of me."

"I'll bet he does. Has he tried to get your clothes off yet?"

"Of course not," she replied indignantly.

"Well, you might want to check out that helicopter. See if it's a stretch one, with a big backseat that folds down. Where exactly is he planning to take you?"

"I don't know. But he told me to bring a passport."

Harvey's eyes grew wider. "That's it. Mexico. Hasta la vista, baby. Pack a diaphragm."

"Harvey, he was joking."

"Right. So was Ted Bundy."

"Harveeeeeeeeee! I'm burning up over here!"

"I guess I'd better take care of Joan of Arc." Harvey shouted, "I'm coming, sweetheart!"

"How nice for you," she replied. "Now get your cute little ass over here."

———

Helen did something uncharacteristic that afternoon. Each time she had a few minutes between attending to clients and dealing with staff, she stood in front of the mirror at her station and fussed with her hair, trying variations on her usual style. One time it was a sweep straight back with the help of some gel, which made her look, she was convinced, like a greyhound. Another time, she tried scrambling her hair, only to realize that was exactly what it looked like: scrambled hair. Her last attempt was spraying in some bright-gold coloring, which, with the red, made her hair look like a USC football helmet. Fortunately, the coloring was removable. She would end the day back to her normal, albeit to her, boring style. It was, after all, how she had looked the three times Paul had seen her.

She chided herself that it mattered not how she appeared in a man's eyes. After all, wasn't meeting someone the furthest thing from her mind just two days ago? Yes, but she had to admit that the idea had begun to move closer to her mind. She found herself on the horns of a dilemma, although she wasn't clear about the metaphor. Why did dilemmas have horns? Who knew? Who cared? In three hours she was going to see this man for the fourth time, and she had better wash out the gold coloring and think about something to wear. What does one wear in a helicopter? Surely not those unflattering olive-green leisure suits with all the straps and buckles. A dress would be out of the question, as would heels. Pants, of course. Flats too. Her black leather jacket? It might add an aviation look. She warned herself to think less of her wardrobe and focus on getting out of the salon and home in time to shower, change, fuss with her hair a little more, and make sure her last will and testament was somewhere easy to find.

At precisely seven o'clock, the doorbell rang. Helen had been waiting in her bedroom, the farthest point in the house from the front door, so it would not seem as though she had been waiting at the door. She stopped on her way through the dining room to circle the table, adding a few extra steps before crossing the living room. She peered through the peephole in the door and saw an eyeball peering back at her. Assuring herself that the eyeball belonged to Paul, she opened the door. She was shocked to see not Paul, but a tall, thin man with curly red hair and a few days' growth of beard, wearing a T-shirt with the logo Lightning Delivery. He held a white padded envelope.

"Package for you. Sign here." He thrust the envelope toward her with one hand and offered a receipt pad and pen with the other.

She took the envelope, the pad, and pen, juggled all three of them until she could scribble her name, and noticed Paul standing a few feet behind the delivery man. He waved at her, smiling. She nodded back.

"I was taken aback by your eyeball" was all she could think to say to the man.

"My eyeball?" he asked.

"You were peering in," she said, pointing to the peephole.

"Just trying to see if anyone was home, know what I'm sayin'? A lot of people aren't this time of day."

"Of course. Yes, thank you," she said, handing the receipt pad and pen back to him.

She saw the sender's name on the receipt, Helen of Troy, and knew immediately it was one of Harvey's little surprises. She tore open the envelope and saw the top of a small box labeled 10 Super-Sensitive Condoms and a bottle of pills, and quickly closed it back up, holding it tightly in her hand.

The messenger turned and nearly bumped into Paul. "Strange night," said the man as he walked back down the sidewalk to his truck.

Paul stepped forward. "Hello."

"Hello," she echoed.

"Important delivery?"

"Delivery?"

She held up the envelope and quickly dropped her arm back down. "Oh, this? No, just something from the salon that someone thought I needed."

She looked at her wrist, which, this time, actually had a watch wrapped around it. "You're on time," she said, seemingly flustered.

"I usually am. Sometimes I'm early, which probably isn't such a good idea."

"Why not?"

"It can look like you don't have enough to do. Or that you're too eager."

"Is either the case with you?"

Ignoring her question, he said, "You look ready for a ride in a helicopter."

They looked like a nightclub act: both were dressed completely in black, she in a black turtleneck sweater, pants, and sensible shoes, he in a black polo shirt, black jeans, and what looked like black bowling shoes. He also wore a black leather jacket.

"Would you like a glass of water?" Helen asked, going back into the house.

But he remained on the porch, not sure whether he had been invited in or if she was planning to bring water out to him. "No, thanks. There aren't any restrooms on the helicopter."

She popped her head back into the doorway. "What did you say?"

"Nothing important. No, I'm not thirsty, thank you."

"Don't you want to come in?" she asked.

"Yes, I do. I wasn't sure that was the plan." And he followed her in.

He looked around the living room, at the step-up dining room and the kitchen beyond, noticing the sheen on everything, nodding. "Everything gleams," he said.

She looked at him, puzzled.

"The floors, the furniture, all so polished."

"Is that not all right?"

"Oh, it's very nice, in fact. I'm admiring it all. You have a lustrous home."

"Thank you. Would you like to sit down?"

"Sure." He chose the brown leather sofa.

"But maybe not." She caught him in midair, her words prompting him to straighten up again. "If it's time to go."

He looked at his watch, which had the right time. "I guess it is."

"Fine. I'll get a jacket." She grabbed her black jacket, which had been hung over a chair in the dining room, hoping he would not notice it, and went to her bedroom.

"That's a nice black jacket," he called out to her. She didn't respond.

Closing the bedroom door behind her, she opened the envelope again and took out the pill bottle. It was labeled Dramamine. She also took out a note in Harvey's familiar handwriting:

> *Your survival kit for tonight—the condoms are tidy little receptacles if you should have to throw up in the air. The Dramamine is for any motion sickness you experience later on in bed. Happy landings.*
>
> XXOXX

In a minute or so, she reappeared in the living room wearing a bright-red jacket.

"That's also a nice jacket," he said.

"Well, shall we be off?" she asked.

He glanced into the kitchen, pleased to see that the flowers he had given her still lived, now in the vase on the counter. He also noticed the lone banana beside the vase, thinking it made for a pleasant still life. "The flowers look nice," he said. "So does the banana."

Paul parked his car out on the tarmac of the Santa Monica Airport, near where a blue-and-white helicopter with the words See It All Air Tours on the fuselage awaited them, its engine idling. A short man in a blue jumpsuit stood outside the aircraft, no more than thirty feet away. Paul waved at the pilot, who did not seem to notice him. It soon became apparent why: when Paul and Helen reached the pilot, they saw that he wore the thickest eyeglasses either had ever seen, so thick they made the man's eyes look grotesquely large. Squinting at his two passengers, he smiled and said, "Evenin' folks. My name's Malcolm. Nice night for flyin'."

Paul whispered in her ear, "Think his last name is Magoo?"

She shrugged, not smiling.

"You can climb aboard. Everything's ready," said Malcolm.

Paul and Helen stopped at the open door, the bottom of which was too high to step into.

"How do we get in?" Paul asked.

"Just use the step box right there," Malcolm said, pointing to the ground below the door, on which stood nothing at all.

"Excuse me," said Paul, "but there's nothing here."

Malcolm looked puzzled and walked close enough to the doorway to fall into it. He bent over and examined the ground. "Damn, I was sure I put it there."

He reached into the doorway and moved his arm around until his hand found something, which he slid out. It was the step box. He placed it on the ground and proudly held out his hand. "There you go."

Paul glanced over at Helen, then helped her climb the step into the helicopter, following her into the cabin. He bumped his head going through the doorway and tried not to wince from the pain.

"Don't forget to duck going in," Malcolm called up.

"Thanks for the warning," Paul muttered.

He found two upholstered seats and gestured for Helen to sit in the one away from the door, next to a large viewing window. He joined her and began to fumble with the shoulder and lap belts.

"That's her belt you're trying to buckle to yours. Cozy, but not a good idea," said Malcolm, who had quietly come aboard. Paul thought it strange that he could see in the darkened interior.

"He could be a bat," Paul whispered to Helen. "They have radar. Let's see if he hangs upside down."

If Helen saw the humor, she did not let on. She continued to look stunned.

"Okay, folks, let's see if we can get this thing up in the air," said Malcolm as he squeezed himself into the left front seat. Above his head was a sign that said "Push Stick Forward to Make Things on Ground Bigger. Pull Back to Make Things Smaller."

"Do you see that?" Helen asked Paul, her voice jumping an octave.

"Relax, it's a joke," said Paul.

Malcolm apparently heard him. "Like my sign? Always gets a laugh. Or sometimes a cancellation. Don't worry about a thing. I've been flying this thing for, let's see … " He looked at his watch. "Just kiddin', folks. Part of the routine."

Paul rolled his eyes at Helen. She turned and looked out the window, as if wondering how to open it.

"Relax," said Paul. "This is going to be fun."

She smiled weakly. But the smile was jolted off her face as the helicopter lurched upward and the ground began to move away from them.

"See?" Paul pointed toward the ground. "Just like it says. Those people down there shaking their heads and covering their eyes, they're getting smaller."

She bolted forward in her seat, looking out the window, and was bolted right back by her harness.

"I assume you've been in one of these before."

"Never. I thought it would be interesting, since you won't have dinner with me. In here we don't have to watch each other masticate."

"At least dinner wouldn't be dangerous," she said, looking a bit pale.

"Why should we worry about danger?"

She ignored the question. "What about your dislike of heights? Doesn't this bother you?"

"Not at all. We're inside."

"I'm not sure I understand the difference," she said.

"I don't think I do either, other than the fact that in here someone else is responsible for what happens to us."

He turned toward the pilot who was squinting out the window through his half-inch-thick glasses.

"How comforting," she said, turning her focus out the window again. "Actually, it's a nice view."

"Look, there's the bay. And the pier's coming up."

"Santa Monica Pier, straight ahead," said Malcolm. "Want a closer look?"

Paul looked at Helen, and she shrugged.

"Sure. How close can we get?" he asked.

"Well, let's see," Malcolm answered and pulled on the control stick, sending the helicopter into a sharp bank to the left until it was on its side, veering across Santa Monica toward the west.

Paul noticed Helen gripping the armrests as though she was going to break them off.

"Are we supposed to be doing this? I feel like I'm going to fall out," said Helen, pressed against the window by the force of the banking.

"Not if you don't open the window," replied Paul, which got him a pained smile.

"Open the window?" called back Malcolm. "I wouldn't do that."

"Just kidding, folks," said Paul.

Helen seemed to relax as the helicopter leveled out and floated through the evening sky. The last light of the setting sun hung over the horizon, sending a pale orange glow onto the calm Pacific.

"There it is, the pier," said Paul.

"That's it," said Malcolm. "Let's go in for a closer look."

He slowed the forward motion and settled lower as they approached the pier. In addition to the lights of the amusement rides, they could make out people strolling along.

"It's beautiful from up here," said Helen.

"Just a few nights ago, we were standing at the end."

"And I was making a complete fool of myself with that fish thing."

"I found it all, well, endearing," said Paul.

"You obviously can be easily charmed."

"I know."

He looked into her eyes, smiling. She, in turn, could only return his look for a moment or two before becoming uneasy. She turned to look out the window again.

"Would you like to stop?" asked Malcolm.

"How on earth could we do that?" Helen said.

"Like this," the pilot replied, and he made adjustments to the throttle as he moved his feet on the pedals, bringing the craft to what appeared to be a full stop as it hovered over the end of the pier.

"Pretty amazing, what these things can do," Paul remarked.

"Look," said Helen. "People are waving at us."

"Happens all the time," offered Malcolm. "They think we're a TV news chopper. Or shooting a movie. Either way, they want to get into the shot. Here, I'll wave back."

He moved the stick to and fro and the helicopter swayed from side to side.

Helen smiled genuinely for the first time all evening. "I see your point," she said to Paul. "It's an entirely new way to see the city."

"This is just the beginning," he said. "What's next, Malcolm?"

"How about a look at downtown?"

"As long as we stay off the freeways."

"I'll try my best," Malcolm said.

The craft floated effortlessly above Santa Monica in an easterly direction, following Pico Boulevard. Paul could pick out every neighborhood along the way.

"High pool count along here," he said, observing the many blue shapes lighted from beneath the surface, sending a message to anyone above that in these homes lived the privileged L.A. class that could afford to own a pool and light it at night.

"The Fox lot," Paul pointed out next.

Helen looked out the window and down at the mini-city that had been created on the sprawling grounds of the lot. There was the famous New York street near the main gate and the rows of enormous soundstages, huge hangarlike stucco buildings with silver arched roofs. In those buildings many of television's more successful shows were filmed or taped. Then there were all the white bungalows that housed the executives of production companies who had "housekeeping deals" with Fox.

"Everyone with an idea or a dream wants to get into those buildings. And to make sure they don't, they have these muscle-bound guards at the gate who learned customer service in Folsom Prison."

"Have you been in there?" Helen asked.

"Folsom Prison? No. But I get mail from there."

"I meant down there, the lot."

"Once, actually. A long time ago. I wrote an episode for a television series and went to a script meeting in one of those bungalows."

"Really? What show was it?"

"It's not important."

"I see. One you're not proud of."

"I was young and naive. Which was my last phase before old and cynical. I actually thought I could raise the bar in episodic television."

"And you didn't succeed?"

"No, I failed, large. It was a story of a man whose courage and values were tested by a gangland murder he had witnessed. Before the trial, he fell in love with a woman. Revealed his dilemma to her: should he risk his life and testify to see justice done or remain silent and safe and have a life with her? In my script, he said a painful farewell to the woman, testified in court, which helped get the conviction, but had to disappear into the Witness Protection Program, never to see her again, which she understood and accepted."

"That's an interesting story. Why do you say it failed?"

"I went to a meeting in one of those bungalows, with the show's producer. Her assistant, a younger man she was married to, and her yappy dog were in the meeting. The producer said, 'We're not in the business of sad endings. Your ending is pathetically morose. But it can be fixed. Just make him choose love over that justice bullshit. That's what our audience wants to see. Don't write editorials. Write fantasies for some poor housewife in hair curlers in Cleveland. Give her an alternative to her potbellied husband asleep in his recliner with a beer can in his fist. That's America, mister, and you'd better write for it if you want to succeed.'

"Her husband just kept grinning and nodding, like those bobbleheads in people's cars. Never said a word. Maybe he didn't know how to. And the stupid little dog looked condescendingly at me the whole time, like he agreed."

"What did you do?" asked Helen.

"I told the woman I would not rewrite the script the way she insisted it be written. I suggested she might want to let her smiling husband have a go at it. Or the dog. 'Do you know what you're giving up for the sake of your damn values, whatever the hell they are?' she asked. Yes, I knew perfectly well what I was giving up, and for that, I would be eternally grateful. Never again would I have to suffer a heartless producer, a witless husband, or a stupid little dog with a bow on its head."

"And you dropped the notion of writing for television?"

"Yes. Actually, television dropped it for me. When you

say no to a well-known producer, it's like refusing to name Communists' names. You get on a list. And no one takes your calls. But I didn't make any calls. I was perfectly content to be an abject failure at that line of work."

"So you wrote for television?"

It was Malcolm, talking over his back. Paul wondered how he could eavesdrop over the din of the engine and the whirring blades.

"No, I didn't."

"But you got into one of those bungalows, you said."

"Just to take out the trash."

"Too bad. I have a great idea for a new series."

"I'm going to guess it's about a helicopter pilot who takes people on tours," said Paul.

"No, actually it's about a guy who goes blind and proves that he can fly airplanes with his Seeing Eye dog in the other seat. It's called *Fritz Is My Copilot*. Fritz is the dog's name."

"I hope you registered it. Someone could steal a hot idea like that. You know how this town is," said Paul.

"No chance. It's registered and copyrighted."

"That's a relief," said Paul, turning to Helen and shrugging his shoulders.

"He wins a big discrimination case against the airlines, the blind pilot does. It's got a real message, don't you think?"

"It definitely does," said Paul.

"We've crossed into Beverly Hills," Malcolm said proudly, as though finding the city at night was a major accomplishment.

"Look, that's your shop," said Paul.

"I don't see it," Helen replied, trying to spot it among the city lights.

"That's it, I'm sure."

Then to Malcolm, he said, "Could we get down a little closer?"

"Sure. I can set down on one of those rooftops. But I think there's an ordinance against that in Beverly Hills, like everything else, you know—smoking, putting for-sale signs in your car."

"Just hovering would be fine," replied Paul.

Malcolm obliged, and the helicopter floated down to within no more than a hundred feet of the ground. People did not bother to look up, since both news and movie helicopters are such everyday occurrences in Beverly Hills. However, one man was looking up. He stood in front of what Paul was certain was Helen's salon, waving his arms as if guiding the helicopter in for a landing.

Paul said to Helen, "That guy down there. He's waving at us."

"That's Harvey. He sees us. I can't believe it."

"Your partner?"

She nodded.

"How did he know it was us? Did you tell him what we were doing tonight?"

"I tell Harvey everything."

"Really. Everything."

She nodded.

"The thing on the subway?"

Another nod.

"The pier, the fish, and the tar pits?"

A series of nods.

"And he hasn't tried to stop you from seeing me?"

"I wouldn't say that."

"So you don't listen to him."

"I wouldn't say that either."

"Oh."

"He obviously finds the whole thing amusing," said Helen.

He thought it would be a good time for Malcolm to move out of Beverly Hills.

Malcolm must have had the same thought. "Next stop, downtown," he said. "That okay with you folks?"

"Okay?" Paul asked Helen, to which she nodded, waving out the window at Harvey on the ground.

"Okay with us," he said to Malcolm.

This time, both of them were prepared for the sharp banking, which left them looking straight down at the salon and the waving Harvey.

"You're very close to Harvey, aren't you?" asked Paul.

"He's very special. And protective of me."

"Does he have any idea of your plans?"

"Which ones?"

"The obvious ones."

"Oh, we're back on that subject again."

"It's pretty easy to get there. I mean, it's not exactly the most common thing in the world, wanting to take the last leap, wouldn't you agree?"

"The truth is, I've never discussed it with Harvey."

"Are you concerned he might take some drastic step?"

"What kind of step?"

"I don't know. He could insist you call one of those help lines for people like us."

"He'd be a little late."

Paul was startled. "Is there something you haven't told me?"

"No," she said, with a shrug. "At least nothing that I think you should know."

"You're not going to beat me to it, are you? I really don't think this should be a competition, like 'Last one off the bridge is a sissy.'"

"What on earth are you talking about? I meant he'd be a little late getting me to call one of those hotlines. I did that months ago."

"Oh, sorry. How was it?"

"As terrible as you might imagine. I was assigned to some man who told me he had made seven attempts before someone convinced him that it was the wrong thing to do."

"Seven is pretty excessive. What was he doing, going out of second-floor windows?"

"I don't think he meant he was doing it wrong," she said with an edge.

"What did he have to offer you?"

"That's it; he really had very little to say about me. He didn't so much as ask why I was preparing for it, whether I had a specific plan, the usual things. It was all about him from the beginning. I was regaled with stories of his four divorces, his job losses, and his failed attempts at breaking into the movies."

"Did you have any advice for him?"

"That's what he was supposed to be offering me."

"That's why I've never tried one of those groups. But I've been thinking of starting one of my own, with a different tack. It would be perfect for that guy who you talked to: a hotline for people who tried to check out but failed, like him, with no wins and seven losses. It's a how-to thing. Lots of helpful advice on how to get the job done—quick, minimal discomfort. Even offer a rating system. You know, a four-tombstone system all the way down to no stones. The pier, for example. Good drama, but not high enough and, of course, dirty water. Give it maybe one tombstone. What do you think?"

"I think you're sick."

"Thank you. I was afraid you'd think ill of me."

"There it is," called out Malcolm. "Downtown Los Angeles, in all its glory."

Paul and Helen both craned to see out the window.

"That building in front of us, isn't it higher than we are?" Helen asked.

"What building?" He paused for effect. "Just kidding. Actually, you're right. We're about ten floors below the roof."

"Are you planning to go higher?" Paul asked.

"Nope," he cheerfully answered.

"That raises an interesting issue," Paul said.

"Truth is, I'm going to circle around it. It's a lot of fun. You feel like you're in a Governor Schwarzenegger movie, floating just outside a big window. Sometimes you really surprise people in their offices this time of night. They think no one could ever see what they're up to, if you know what I'm sayin'." He winked knowingly.

"We get the picture," said Paul.

To Malcolm's dismay, and Paul and Helen's relief, there was nothing going on in the upper floors of the building other than a woman emptying trash baskets and a man vacuuming the floor.

"Just like you see on TV and in all those movies, L.A. at night," said Malcolm. "And over there's the new symphony hall. Looks to me like the guy who designed it had a real bad hangover. Or he wanted to get even with Disney, if you want my opinion."

"We don't," Helen whispered.

"Frank Gehry, one of the world's great architects, did it," said Paul.

"To each his own, I always say," answered Malcolm. "There's the court building where they had the O. J. trial."

Paul anticipated some more trailer-park wisdom, so he changed the subject. "That's interesting. What's next, the Valley?"

"Yessiree, no tour of L.A. is complete without it."

Another veering turn and they were floating back over the city toward the north.

"That's the Santa Monica Freeway down there," Malcolm offered. "Or maybe it's the Hollywood. Could even be the four-o-five, for all I know. They all look alike."

They floated past a sparsely lighted area alongside the freeway. Paul tried his hand at tour guiding: "That's USC down to the left."

"No kidding?" exclaimed Malcolm.

"And up there is the L.A. Times Building and MLK Hospital," Paul added.

"I better be careful. You could take my job away," said Malcolm.

"You're safe there. I've never flown anything."

"Like I said, you could take my job away."

The ride was smooth and the air unusually clear.

"There's the Hollywood sign, coming right at us," said Paul as one of the most frequently photographed sights in all of California loomed closer. "A lot of people think it was put there to call attention to the movie industry. The truth is, it was originally a sign for a real-estate development, Hollywoodland, back in the 1920s, I think. Eventually, the last four letters, *LAND*, fell off the cliff. Or were pushed. Or jumped."

"We're crossing Cahuenga Pass," declared Malcolm. "We should feel a little bump when we go over the crest. There's always a thermal."

On cue, some invisible force jolted the helicopter, sending a shudder through the craft. As they came still closer to the sign, Helen was transfixed on the white block letters cut into the darkness. She felt a second, stronger tremor. The sound of the motor changed from its hum to a series of surges, almost groans. Suddenly there was no engine sound at all. Malcolm frantically flicked switches and moved a knobbed lever next to his seat forward and backward, shaking his head. He fought the control stick as the craft began to wobble back and forth. Helen stared out the window at the Hollywood sign, which was coming closer all the time. A tingling ran through her body, an alarm system foretelling a calamity. The pilot cried out, his terrified voice echoing, "I can't get it started. We're going down, my God, we're going down!"

Now Helen was outside herself, as well as outside the helicopter, as she watched it head directly into the Hollywood sign. There was a moment, a fraction of a second, in which the image froze in place, in which there was no sound. And then, the horrific impact as the helicopter hit the last letter of the sign, the *D* bursting into a ball of flame at the instant of impact. Now the sign read *HOLLYWOO*, and where the *D* had stood there was only an orange flame illuminating the night sky.

"What are you staring at so intently?"

Paul's voice jolted her out of her reverie. "I was thinking of something about the sign down there."

"And now we're coming over the Hollywood Reservoir," Malcolm announced. "The dam is pretty famous. It's been used in a lot of movies about earthquakes. You know the scene, the crack in the concrete gets bigger and bigger, and then everything breaks loose with a big flood."

Paul could make out the shoreline, which was ringed by streetlights, and then the spillway, topped by a narrow road. Malcolm was right; he'd seen the dam, made to look much larger than it was, in some pretty bad movies.

He felt another bump, stronger than the previous one. Paul knew what the shrill whining sound from above meant. The helicopter pitched erratically to and fro as the whine became louder. He felt the craft go into a slow rotation on its own axis. The whining of the motor turned into a piercing scream as the spinning continued. He looked down at the top of the dam, which was coming closer as the craft lost altitude. From the small house on the spillway top a man emerged and looked up to the sky at the whirling helicopter, which seemed headed straight for him and for the spillway. The man started running toward one end of the road and the safety of the adjacent hillside. Now Paul found himself watching the scene as if it were one of those bad movies. He could see the helicopter in which he was trapped whirling and pitching like a toy, headed for the spillway. There were no cries of panic, no screams of terror as the doomed helicopter closed the final distance between it and the dam. Then, the fireball. The man who had run to the end of the road raced back to the site of the crash, frantically yelling into a cell phone. He stopped short of the burning wreckage and looked down at his feet, between which a crack had appeared in the concrete roadway. He looked frantically to the left, then to the right, and jumped away from the crack just in time, as it began to widen. He ran to the railing at the road's edge and looked down at the spillway. The crack that had appeared on the road was dancing down the face of the dam, widening as it went. Then, in one explosive burst of shattered concrete, the entire dam gave way to a furious rush of water. In seconds, the spillway was torn completely open and the torrent rushed down the valley, through which, only seconds before, a narrow stream had run. The ball of flame, which had been the helicopter, rode the rushing waters downstream while above, on a remaining parapet at the edge of what had been the spillway, the man who had witnessed the catastrophe held fast to a tree limb, looking down at the fireball and the newly formed rapids. "No one could have survived," he said into his cell phone. It struck Paul that the man bore a striking resemblance to Charlton Heston, particularly in his determined grimace. "I'm going down there anyway. I know it's a risk. But someone's got to do it."

"But someone's got to do it," echoed Malcolm, startling Paul out of his movie.

"Do what?" Paul asked.

"I was explaining how I have to work nights, since I'm the only pilot they have. Not that I'm complaining."

"Do you ever get into a spin in this?" Paul asked.

"You mean when the whole things starts to twirl around?"

Paul nodded.

Malcolm shook his head. "No way. That happens, you're out of luck. You'd end up corkscrewing right into the ground."

Paul leaned toward Helen. "Something we haven't thought about. Corkscrewing right into the ground."

"Or into the Hollywood sign," she said.

"That's interesting. Wonder which letter you'd hit."

"The *D*."

"The dam is what I was thinking. Charlton Heston grimaces and comes to the rescue. With several guns, of course, that can only be pried from his cold, dead hands."

"Excuse me, folks," said Malcolm. "We're getting a little low on fuel. Think we ought to head back. I don't think we'll find a filling station up here. I thought we'd circle over to Malibu and then up the coast to home. Okay?"

Paul made a circle with his thumb and index finger, but, of course, Malcolm did not see it.

"Is it okay?" he repeated.

"Yes, it's fine," Paul said.

The rest of the journey took them along Mulholland Drive, with a spectacular panorama of both the sprawling San Fernando Valley to the north and the entire Los Angeles basin to the south, then to Malibu Canyon, which they followed down to the sea. They turned back over Malibu Colony, the gated community of multimillion-dollar beach houses so popular with the entertainment industry, and headed along the coastline back toward Santa Monica.

"They don't look all that expensive from up here," said Malcolm, nodding down toward the homes, which seemed to be attached to one another in one contiguous show of excess. "Guess it depends on how you see it."

"Have you been in any of those places?" Paul asked Helen.

She nodded slowly, deep in thought.

"Want to talk about it?"

"Not especially."

"Must have been quite a party."

"It wasn't a party."

He waited for more.

"It was a memorial gathering, for my husband."

"I'm sorry."

"You needn't be," she said, looking out the window, not at anything in particular, it seemed, but more an attempt to avoid eye contact with him.

"It was a nice tribute to my husband. But it was difficult to be there. You have no idea how stars who are so glib on camera can be so totally at a loss for real words. It became especially painful when one would try to top another with things like 'He was a man for all seasons.' We have no seasons here. Or the actor who looked at the sky and said, 'He's in a better place now, a place that awaits us all one day.' How would he know? Has he been there?"

"Please tell me you're making that up."

She shook her head.

"No one would actually say that."

"Not only did someone say it, but a screenwriter, a famous one, asked if he could use the line in a script he was writing. 'Pearls like that don't come along every day,' I believe he said. I think it was that day, at that gathering, when I first started thinking about—" She stopped.

Paul fell silent. He leaned toward her in an attempt to put his arm around her shoulders, but the seat harness restrained him, making him feel all the more inadequate.

"As they say on the set, that's a wrap," said Malcolm as they turned back toward the airport. "I've been on a few in my time. Sets. Did a fair amount of stunt work in choppers."

Paul did not want to know why he no longer worked in movies.

"I sure hope you enjoyed our little tour. If you did, I'd appreciate it if you'd tell your friends about us. We do tours of the stars' homes, weddings. You name it."

"Weddings?" Paul asked. "You perform them in here?"

"Oh, no, nothing like that. We take photographers over them. You know, when it's a celebrity wedding and no press is allowed in."

"Prurient," said Helen.

"Who?" said Malcolm. Getting no response, he reached his hand back, holding a few business cards. "Here, take a couple of cards. You never know when someone might need us."

Paul took the cards and looked at one. "This says Ecsta-Sea Boat Charters."

"Oh, hell, I gave you my other cards. Well, go ahead and keep 'em. I skipper pleasure boats too."

"Also for spying on weddings?" said Helen.

"No. It wouldn't work. Actually, we can do weddings out on a boat. The whole thing, including a honeymoon cruise. One-stop shopping. You two might just want to keep that in mind, know what I'm sayin'?"

"What about jumping?" Paul asked.

A puzzled Malcolm said, "Did you say jumping?"

"Yes. Do you take people up to jump out?"

"Out of what?"

"The helicopter," said Paul, getting a poke in the ribs from Helen.

"I don't think we're licensed for that."

A shrill sound reverberated through the cabin and a red light began flashing on the pilot's console. Malcolm reached out and flicked a switch, stopping both the light and the sound.

"Anything wrong?" asked Paul.

"No. Just a warning. We're about out of fuel."

"Do we have enough to get back?" Helen asked.

"Doubt it."

He waited for the look of shock, which did not come.

"Oh, you mean back to Santa Monica. Sure. I was think-ing you meant back up to the Valley or something. Relax. We're there. I just like to kid around. Livens things up."

Paul and Helen both looked out the window at the airport tarmac, which was coming up quickly. They also noticed a sudden change in sound. Actually, it was an absence of sound. Then they were thrown upward and lurched back down with a creaking jolt.

"I keep telling them to fix that bump in the tarmac. How'd you like our powerless landing?"

"The engine quit?" Paul asked.

"No, the fuel did. The last thirty feet, we were on selfrotoring. The blades continue spinning to let us down."

"I can't believe you used up all the fuel," said Paul.

"Only what was in the tank," said Malcolm. "We still had the reserve. But I try not to use it. It's a little game I like to play with the fuel guy. If I can run dry before hitting the ground, I win. If I still have fuel when I land, he wins."

"That's great. But what if you run dry before you reach the airport?"

"Oh, then nobody wins. But don't worry. All I have to do is flick this switch to put it on reserve."

He looked around the instrument panel, squinting and nearly touching it with his head.

"Let's see, where is it? No, that's not it. Well, it's here someplace."

After paying for the tour, which included watching Malcolm fiddle interminably with the credit card and drop it a few times before swiping it, Paul thanked the pilot for the interesting ride and assured him he would tell people about the experience. As he and Helen drove away on the tarmac, he noticed Malcolm waving good-bye, although the wave was directed toward a parked airplane, not the car.

"Can he see at all?" Helen asked.

"I think it could be part of his shtick. Maybe he thinks it will help sell his blind-pilot script."

"Then he should have his Seeing Eye dog with him," said Helen.

"Good idea. I'll mention it the next time I book him."

"You actually would?"

"Just kidding," he said in his best Malcolm imitation. "Are you hungry?"

"Why do you ask?"

"It's not rhetorical. I thought you might like to stop for something."

"For what?"

"It *is* dinnertime. I know how you feel about eating in people's presence, but I could find a dark place. Or I could promise not to look at you."

"Thank you, but I should get home to the dog."

"Dog? I didn't see one."

"He wasn't there. The walker had him."

"You have a dog walker?"

"Is that unusual? Don't you have one?"

"I don't have a dog."

"They can be good company."

"I know. I planned on having one. But that dog I told you about apparently thought a lot less of the idea than I did, mistaking my arm for a stick to chewed on."

Helen laughed, that snort of hers that Paul found endearing. "Well, I'm sure my Tabby wouldn't do that to you," she said.

"You have a cat too?"

"No, just a dog."

"Named Tabby. I see." Which he did not.

"Thank you for the tour," Helen said as Paul pulled up to her house and parked. "It was very nice."

"Sorry if our pilot was a little over the top."

"Of what?"

He ignored the question. "I hope we can do this again."

"Sit here in the car?"

"You *are* playing with me, aren't you?"

"No. It's just that I tend to be at a loss for words when I'm sitting in a man's car, in the dark, in front of my house," she said, looking self-consciously at her hands.

"I'm sure you know I'm attracted to you," he said.

"I'm not certain. But I admit the notion has crossed my mind."

"And what do you expect me to do about it?"

She shrugged, still concentrating on her hands. He reached down and placed a hand on top of hers. She smiled, but only for a moment.

"You know, this is awkward," he said. "I've told you I'm attracted to you. Now I've put my hand on yours. What do you think happens next?"

She finally looked up at him, directly into his eyes. He cocked his head, waiting for a response.

"You might try to kiss me, I suppose."

"Would you resist?"

"I don't think so. Would it be open? Your mouth?"

He stopped just short of bending closer to her face. "I've never been asked that before, at least not as an adult. Do you have a preference?"

"Until we know one another better, closed might be best."

"You're probably right," Paul said. "No sense taking a chance on getting my germs."

"That's not what my concern is. Open mouths are a step to something else."

"That's what I'm told. We are consenting adults, after all."

She half nodded, half tilted her head in contemplation, while he slowly moved in and guided his lips to hers. They touched as though they had been magnetized. He held his breath and basked in the soft warmth of the kiss. His lips began to part, but he maintained control of them. Her fragrance made the tentative sojourn sweeter than he might have imagined.

Meanwhile, Helen viewed a little vignette of her own as Paul's face came closer and his lips docked against hers. She saw, in full, vivid color, a woman hanging by her fingers from the edge of a cliff that dropped off straight down thousands of feet to a canyon floor. The woman silently said *I can't hold on.* On closer view, Helen noticed that *she* was the woman, dressed in mountain-climbing clothes, her feet dangling in thin air. A man ran to the edge, stopped, and looked down at her. The camera's reverse angle revealed Paul, also dressed in mountaineering clothing, with ropes and metal gadgets clanging from his waist. He got down on his knees, then on his stomach, and inched closer to her. He reached over dangerously, his entire torso beyond the edge, and, instead of offering a hand or a rope as a normal hero would do, he stretched out enough to reach her lips with his. The kiss, incredibly enough, became a strong enough bond to hold Helen. She relaxed her grip on the cliff's edge and dangled there in a lip-lock, her eyes closed, calm overtaking her. But then, suddenly, Paul opened his mouth to say something. "Dinner?" Before the first syllable left his mouth, Helen was floating through thousands of feet of air. Paul watched her descent and yelled, "I shouldn't have opened my mouth!"

"That was very nice," said Paul, trying to catch the breath he had held throughout the long kiss. "Even with our mouths closed."

Helen blinked a few times. "Lucky for us," she said, straightening her clothes, which had not actually been rumpled. "I should go in. Would you like to come in for a peanut butter sandwich?"

"I'm really not hungry, not for peanut butter."

"I don't know what else I can offer you."

He grinned and hoped it wasn't a leer. She studied him. Maybe it was a leer.

"Your company for a little longer would be nice," he said.

"Will you kiss me again?"

"I'd be happy to." He leaned in.

She leaned back. "I meant, is that what you'll do inside?"

"It's what I'd certainly like to do. It beats a peanut butter sandwich."

Opening his door and getting out, he suggested, "Why don't we continue this nonconversation inside?"

Then he surprised her, walking around to her door, opening it, and offering his hand.

"That happens to be a nice gesture one rarely sees anymore," Helen said appreciatively.

—

They walked up to the house together, and Helen stopped at the front door, keys in hand. She turned to Paul. "This is where men who open doors for women usually say good night with a gentle kiss. Mouths closed."

"But I thought you invited me in."

"Yes, I did." And she unlocked the door. "I should go in first."

It took about one second after he set foot inside the house to realize why she wanted to proceed him. That was all the time that passed before a giant black animal galloped across the gleaming living room floor toward him. His life didn't flash before his eyes, only the small part of it in which he had offered his arm up to the large charging dog at the Los Angeles Pet Adoption League.

"This is Tabby," said Helen, much too matter-of-factly considering the animal seemed about to devour her guest.

But the dog, a sleek-coated Great Dane, skidded to a stop just short of Paul. It stood a good three feet tall, which put its muzzle precisely crotch high, where it lunged with its nose, forcefully enough to evoke a gasping sound from Paul and send him back against the door.

"No need for alarm. It's his way of greeting you," said Helen.

Paul looked down at the dog. It seemed to have no plan for backing away, but merely looked up past Paul's crotch and into his eyes.

"Shaking hands would be nice," Paul said.

"Tabby, be a good boy now," said Helen.

The dog turned to look at his mistress, and Paul took the opportunity to move away. But he got only a step away from the door when Tabby turned back and gave him another jab at fly level.

"Sit, Tabby."

The dog followed the command and sat directly in front of Paul, staring him down.

"His mouth is open. I don't think that's a good sign," Paul said.

"He might sense you don't like dogs."

"I like dogs—the ones that don't see me as a snack."

"Oh, he'd never bite, unless he sensed I was in danger."

"Good. Maybe you ought to explain to him that I'm not going to maim you."

"Lie down, Tabby," she said.

And the dog obeyed, but it chose to do its lying down across Paul's shoes, which he slowly slid out from under the animal's body and moved away.

"Have a seat," Helen said.

"Are you talking to me, or to little Tabby?"

She pointed to the brown leather sofa. Paul sat down on

one end, eyeing the dog, which sat directly in front of him. The animal was even taller in the sitting position. This time, his muzzle was level with Paul's throat.

"Maybe he'd like that peanut butter sandwich, or a young calf, for a snack."

He noticed that the dog never blinked while staring into his eyes. And he wondered if dogs blinked at all.

"I'm sorry if he makes you uncomfortable. Come on Tabby, it's time to go to your room."

"He has a room?"

"My bedroom, actually. But he thinks of it as his."

"And who would want to argue with him?" Paul asked, trying not to make any sudden movement, watching the eyes that fixed on him like lasers.

Helen clapped her hands and, to Paul's amazement, the huge animal got up on all fours and marched across the wood floor to the open door of the bedroom, stopping to turn back and look at Paul once more before disappearing. Helen followed the dog and closed the door.

"I've had him since he was a puppy," she said, sitting down next to Paul.

"I can't imagine a dog like that ever being a puppy. It's like trying to picture King Kong as a little monkey."

"Would you like some water?"

"No, thanks. I'm feeling pretty well hydrated."

"I could offer you a glass of wine, if I had some. But I don't."

"That's right. You don't drink."

"Is this one of those awkward moments?" she asked, looking down at her hands again.

"To be totally truthful, most moments I'm with you have a certain awkwardness to them."

"I'm sorry." She seemed to pout.

"It's not you. It's me."

"Really?"

"No. It's a joke. The breakup line. You haven't heard it?"

"I haven't had a breakup."

"Well," he sighed, "yes, this is one of those awkward moments. We kissed in the car. It was very nice. But awkward. We came in here. I had hoped to kiss you again. Maybe even get as far as open mouths. Slightly, not too wide. And then, there's the big dog with a little cat's name who seems interested in my crotch, platonically, perhaps, but it's all on the awkward side, yes. Very awkward."

She looked up from her folded hands directly into his eyes. He waited for an argument, a rebuke, even a reappearance of the giant dog. But none of those things occurred. She remained still and silent. Then she did the last thing he would have expected, yet the first thing he hoped for. She threw her arms around his neck and pulled his face close to hers, still staring at him in silence. Her lips parted, and she closed the distance between their faces. She kissed him fully, warmly, deliciously. His lips opened. He felt the tip of her tongue dart outward and just slightly into his mouth. His tongue greeted it, touching it gently. It would have been a challenge for either of them to say how long they stayed in the embrace, in the kiss. It could have been several seconds; more likely, it was more than a minute.

Eventually, they parted.

Paul was the first to speak. "Now that's a kiss."

"I'm afraid it was lustful," she said.

"Kisses generally are. They're a prelude."

"That's a man's view. Why can't a kiss just be a kiss?"

"You think I have an agenda? Of course I do."

"Don't be defensive," she said.

"We might be better off not talking," he said, pulling her closer and moving in for another kiss.

She dodged him, turning her head, and his lips landed on her ear.

"Now that's what I call awkward. Why are you playing dodgeball?" he asked.

"Conflict."

"Between us?"

"Between the two of me. On the one hand," she said, holding up her right hand, "I like the way it felt when you kissed me. It made me tingle."

"And on the other?"

"A warning: Stay back. The tingle will be short lived."

"I prefer the first hand. Why can't you accept that things might work out to your liking?"

"I find that an interesting question, coming from you."

"Hey, I'm just a cockeyed optimist."

"Searching for a better way to end it all."

"To each his own optimism. There was an old Indian chief who sat in the sun, looked around, satisfied with his world, and said, 'This is a good day to die.'"

"That's my point. You get me tingling, and we both know it's just going to end."

"Why can't we take the existential path?" he asked.

"So what you're really saying is, it's all right to kiss, mouths open, and then it's all right to move along to something else, like the end."

"Sartre couldn't have said it better."

He leaned toward her again, this time more slowly. She didn't turn away. She waited for him to kiss her again. It was more intense than the previous kiss. This time, their tongues played with one another. Their breathing was quicker, deeper. He felt her relax in his arms, all resistance melting. He moved on top of her. She moved her lips away from his and looked deep into his eyes.

"This isn't a bed," she said, breathing deeply.

"But it's comfortable."

"In the other room."

He looked over her toward the closed bedroom door. "That's where the dog is."

"I know. I can put him away."

"No need to be that drastic," he said, between his own deepened breaths.

He kissed her again. She pressed up to him again. Their mouths opened still wider, their breathing frenetically synchronous.

She spoke, into his mouth this time. "I meant I can put him in the bathroom."

"Fine. Whatever moves this along."

"We're talking into each other's mouths."

"Yes," he said, and their lips joined again. "You have sweet breath. Like a lotus. Not that I've tasted a lotus."

He warned himself to stop struggling to make conversation, which would only come out sounding stupid.

She pulled back yet again, her face flushed deep red. "Are you trying to take my clothes off?" *Lotuses, for God's sake.*

He realized that his hand had worked her blouse halfway up her back. She stiffened.

"Sorry, my hand got lost. But the truth is, I'd like to take your clothes off. I'd probably like it even better if you took them off. But now *I'm* conflicted. I'm not sure which of us should do it. How do you vote?"

"The bedroom."

"The bedroom it is, by acclamation." He loosened his embrace and fell silent. His expression changed from eagerness to dismay.

She cocked her head.

"I didn't bring anything," he said. Confessed, actually.

"Like what?"

"You know, what's needed at a time like this."

She waited.

"Protection."

"You mean condoms?"

"Yes, that's what I mean."

"You don't have any?"

"Not with me, no."

"You don't carry them with you, like most men do? In the glove compartment?"

"Of course not. I graduated from high school a long time ago. But this whole discussion is a real mood breaker. Here we were, letting things go their natural course. A man, a woman, and now—a condom."

He stopped long enough to notice that Helen was looking at him as though he were some sort of alien speaking in a cryptic tongue.

"Sorry, I got carried away," he said. "Can we get back to where we were?"

She said nothing, just continued looking at him. He encircled her with his arms again. Another kiss, and it seemed as though they had found their place again. But she suddenly bolted upright, just as his hand was working her blouse upward once more.

"It really shouldn't be a problem," she said.

"What shouldn't?"

"The things."

She stood abruptly and, in the process, left him off balance and sliding down onto the gleaming wooden floor. He watched her pit-a-pat across the room, admiring the rhythmic way her hips moved. She stopped at an antique wooden cabinet and opened a drawer, pulled out a shoe box, and turned back to him.

"I have a supply," she said, to his astonishment.

Paul paused, dumbstruck, staring at the shoe box.

"You seem troubled. Why?"

"A whole box of them?" His voice was noticeably higher. He didn't bother to get back up on the sofa, as though he had forgotten where he was.

She nodded and opened the lid. She reached in and pulled out a handful of foil packages in a panoply of vivid colors, then let them drop, one at a time, back into the box.

"I can't believe you have a whole shoe box full of condoms," he said.

"And why should that be so hard to believe?"

He noticed the fork of hair had popped up again.

"I'm not sure. It's unexpected."

"You said you have some at home," she said, holding the box almost defiantly.

"Well, yes, I do. But not that many."

"You might want to pick yourself up off the floor and explain why you should have a supply and yet are shocked that I have my own. Wait, I think I understand. You think it's a mark of promiscuity."

"No, that's not it."

He finally gathered himself up and back onto the sofa.

"That *is* it. I'm some sort of loose woman. I should wear one of these things to warn the world, like a red *A*. Let me see," she said, rifling through the box. "Yes, here it is, a bright-red one. I can put it on my forehead. There," she said, holding the red square package to her head.

"You're definitely overreacting, not to mention looking ridiculous holding that thing to your forehead. I expressed a little surprise, that's all. How did we get off on this tangent anyway?"

"I think it had something to do with your pushing my clothes off me and those long kisses, not to mention your wont to slide on top of me."

Wont? She was talking like a Victorian novel again.

"Maybe this wasn't such a good idea," he said.

"Perhaps not." She looked at her wrist. "Besides, I have to get ready."

"For?"

"My next appointment. The Los Angeles Raiders."

"They're in Oakland."

"I don't care where they are. They're coming here. That's why I have to keep so large a stock," she said defiantly, picking up another handful of little packages and dropping them into the box.

"Then I guess I'll leave."

"Fine. Unless you want to try out for the team."

"Why are you so angry?" he asked.

"Do you know why I have this collection?"

He shook his head.

"Then I'll tell you why. I volunteer for L.A. Project AIDS. One of our activities is distributing condoms. In schools, on college campuses, on street corners, to homeless people. It's a pathetically small thing to do, but people are dying out there, including friends of mine. I have to do something. Can you understand that?"

"Completely." He said it so softly, she barely heard. "I'm sorry."

"As am I. For the briefest of moments, I felt something I had not felt in a very long time. But, as is usually the case, reality visited itself."

"Self-pity isn't the answer."

"I'm sorry, but I don't recall asking a question."

"And that's my exit line."

He turned and went to the door, where he stopped briefly. Turning back to Helen, who still held the shoe box, he said, "I'm sorry."

She slowly shook her head. She had a look of vulnerability that urged him to go back and hold her once more. But he knew better, and simply left.

Chapter 11

"You look like crap."

"Thank you, Milton. You have a nice way with words," said Paul, sitting uncomfortably in front of Milton's desk.

"I'm sorry, but you look like you've been up all night. At least I hope it was for a good reason. Finally get laid?"

"No," said Paul. "That's part of the problem."

"I told you there's no future with that woman. What's her story, anyway?"

"Helen of Troy."

"She's an actress?"

"A hairdresser."

"What am I missing here?"

"She owns a salon. It's called Helen of Troy."

"And she turned you down."

"That's what I like about her."

"Besides the fact that she's rejected you, what else draws you to her?"

"We like to do the same things."

"Like what? Go out for nothing to eat?"

"We both know what we want out of life," said Paul,

smiling at the irony of his own words.

"Care to share that?"

"Not a good idea."

"Did you bring a column for me?" Milton sounded like a father asking a son about his homework.

"Sorry. It's a little slow in coming. I'm working on one about a woman whose husband sneezes during sex, but I'm kind of plugged up today."

"I really don't think I can tell our readers that there's no Man to Man today because Paul is constipated."

"I'll have one this afternoon."

"You plan on buying one, finding one, or, miracle of miracles, writing one?"

Paul chose to ignore the taunt. "What do you think it means when a woman keeps a shoe box full of condoms around the house?"

"Jesus Christ, don't tell me that's your next column."

Paul shook his head. "I'm curious. What would you think?"

"Well, she's either a very busy woman or a hopeful one. Why? The hairdresser collects condoms?"

No answer.

"Hey, some people collect stamps. I don't know what the hell it means. Did she bring her collection out to show you?"

Only a shrug.

"Did she want you to try some on?"

Nothing.

"Hey, don't be so talkative."

Another shrug.

"Okay. So tell me, what do *you* think it means?"

"Actually, she told me why she had them."

"And?"

"She's been touched by the AIDS epidemic. She volunteers in the movement." Then Paul paused, showing just a little guilt. "The truth is, I was a total sexist fool. And I doubt she'll ever want to see me again."

"And I'm getting the feeling I might not see a column again if we don't get you snapped out of this funk you're in. Where's this place she owns?"

"Beverly Hills."

"You been there?"

"Yes."

"Okay, you're going back there. Now. With me."

"What for?"

"I need a haircut."

Paul surveyed what little brown hair remained on Milton's balding head and made no comment.

"A trim. They do men, don't they?"

Paul recalled Harvey's response. "Every chance they get."

"Come on. Something's got to get you unplugged."

"A haircut?"

———

Paul, wearing a smirk, pulled the car to the curb in front of Helen of Troy.

A young man in a red vest and black bow tie smiled broadly, waving Paul to pull forward.

"Valet parking. For a haircut," said Milton. "What next, valets at Seven-Elevens?"

"Yes, sir. We do one up on Little Santa Monica," chimed the happy valet. "Tell them Frank sent you. You'll get a VIP spot."

"How's the screenplay going?" Paul asked the man.

"Not bad. Having some second-act problems."

Relinquishing his car to the valet known as Frank, Paul led Milton to the front door of the salon.

Milton said, "You know that guy?"

"No."

"Then how the hell did you know about his screenplay?"

"It's a touch I have," said Paul.

Inside they were greeted by the sights and sounds of a busy weekday morning. Voices, mostly female, buzzed over the hum of the ubiquitous hair dryers.

The receptionist seemed to recognize Paul from his previous visit. "Looking for Helen?" she asked.

"A haircut, actually," said Paul.

"Do you have an appointment?"

"No. But it's not for me."

The receptionist looked at Milton and then down at her desk, trying to conceal a smile. She picked up the phone, pressed a button, and looked at her nails. "Someone to see you out front. Your friend with the jack." Which got an exchange of glances between Paul and Milton. "And he's with a walk-in, for a haircut. Sure." She hung up the phone. "She'll be right out."

It took only a few moments for the stainless-steel door to open and for Helen to appear. "Good morning," she said to Paul, neither overtly friendly nor cool. Businesslike.

"Hello, Helen. This is Milton. He needs a haircut."

She smiled and held out her hand. "A pleasure." She turned to the receptionist. "Is Harvey available?"

Glancing at a large pad on her desk, she said, "Looks like it." She picked up the phone again. "Harvey? Can you come up front? A walk-in." She hung up.

"So how are you today?" Paul asked Helen.

"I'm well, thank you. And how are you today?"

"Well, thank you."

Milton watched the two of them in their verbal dance, shaking his head. The receptionist caught him and smiled understandingly.

"Nice place you have here," said Milton.

"Thank you," said Helen.

"Awkward conversation, we're having," said Paul.

Milton and Helen both turned to look at him.

"Well, it is. Everybody's well today. It's a nice place here. The weather's pleasant too. Beyond that, what are we going to talk about?"

"Would you like to talk about last night?" Helen asked.

Paul leaned back as though he might fall over.

"Why not?" chimed Milton. "We're all adults here. Let's talk about last night."

"Did he tell you about my collection?"

That peaked the receptionist's interest too.

"As a matter of fact, he did."

"Milton, come on," said Paul.

"It's all right. As Milton says, we're all adults," said Helen. "We can speak openly about condoms."

Which aroused even more interest from the receptionist, along with a wry smile.

"I can't believe this conversation," said Paul.

"And why not?" asked Helen.

"Why not? Some things are simply personal and are best kept that way."

"And not discussed publicly?" she asked.

"Exactly."

"Including in newspapers?"

He started to answer, but stopped himself. Milton smiled and raised an eyebrow.

"I think that's definitely a gotcha," he said.

Helen smiled triumphantly. Paul smiled disdainfully. And Milton? He just winked gratuitously.

"He wants a haircut," Paul said to Helen.

"And you want a change of subject. Which is fine. Here's Harvey."

The two men turned to see Harvey come through the door and announce, "Who's in need of a haircut here?" Paul found the scene playing like drawing room comedy. Harvey surveyed both heads. "I'm so glad you don't do a comb-over," he said to Milton. "You show class for a balding man."

What surprised Paul was Milton's reaction. Instead of being flustered or put off by the candor, he nodded and said, "Thank you. I'm Milton."

"And I'm Harvey. I do the men around here."

Milton nodded again, with a look that once more puzzled Paul. If he hadn't known Milton better, he would have described it as bordering on beatific. He also thought he saw a slight reddish tinge on his editor's face, equally out of character. Not once had he ever observed Milton blush at anything.

"I'd never do a comb-over," a flustered Milton finally sputtered, forcing his voice down to an even more gravelly than normal timbre. "Like I say to the guys at the gym, go with what you've got."

"Oh, you work out," Harvey said approvingly.

Paul saw Helen roll her eyes at her partner while Milton jutted out his jaw and nodded.

"Well, come on back and we'll get you spruced up," said Harvey, turning to the side, holding out his hand, and bowing like a maître d'.

"Why don't you two try and settle that business about last night?" Milton said to Helen and Paul as he preceded Harvey through the stainless-steel door.

"Can we find somewhere just slightly more private, perhaps a crowded bus?" said Paul.

"If you'd like," replied Helen. "Am I clear?" she asked

the receptionist.

"Perfectly" was the answer, accompanied by a knowing smile.

Out on the sidewalk, Paul sighed deeply, looked around, and then squarely gazed into Helen's eyes. "I'm sorry. I acted stupidly last night."

"You only acted like a man."

"I pride myself in being neither sexist nor misogynous. And then I end up being both in your living room."

"You're neither. You just hit a spot that can easily be bruised. I'm sorry if I overreacted."

"And I'm sorry if I underappreciated."

They looked at one another, saying nothing.

Paul finally broke the silence. "How long will Milton be?"

"The haircut will take about ten minutes."

"Oh."

"And the conversation another forty," she said.

"Take a ride with me then?"

"Where?

"Ever been to the steps?"

"As in Russia?"

"Santa Monica."

"I didn't know there were any."

"Steps, that go up." He moved his hand in the familiar arcing motion. "I think you might like them."

He got the attention of the smiling valet by waving his ticket. The man was off in a jog to the nearby alley and returned in less than a minute with the car. Paul held the door for Helen, whose smile indicated that she appreciated the gesture. The valet held the driver's door open with his hand outstretched, into which Paul placed two dollar bills.

"The steps are all the rage for fitness buffs," he explained as he drove along Santa Monica Boulevard. "And for singles."

Stopping for a red light, he looked up to see, once again, the billboard promoting music "for lovers only."

"So pretentious," he said.

"Who is?"

"That billboard. As if romantic music and a nice sunset are all it takes to establish a meaningful relationship."

"Wasn't there a time when you felt yourself swept up in that sort of situation, where everything around you looked beautiful?"

He remained silent for a moment or two. Then, "As a matter of fact, yes." He reflected on the previous night on the sofa, before the absurd dialogue about condoms. He kept the thought to himself, of course. But he wondered if she might, just possibly, be thinking something similar.

"I don't suppose there would be any point in telling me about that time," she said.

"Probably not. Anyway, these steps are busy day and night."

At a certain point on westbound Santa Monica Boulevard, the proximity of the ocean becomes clear, long before it can be seen. The street gently slopes upward toward the horizon point, where it drops down again, creating a false feeling of land's end. The sky somehow becomes larger. And the senses play tricks; every time Paul reached that point, he was convinced he could smell the salt in the air, even through the exhaust fumes that hang on the busy boulevard.

True land's end is at Ocean Boulevard, where a grand vista presents itself, a sight that never becomes commonplace even to those who have seen it a thousand times. Beyond the greenbelt pedestrian park that sits atop the seaside bluffs, the precipitous drop-off to the ocean below gives a feeling of being perched for a launch toward the horizon, which can be seen for more than twenty miles from the high vantage point.

Paul turned right and drove north until they crossed San Vicente Boulevard, and then he took a right turn into a narrow residential street that wound its way to the bottom of the bluffs. Another right turn took them up a few densely treed blocks. He pulled to the curb and nodded toward a very steep concrete stairway that disappeared into the trees a short distance above.

"There it is. The stairway to nowhere in particular, the same place the L.A. subway goes."

Helen studied the scene: Men and women, young, middle-aged, and even a few seniors, all in the process of climbing up or jiggling down. Most wore athletic clothing and running shoes and carried the obligatory water bottles. Breathing was generally labored; sweating was common. Traffic rules appeared to be obeyed: climbers on the right, descenders on the left, passers in the narrow middle. A small crowd was gathered at the bottom; some stretched in preparation for the climb, others panted or swigged water after finishing, and a knot of people just seemed to be socializing with one another.

"I once heard more than a thousand people a day use them," said Paul.

"It's safe?"

"I'm sure," he said. "Maybe a turned ankle now and then, shin splits, and the occasional fall from watching people instead of steps. The only real problem is heart related, and I don't mean in the romantic sense. I understand there are a few cardiac arrests a week. It's interesting. You'd think people would realize racing up steps puts an enormous strain on the heart. But then, maybe some people *do* realize it. Think about it; it's simpler than jumping off or in front of things. More natural. And it sounds better, more heroic: 'So-and-so suffered a fatal heart attack while vigorously exercising on the challenging Santa Monica steps.' Want to give it a try?"

"Toward what end?" she asked.

"That's funny."

"It wasn't meant to be."

"Sorry. Try it, though. It's a nice workout."

"All right."

He was surprised she agreed, and pleased, of course.

At the bottom of the steps, where people totally ignored them and the fact that they were not dressed in workout clothing, they waited for a break in the steady flow of traffic, since most of the climbers would turn around at the bottom step and head right up again. When two people stopped in near collapse, there was room to jump in and start up. Paul nudged her elbow, guiding her onto the bottom step, and followed her, one step below.

"Okay. Just keep the same pace as the man in front of you."

"If—you—do—you'll—keel—over," the man, overhearing him, huffed.

"I feel if I don't concentrate, I'll miss a step, and everyone will go down like dominos," said Helen, her breath only slightly labored.

As they progressed upward, Paul noticed she had found a rhythm consistent with the huffing man ahead of her. Paul followed suit, and the three of them made a synchronous ascent.

Until, at a landing not very far up the hill, the man in front grasped the iron railing and pulled himself out of line. His face was ashen and his breathing was very labored. He shook his head, saying nothing, and waved them on.

"You okay?" Paul called back.

"No. But—I—never—am—when—I—do—this."

The man sounded as though any one of his sucking breaths could easily be his last. But as Paul turned around, he saw him still standing.

"How are you doing?" Paul asked Helen.

"I'm breathing," she puffed.

"Good sign."

And they continued on. Barely halfway to the top, their faces glistened with perspiration while their breathing gave way to gasping.

"Five round-trips would do it," Paul said.

"Five? It would kill me."

"That's what I said."

"It was a figure of speech," she said. "Truth be told, I'm too healthy."

"You need to train, like I do. Lots of fat. Cholesterol. Eggs, butter, red meat. Clog those little arteries."

"You can't be serious," she panted.

"Natural causes. Solves a lot of problems. Looks much better in the obituary than, well, you know."

"Is this a sitcom?" came a voice from above Helen, from an easy-breathing yuppie.

Helen said nothing.

"A new reality show," Paul called up to him.

They negotiated a right-angle turn in the steps and finally came within sight of the top, where several climbers were in positions ranging from stretching to near collapse, catching enough breath to begin the return descent. Paul felt as if his knees had been beaten with a baseball bat. His temples throbbed. His heart raced at the rate of three beats to the count of *one-one-thousand*, a pulse rate of 180, he estimated, wondering how high it would have to go to strike him down in his tracks.

"We made it," panted Paul, barely audible. "You okay?"

Helen could only nod, wide-eyed.

"You look good in sweat."

"A regular Cyrano," muttered the middle-aged man,

who had made it to the top and was bent over, hands on his knees, mouth sucking for air like a dying halibut.

"Let me know when you're ready to go down," Paul said to Helen.

"Tomorrow?"

"Nothing to it, going back down. Just shin splints, maybe."

She wiped perspiration from her eyes with the back of her hand, stepped onto the landing, and started down behind a man in running togs who had reached the top and stepped to his left to begin the descent—backwards.

"Who likes a show-off?" Paul whispered in Helen's ear as he fell in behind her.

"Hi," said the backward stepper to Helen, not even breathing hard. "I'm Phil."

"I'm dying," said Helen.

———

Helen sat on the floor of her station in the salon, her breathing labored, legs stretched out in front of her, with her back propped against the wall and her face still glistening. Paul sat next to her, in similar exhausted repose, his shirt wet, his hair plastered against his forehead.

Standing above them were Harvey and Milton, both smirking.

"We should never have done it a second time," said Helen.

"Dare I ask what you did a second time?" asked Harvey. "And where you did it?"

"The steps," she answered.

Turning to Milton, Harvey said, "Guess we have to give the devil his due. Twice. And on steps."

"We were climbing them. For exercise," said Helen.

"In Santa Monica," Paul added.

"You were out in the heat of the day, climbing steps in Santa Monica? I don't get it," said Milton.

"You should try it. Great for the heart."

"Yeah, if you want to stop it."

"Whatever launches your boat," said Harvey.

Paul studied Milton. "Get your hair cut?"

Milton nodded. "That's a sign of a good one, when you can't tell."

Helen looked at her wrist. "I've got an appointment in ten minutes." She tried in vain to get up from the floor. Harvey held out his hand to help her.

"You look like hell," he said.

"Thank you."

"And it's about time." He turned to Paul. "Nice going, stud."

Flustered, Paul turned to Milton, who winked at him.

"Did you just wink at me?"

Helen looked in the mirror above her client chair. "My God, I *do* look awful. I'll take a quick shower."

"Alone," said Harvey. Now *he* winked at Paul.

"I'll call you later," Paul said to Helen as she was leaving.

"You might want to try Cedars-Sinai. The E.R.," she called back to him.

Harvey followed her to the back of the salon. "I need to talk to you," he said.

Helen stopped. "About what?"

"Your friend's friend. The one who hasn't needed a haircut in ages."

"Milton? What about him?"

"He hit on me."

"He what?"

Harvey nodded.

"He's gay?"

He nodded again. "Behind the beer-drinking and the ball-game-watching lurks a man in a closet."

"He asked you out?"

Another nod. "He didn't say, 'How about a date, honey?' But he invited me to the Hollywood Bowl. To see Yanni, for God's sake."

"What did you say?"

"What the hell am I supposed to say? That he's barking up the wrong tree? You think he'd believe me, the way I flit around the place? I told him I already had plans. My book club meets on Wednesdays. Then he says he's always wanted to join a book club. You started this whole thing, meeting that weird guy who tries to kill you on some goddamn steps. This is L.A., baby. He could be the stairway stalker, for all you know. And now I've got his friend trying to pick *me* up. Yanni!"

"Perhaps I should talk to Paul about this."

"You can't out his boss. Maybe I can fix the poor guy up with that repressed weight lifter who comes in every week. Who knows, they might end up coming out together. At the Hollywood Bowl."

"Paul told me he finds me attractive when I perspire."

"He actually said that?"

"I think it was, 'You look good in sweat.'"

He put his hands on her shoulders and stared into her innocent eyes. "Sweetheart, you know how much I love you. That's why I want you to think very carefully before you sweat with someone like him."

"It was the steps, I told you."

"You're not standing on any steps now, and yet every time you mention him, you get all red, and probably wet."

"That's vulgar."

"I know. And it turns me on."

She playfully pushed him away. "Besides, I've started tingling again."

"Oh, so now it's tingling *and* sweating. What's next? Swooning? Tingle, sweat, and swoon. Sounds like a talent agency."

"Did Milton say anything about Paul?" she asked.

"Not much. He said it was his idea to come down here. He wanted to meet you because he was worried about his star writer, that he was being distracted, by you, of course. This is a guy who takes you out for nothing to eat, on a helicopter ride with a blind pilot, and now up and down a bunch of stairs that almost give you a heart attack. He's distracted?

Try demented. And you know what Milton thinks? His poor friend just needs some sex. I told him he needs some Prozac."

"Did he say anything else?"

"Not about his boy. When I made the mistake of telling him his balding head makes him a good-looking man—you know, the usual bullshit we feed people—he changed the subject. Then it started: the questions, the small talk, and all of a sudden it was about an evening under the stars. Of course, when I turned him down, he did a lot of backpedaling, like he just had this extra ticket, and he started talking like a jock again. I feel for the guy."

She smiled and raised an eyebrow.

"Oh, don't start that shit. It's a figure of speech."

———

"So, what did you accomplish?" Paul asked Milton as they crawled through traffic on the Santa Monica Freeway.

"I told you to take surface streets."

"They're worse than the freeways. What did you accomplish?"

"What do you mean? Look at that schmuck in the carpool lane." Milton raised his middle finger toward the man in a huge SUV, who let go of the steering wheel and one-upped him with two middle fingers.

"Jesus, Milton, that's what gets people shot," said Paul as he swerved into the far-right lane, out of sight of the scofflaw.

"I don't give a shit. He's driving his damn SUV in the

HOV."

"So he'll be SOL if he gets caught by a CSP. I repeat, what did you accomplish, other than a haircut?"

Milton reflexively touched his sparse hair on one side. "The guy's good, this Harvey."

"I can see. Did he shed any light on things? That *is* why you wanted to go there."

"Not a lot. He thinks you're dangerous. Helicopter rides with pilots who can't see, hanging out on piers—you know, little things. And now I'm sure the step thing you did confirmed it for him. But I told him you're not really all that dangerous. Just demented. What do you know about this Harvey anyway?"

"Less than you do, I'm sure."

Milton snapped his head around. "What do you mean by that?" he asked, a little too loudly.

"Relax. I just mean he had you in his chair for close to an hour. You must have gotten to know him."

"Hey, it was a haircut, that's all."

"Don't be defensive."

"What the fuck are you talking about, defensive?"

Paul smiled and shrugged. "So he didn't give you any new insight? I'm referring to the reason you went down there in the first place."

Milton had to think. "Oh, well, not anything you don't already know. I asked him about her condom collection. He didn't know about it, but he thought it was funny, that maybe the more you have, the safer the sex is going to be. Which I don't get. It's not like you can use more than one at a time. Unless you're having a whole football team over."

Paul nearly swerved into the oncoming traffic when he turned to Milton in shock. "What the hell is that supposed to mean?"

"Hey, don't get defensive," Milton said through a sly grin. "He also thinks you have some weird ideas about dating, which I find interesting for a nationally syndicated relationship advisor. The La Brea Tar Pits aren't exactly the Hollywood Bowl."

The chiming of Milton's cell phone got them off the subject.

"I hate those things," said Paul, watching Milton flip open his phone, read something on its small screen, and then close it again. "They eat your brain away."

"You think there are little aliens inside?" said Milton.

"Worse. Why didn't you answer?"

"Wrong number."

"How do you know?"

"It was my ex-wife."

"So you don't think she meant to call you?"

"Of course she did. But I've asked her a hundred times not to call me on my cell phone from New Jersey. When I explain it costs me two bucks every time, well, you can guess what she does. Calls from New Jersey. At least five times a day."

"A woman scorned."

"No, a woman obsessed. It's what women do."

"That's pretty sexist of you."

"Come on, you know as well as I do that there are some things only a woman will do. Like throwing all your shit out on the street, changing the locks, and then hating you for leaving. That's deranged."

"What about a man who throws out a woman he's sleeping with because he finds dresses in his closet and makeup in his bathroom?"

"That was a matter of principle. She never asked me if she could leave all that stuff, I told you. She was surreptitiously moving in."

"So when a man does it, it's principle. But when a woman does it, it's deranged."

"I didn't put her stuff out on the street. And I didn't change the locks."

"That was noble."

"Do me a favor. Save your judgments for the column, which, I assume, you're still writing."

"I told you, I'll be caught up by today."

"If you're not taking your girlfriend on a parachute jump."

Paul thought for a moment, curious. "Where can you do that?"

"You serious? Because I wasn't."

"Why not? That's a fascinating idea."

"Oh, sure, if you want to end up splattered on a field somewhere. Check your contract. You can't do things that would be considered dangerous by insurance companies."

"How dangerous could it be?"

"Plenty."

"Really?" said Paul, suddenly interested. He had a momentary flash of a man and a woman sailing, in slow motion, downward through a blue sky, pulling at their closed parachutes in frustration, then looking at each other and smiling broadly as they continued to plummet.

"Does Helen ever talk about her partner?"

"Who?" He was slow coming out of his thoughts.

"I imagine she only has one. The guy who cut my hair."

"Harvey? Oh, sure. They're very close. Sometimes I wonder if they have something else going on besides business."

"No way," protested Milton.

"Why not? They spend more time together than most couples."

"It's just, I don't know, not in the cards."

"Oh, I get it. It wouldn't work. He's, well, you know—" Milton waited intently.

"—too young."

"Exactly. Definitely too young." Milton cleared his throat. "So, how about those Raiders?"

"What about them?"

"They're looking good, those guys."

"They haven't started playing yet."

"I know that, for God's sake. I'm just saying, they're looking good for next season."

"Why?"

"Never mind. Read the sports pages, like I do."

Paul wondered why Milton was acting so strange. *The man meets Helen. Then he meets Harvey. Harvey gives him a haircut. He works in a salon and wears tight pants. But he's not gay. Milton thinks he is, though. Go figure that one out.*

Milton turned to him and asked, "You think this Harvey is, you know … " And he made a twisting motion with his outstretched hand.

"Why? Because he's in the salon business?"

"I'm just asking your opinion. Making conversation."

"I have no way of knowing what his sexual orientation is, Milton. And I don't care. He's Helen's partner and friend. That's all I know. All I need to know."

"Jesus, I ask a question, I get a lecture."

"Anyway, what difference would it make if he is? Would his haircuts not be as good?"

"Okay, okay, sorry I asked. Just drop the whole thing. Think about the column—no, the columns—you owe me. And, by the way, you're a fine one to be lecturing. As I recall, you were really into that lesbian business, that sailor who walked in on his wife with the other woman. I was the one who had to stop you from running that garbage, if you recall."

"I wasn't being prurient about it. Just dealing with reality."

"Bullshit. You *were* being pure-ient."

"*Pru*rient," he corrected.

"That's what I just said. What the hell's the matter with you?"

Paul was half tempted to answer the question, but he thought better of the notion. How could he begin to explain what was wrong with him? It would have been far easier, and consumed much less time, if the question had been what was right with him. And the one thing that had the greatest prospect of being right was so tenuous it was best left undiscussed. Instead, Paul drove the rest of the way back to Milton's office in silence, which seemed agreeable to Milton, who was deep in thought himself. Paul thought about Helen and how unapproachable she continued to act. While she agreed to see him when invited, she had a way of placing herself in an impenetrable bubble when they were together. But who was he to talk? Hadn't he become the original bubble boy himself?

"There's nothing wrong with me," he finally said.

"What are you talking about?"

"You asked me what the hell was wrong with me."

"I did?"

"Yes, you did. And I'm telling you there's nothing wrong with me. Anything wrong with you?"

Looking absently out the window, Milton ignored the question.

"Maybe you need to follow your own advice."

Still no response.

"You know, get laid."

Milton finally spoke. "I don't recall sending a letter to Man to Man." Looking back out the window, he said, "I've got a couple of tickets to the Bowl tomorrow night. Want 'em?"

"Thanks, but I've got plans." It wasn't quite a lie, since he did have plans: to call Helen and ask her out again. But certainly not to go to the Hollywood Bowl.

Milton shrugged. He was clearly troubled about something, and Paul wished he could help, but knew he could not. Considering the eight years during which they had had almost daily contact with one another, Paul found the man to be an enigma. He eased the car to the curb in front of Milton's office building and turned off the ignition, not wanting to release any more gases than necessary while idling.

"Do you realize you're in a bubble?" Paul asked.

"A *what?*"

"Who's the real Milton?"

"Very funny."

"No, I'm serious. I was just thinking. For all the years we've known each other, there's a boundary you put up."

"That's just so much psychobabble. Bubbles, for Christ's sake."

He noticed an official-looking woman in a gray-blue uniform and white cap holding a minicomputer in one hand and pointing to the No Parking or Standing Anytime sign with the other. He leaned out the window.

"Just dropping him off."

She ignored him and started pressing numbers on her computer.

"She's giving you a ticket," said Milton.

"Ma'am," he called out to her. "I'm not parking. Or standing. I'm dropping. Would you give me a break, please?"

She shook her head, and a small piece of white paper crawled out of her computer. She tore it off, stepped to the driver's side of the car, and handed it to Paul. "Have a nice day, sir," she said, and sauntered off.

"Come out of your bubble," Paul shouted to her. "Let go of your aggression!"

She continued walking away, but raised one white-gloved hand and wiggled her fingers.

"She likes you," said Milton.

"Yeah. And her affection's going to cost me fifty dollars."

Milton grabbed the ticket from Paul's hand, looked at it, and shook his head. "I'll take care of it."

"You can fix tickets?"

"No. But I can expense them."

"That's very nice. You see, that could just be the real Milton inside."

"Bullshit. It's the Milton who wants his columns."

"No, I think you want to commit random acts of kindness."

"Fuck you" was the response. Milton strained to get out of the low-riding sports car. "You ought to get yourself a real car, that people can actually get out of."

"Have a wonderful day, Milton."

Straightening himself, Milton walked toward the building, tossing a middle finger over his shoulder.

"Same to you, asshole," said a nearby bicycle messenger looking up from a large envelope and apparently thinking the digit had been aimed at him.

You really have to love this city, Paul said to himself. *But it requires so much effort.*

Chapter 12

Paul felt sufficiently guilty to sit down to his computer and try to catch up on the column. He refused to believe his tardiness was Milton's primary cause of distress, but it probably contributed to it. Here he was, neither Catholic nor Jewish, yet he always managed to find himself guilty of just about everything, including missing one of Milton's deadlines. Why? Were some unknown guilt genes lurking surreptitiously within him, genes that had no place in white Protestant bodies?

The phone rang. He hopefully anticipated Helen's voice. But the hopes were dashed by the officious voice of Julie, his doctor's nurse.

"Good afternoon, Mr. Malouf, Doctor asked me to call to set up an appointment. He wants to check your cholesterol numbers. Can you come in next week?"

"Actually, I was wondering if we could wait a little longer."

"I suppose we could. Are you unavailable all next week?"

"No, not at all. But I'd like to wait for something I'm doing to take effect."

"I see. You've changed your diet?"

"Yes, I have."

"Well, Doctor will like that news."

Which made Paul chuckle to himself. If only *Doctor* knew about the kind of diet change he'd made, about the exponential rise in fats and cholesterol he'd introduced to his refrigerator and his system. Not to mention the cigarettes. He wondered if Nurse Julie might have any suggestions for stopping the choking and gagging when he tried to inhale, but, of course, that would be news Doctor would *not* like hearing.

"Well, now, you just keep right on with what you're doing and give us a call when you think you're ready to see the results."

"I'll do that. Thank you."

"Bye-bye, now," chirped Julie.

He called up his saved e-mail file to browse through letters he kept for possible future use in the column. He came across a deliciously ironic favorite that he had been tempted several times to use. But, knowing Milton, Paul had thought better of it. It was from a man who identified himself only as Perched in Chicago. It read, in part:

> *Dear Paul,*
>
> *I imagine the subject of my letter will trouble you, perhaps even anger you. My problem is not one of relationships. I'm a sixty-year-old healthy man with, my doctor tells me, plenty of longevity ahead of me. But therein lies the problem.*

Three years ago, I resigned from a company that I found was ripping off its customers, a stock brokerage. I guess that makes me a whistle-blower. But some people view me as a life blower. I blew my retirement prospects, and when I left the company, my severance amounted to three years of reduced income and no retirement benefits. I now have one year of money left. After that, I will have nothing to pay for food, shelter, and some form of recreation. I will not live under a bridge or the roof of my only child. So, I have a plan. I will check out. Take the plunge. Or the exhaust pipe. Or maybe some shot in the arm. My problem is how to deal with the pain my final action will inflict on those who will survive me, my daughter and my small circle of friends. How can I prepare them? What sort of message can I leave that might help them understand? Even though I won't be here to witness their pain, I can't bear the thought of it. Why does society refuse to accept the notion of ending our lives when we feel it's time, while we still have the choice to make for ourselves? Again, forgive me if I offend you. I'm sure you are far more concerned with life than with ending it, like most people. I'll understand if you erase and forget this letter.

Perched in Chicago

If the poor man only knew. Of course, Paul had never included the letter in a column, knowing full well how it would sit with Milton. It would not. Instead, Paul had sent the standard reply: "Thank you for your interesting letter. Unfortunately, we are only able to publish a few of the thousands of submissions we receive. Please feel free to write again with another issue you wish to discuss."

How is that going to work? Paul wondered. *He's going to the only place left that can't be reached by e-mail.*

Paul picked up the phone and dialed the number of Helen's salon. The receptionist, whom he seemed to be entertaining on a regular basis, laughed after he announced, "Hello, this is Paul Malouf calling for Helen, please."

"I'll see if she's available. And ambulatory."

"That's not funny," said Paul.

"I thought it was. They're calling you Stairman here. Better than the jack guy, I guess. Hold on."

After a brief wait, he heard, "This is Helen speaking."

"I know. How are you?"

"A little tired, but otherwise all right."

He waited for the reciprocal questions, but none came. "I'm a little tired too. Is this a bad time?"

"For what?"

"To be calling you."

"Actually it's a welcome interruption. I've been listening for the past hour to a woman who's having an affair with a plumber to get even with her husband, who's having one with a rock-and-roll singer, a client of his."

"How is she managing that?"

"She keeps breaking things, like her garbage disposal and the dishwasher, and he keeps coming to the house. Do you have any idea what 'plumber butt' is?"

"I think so. It's what you see when a plumber bends down under the sink and his pants slip down, exposing his rear end."

"She tells me the man has one, and she likes it. I think I may be ill."

"I'm sorry. But the reason I called is I want to invite you out, tomorrow evening. Are you free?"

"I think that would depend on what you plan to put me through. Does it involve climbing anything?"

"No. Dancing."

"Did you say dancing?"

"Yes. Do you ever do it?"

"Not in a very long time."

"Maybe this is a good time to get back to it, then."

There was silence on the other end. Paul waited. Finally, he said, "Still there?"

"Yes, of course. I was trying to imagine—well, to picture—dancing."

"Is that a yes?"

"Well, no. But, yes, I accept your invitation. For dancing. Thank you."

He thought it might never get easy, communicating with Helen. But it was still worth the effort.

"You're welcome. I'll call for you at seven-thirty."

"You'll what?"

He thought he heard a faint snort.

"I'll call for you. Seven-thirty." What was so odd about that?

"I'm sorry, but that's an interesting way to put it. Calling for me. Actually, it's nice. Quaint, calling for people. And you have calling cards."

"I don't have to be quaint. I can just say, 'Hey, baby, I'll swing by and grab you at seven-thirty. Be ready.'"

"I prefer quaint. Please call for me."

"Okay, then, I'll be by at seven-thirty tomorrow."

Helen stood smiling in the employee lounge, holding the telephone close to herself.

"What's that about? Or, I should say, who's it about?" said Harvey, who was standing behind her.

"It was Paul."

"Is it by land, by sea, or by air this time?"

"Dancing," she said, smiling like she had won a prize.

"It couldn't be him. That's far too normal. Where's he taking you?"

"He didn't say. Maybe it's a surprise."

"I'll bet it is. You best be on your guard, girl."

"Why? He's been a gentleman from the start."

"Jack the Ripper had nice manners."

"You're far too protective of me, Harvey."

"And you're far too trusting. After all, you met the guy on a subway platform."

"Perhaps he'll ask his friend Milton to come along. And

Milton, in turn, could ask you to join us."

"Sweetheart, when I go dancing, it's dirty. And it's not with a man. Although it'd almost be worth it to put some moves on the poor guy, if he's in good health."

"Be nice to him. He's just trying to face up to who he is. I'm sure it's not easy."

"Never is." He studied her face. "You know, I get the feeling you're getting the feeling about this Paul person. Every time you talk about him, your face looks like you're getting roseola. And look how you're holding the damn phone. You'd think he's inside it. You might be falling in you-know-what."

"You know that won't happen again."

He held out his arms and encircled her with them, pulling her closer, gently. "If I felt the guy could be trusted, I'd almost encourage it. It's time to give it another try."

She buried her face in his shoulder, as if she could hide what she was feeling. She still ached from loss, something she was well accustomed to. But now, along came a wanting as well, and she was aware of a struggle beginning.

———

The phone call somehow energized Paul. He was able to focus on the task at hand, finishing one column that day and getting a good start on another, which he was sure he could complete the following day. It meant staying with it through the evening, which he didn't especially mind since he had no plans other than visiting a local cafeteria for a large helping of fried liver and onions. He had read that a single serving of organ meat contains more cholesterol than half-a-dozen eggs.

Walking home from his dangerous dinner, Paul tried smoking a cigarette and managed several shallow puffs without gagging, a sign his system was acclimating to its new invader. He passed a tavern in front of which stood a small knot of men talking and smoking, the latest L.A. street scene: socializing outside bars in which smoking was prohibited. One of the men noticed his cigarette and greeted him with "Hey, how's it goin'? Want to join us?"

He thanked the man, explaining he had to get back to work.

"You gotta take a smoke break once in a while, don't forget that. You'll live longer," the smoker replied.

As he approached the walkway in front of his building, Paul noticed a woman sitting on a suitcase with her back toward the street. She focused on something she held in her hands. He assumed she was waiting for a cab or an airport shuttle pickup. The light was too dim to see if it was a neighbor he knew. Then, as he started up the curving brick walkway, he sensed a fragrance on the air that had a definite familiarity to it, but not from any of the flora planted around the building. It was an essence. A perfume. Suddenly, he was struck by a bolt of recognition. He had bought that perfume, many times. He stopped just long enough to consider turning around and leaving. But where would he go? Back to the smokers? For another serving of fried liver? No, he had to face who—and what—was about to confront him. Paul hoped against hope that it was a coincidence, that scores of people wore the familiar scent. He stopped just feet from the woman and saw that she was engrossed in a paperback book. Now he could see her profile, a beautiful one, but one that sent a shock wave through his entire body.

"Sam?" he said weakly.

The woman closed the book and turned to him. "Paul. Where have you been?"

She made it sound as though he had been gone for an hour rather than two years.

"At dinner" was all he could muster.

"I don't mean that, silly. Why haven't I heard from you?" With that, she got up from the bulging suitcase and threw her arms around him.

His back went rigid and his arms stayed at his sides.

"What's the matter, you can't give your wife a hug?" she pouted.

"Former wife. What are you doing here, Sam?"

She finally got his message and released her grip on his neck. "I'm in a little bind."

"Money?"

"No. I don't have a roof over my head right now."

"Something happen to the house?"

"Yes, in a way. But it's not something I really want to talk about out here. May I come in?"

"Visiting hours are over."

Why now, of all times, did Sam suddenly plunk down

into his life? He looked into her face, which, in the soft bluish light, was attractive as ever, but also as cool as he painfully remembered. An image of Helen superimposed itself over Sam, hair standing at attention, full lips poised halfway between a pout and a smile.

"Well, are you going to invite me in or not?" The tip of her tongue darted out and swiped across her lips. It was her old trick of promising various erotic delights if she were to get her way.

He sighed deeply and turned away to face the building call panel. He silently punched in his four-letter code, *JUMP*, which triggered a buzzing sound in response. He opened the door, started to go through it, and stopped, then held it wider, staring at Sam in a silent, begrudging invitation to enter.

"So this is your bachelor pad," said Sam when they entered his apartment. She surveyed the rooms with a familiar air of disapproval.

"No, this is my home. Glad to see you haven't changed."

"You don't think I look older?"

"I didn't mean your appearance. Always the critic."

"And you're still defensive."

"Well, when one lives under constant siege, one tends to build defenses."

"Come on, let's not spoil anything," she pouted.

"What is there that could possibly be spoiled?"

"We haven't seen each other for so long. I came here in friendship."

"No you didn't. You came here in need of something. What is it?"

"Okay, I'll be honest with you."

"Well, something *has* changed."

The cut either went past her, or she chose to ignore it.

"I have no place to stay. Can I camp here for the night?"

"That's really not a good idea, Sam."

"Oh, come on, why not? It's not like I'm some stranger."

"Nor is it like you're an old pal, is it?"

She took off her jacket to reveal a beige satin blouse, open well into her cleavage and defining the shape of her nipples. He had to admit to himself that she had not lost her ability to arouse a man, even a man who had hoped never to see her beautiful face and body again.

"What do you think? Do I look the same?"

"Yes, Sam, you look just as desirable as you did the night we met, when you seduced me on the golf course. And if you're wondering whether it would work again here in my apartment, no doubt it would."

She smiled provocatively.

"*If* I were stupid enough to allow it, instead of smart enough to avoid it as, I can assure you, I am."

"You're sure of that?" And she opened one more button on her supple blouse, revealing no bra beneath. "Your words tell me you *are* sure. But your friend down there says something else."

His face turned crimson as he sneaked a glance at himself. Yes, she had managed to create a telltale bulge that he could not wish down. And it only angered him further.

"So," she cooed with a leer, "what are you going to do with that? Waste it?"

As she inched closer, he could smell the white wine on her breath. *Things don't change*, he told himself. "Have you had a full bottle yet?"

She ignored him and, instead, slid her hand down his chest, across his belt to the bulge.

He took her wrist, removed her hand, and let it drop to her side, where it dangled. "Sorry, Sam, it's not going to happen."

"Have you gone chaste on me?"

No response.

"Are you in love?"

Still none.

"Not gay, are you?"

"And what if I were? The truth is, I'm seeing someone," he said.

"How's the sex?"

"I wouldn't know."

"I thought you said you're seeing someone." She raised an eyebrow and flicked her tongue along her upper lip again.

He shook his head. "I'm sure it's not something you can grasp, the idea of seeing someone and not having sex."

"You have to admit it's a little unusual, don't you think?"

"I suppose it is. It's also my business."

"And none of mine?"

He didn't have to answer her. She moved away and looked around the living room.

Her eyes fell on the Kevorkian poster. She studied it, puzzled. "Who is that?" she asked.

"Jack Kevorkian."

"An actor?"

"A doctor."

"That's it? He's a doctor and you have a poster of him? What kind of doctor?"

"Don't you read the papers, Sam? Jack Kevorkian. People call him 'Doctor Death.'"

"Why?"

"It's not important. What *is* important is what brought you here. You told me you can't stay at the house. What happened? Problems with the tennis boy?"

"You could say that."

She seemed to shed some of her self-confidence.

"Have you left him?"

"Not exactly. He wandered off."

"So why can't you stay in the house?"

"He's still in it."

"But it's your house. Remember, I signed it over to you, which was an idiotic thing to do, according to my friends and my attorney. At least you ought to live in it."

"I made a mistake."

He waited.

"I signed something a few months ago. He told me it was a technical thing he needed to finance his new business. When I told him to get out of the house yesterday, he pulled out the paper I'd signed."

Her voice dropped to a barely audible level. "It was a quitclaim I'd signed. He said he knew I would throw him out on the street someday and he had to protect himself."

"Jesus Christ, that was our house. I gave it to you. Now you go and give it to some tennis bum. What on earth came over you?"

"You know I'm not good about things like that."

"Look, you can get that quitclaim voided. Talk to a lawyer first thing tomorrow. You can probably file charges against the guy. He stole your house. Meanwhile, just move back in and tell him it's your house. Call the cops if he gives you any trouble."

"I can't get in. He changed the locks. And besides, he's got someone with him. I wouldn't want to be there if I could."

"He's got a girlfriend there?"

She nodded.

"I see why you fell in love him. He really knows how to mistreat a woman."

She mustered every atom of helplessness in her body and put it in her expression, looking up at him like an impounded beagle puppy. "Can't I stay? I can sleep on the sofa if you don't want me in your bed."

The thought of her in his bed did little to tamp what she

had ignited, although his mind claimed no responsibility for what his body was doing on its own.

"Okay. The sofa. And just a couple of rules."

She waited, her head tilted.

"No blouses that showcase your nipples. They're to be fully buttoned. And none of that tongue business. In other words, stop doing what you do so well. The seduction. It's what got us together in the first place and what drove us apart in the last place."

"I can't help myself. I'm a sensual woman."

"I had another adjective in mind, but no need to go into that again."

He left the room with Sam standing in the middle of it. In the hallway to the bedroom, he opened the linen closet and retrieved a comforter, two sheets, and a pillow. He carried them back into the room, only to find Sam sitting on the sofa, legs crossed, her arm extended along the seat back, which stretched the satin blouse event more taut across her nipples. He looked away and dumped the pile of bedding on the sofa beside her.

"The bathroom's down the hall. If the door's shut, I'm in it, and you shouldn't be.

"There's a coffeemaker in the kitchen set to go off at six in the morning. Other than that, there's food in the fridge if you're hungry."

"Are you leaving?"

"For a while."

"Got a date?" she cooed.

"No. I need some things at the store."

"What things?"

"Just … things."

He knew he could think of something he needed. Truth was, more than anything else he needed to get out of the house, forget about her breasts, and talk himself out of temptation.

He drove to the drugstore, where he knew he could find something he needed. Antacids. He had a giant bottle in the cupboard, but it was always a good idea to have an extra one, especially given his houseguest problem. *Wait*, he thought as he walked through the door of the store. *Saltpeter. Is it still made? Is it sold in stores? Or is it only available in prisons and on naval ships? Oh sure*, he told himself, *he was just going to saunter up to a pharmacist and ask for a bottle of saltpeter, or a box, or whatever it came in, if it came in anything at all.* He ended up settling for the big-value jar of Tums Ultra Maximum Strength and a toothbrush, in case Sam didn't have one with her, to avoid the question of letting her use his, which would be entirely too close for comfort. When he walked past the sizeable display of condoms, he smiled to himself, thinking of the absurdity of the argument he had had with Helen over her collection.

"Did you find everything you needed?" chirped the friendly young woman who checked him out.

There was no way on earth he could answer her honestly. *No, I didn't find the saltpeter.* Which undoubtedly would have been followed by an announcement over the public address system for all the world to hear: *Customer at register three needs saltpeter.* So he lied. "Yes, thank you, I did."

Back in his car, he decided it was too early to return home. Sam would not have done him the kindness of going to sleep. It was far too early, and she was far too manipulative for that. So he chose to take a ride. He opted for the slower, winding route on Sunset Boulevard toward the ocean, with no particular destination in mind. It was a drive he enjoyed taking whenever he had time to kill. Turning onto Sunset at Beverly, he drove past the bottom of the strip's commercial district where a Hamburger Hamlet restaurant stood in tribute to L.A.'s love affair with ground beef on a bun. In a city where stars and lawyers could afford the most elegant and expensive meals, there was still a loyalty to the common man's food of choice, the gourmet hamburger.

Now the famous boulevard turned into a demilitarized zone separating the flats from the hills. To the left lay the more modest of Beverly Hills homes, in the one- to two-million-dollar range. Up to the right were the mansions and palaces built with the riches achieved by the successful and the famous of the movie, legal, and, on occasion, illegal industries of Los Angeles.

As the road sloped downward, so did the value of the real estate. After Westwood and the sprawling campus of UCLA, beyond the gates of Bel Air, prices dropped as quickly as the altitude. Just across the San Diego Freeway, in a section of Brentwood, there even were apartments, which had somehow been sneaked onto Sunset Boulevard, in the dead of night, no doubt.

Pacific Palisades became upscale again, but not to the level of upper Sunset. Here there were homes that poverty-level families could afford, those earning less than five hundred thousand dollars a year, that is. The quaint village center looked as though it had been built as a movie set to portray small-town middle America.

The boulevard ended unceremoniously, and inelegantly, in one final sweep past more apartment buildings and a strip of stores, filling stations, and fast-food restaurants, stopping just short of the ocean at land's end and the Pacific Coast Highway.

Paul turned north on PCH, as it was called in the city that prefers to abbreviate everything. The traffic was light and the air was clear, two uncommon phenomena. Ahead lay a sweeping curve of the shoreline marked by a continuous string of orange vapor roadside lights, to the left of which lay the dark void of the sea. He rolled down his window to smell the salted air and hear the occasional crash of a breaker on the shore. He turned into a public parking lot at Will Rogers State Beach and parked the car facing the bay. With his headlights off he could stare out into the blackness, from which definition eventually came once his eyes adjusted. White froth appeared at the crest of slow-rolling breakers headed toward the rocky beach. The wet tips of black rocks embedded in the sand a few yards offshore also became visible. There was a comforting solitude to the view. It was exactly as it must have been before the vast stretch of America's western edge had been discovered and developed, denuded of much of its natural glory.

His thoughts turned to the prospects the beach and the waters beyond it presented. Unlike the pier in Santa Monica and the subway station in the city, anything he did there would go unnoticed, except, perhaps, by the shorebirds strutting along the sand and the sea lions feeding on darting silverfish beneath the water's surface, none of which would pay the slightest attention if he were to invade their space. He wondered how far he would get walking into the water before the bottom would drop off deeper than his height. Then what? Would he bob on the surface until the weight of his sodden clothes carried him down? He closed his eyes and tried to imagine what it might feel like. Would his body's instinct to survive take over and drive him, flailing and gasping, to the surface? Or could he induce a passive state, letting the sea have its way with him? It's the sort of thing a person can't know until it's too late to do anything about it. How humiliating it would be if the survival instinct won out and he somehow managed to thrash his way back to shore, where he would lay exhausted on the sand, choking for air and regurgitating his dinner of fried liver.

He heard a loud tapping, which, in his semisleeping dream state he took to be the sound of flotsam hitting the black rocks.

"You okay?"

It was a voice that came from somewhere nearby. Then came a bright light penetrating his closed eyelids. It took a moment to remember he was sitting in his car, not lying on the beach. He opened his eyes and was blinded by a powerful beam coming from outside the car.

"You okay?" the voice repeated.

The light moved away to scan the passenger seat. The reflection illuminated enough of the man outside to reveal a shining badge. Sitting forward, Paul could also see the dimly lighted interior of a police car. He leaned out the window and spoke to the face that now emerged from the darkness.

"I'm fine, thank you, officer," Paul finally said to the face.

"You looked like you might have passed out."

"No, just taking a little rest."

"Been drinking?"

"No. Just enjoying the drive. And I decided to stop and look out at the bay. Before I knew it, I was drifting off. Is that a problem?"

"Only if there was something wrong. We never know what people have in mind when they pull in here at night. Usually they're not alone. Couples, you know. We like to keep an eye on everybody. Sometimes there's trouble, especially when people are alone."

"What kind of trouble?"

"You know how it is. Things go wrong for somebody. Maybe money problems. Work. Divorce. A person might drive down here out of desperation. Maybe he's got a weapon and thinks about using it. Or he leaves the motor running and rigs up a hose to the exhaust."

"Well, you don't have to worry about me, officer. I don't

have a weapon or a hose."

"So, what do you do?"

"About what?"

"For a living."

"Oh. I write. For newspapers."

"No kidding. A reporter?"

"Not quite. I do a column."

"What about?"

"Problems. For men."

A bolt of recognition hit the officer's face. "Wait a minute. Your name Paul by any chance?"

Paul shrugged and nodded self-consciously.

"I'll be goddamned. You're the guy in the *Times*. Man to Man. That's you, right?"

Another shrug.

"This is crazy."

"Why is it crazy?"

"Because I wrote you, about six, seven months ago."

"Really? Did I answer you?"

"Yeah. You answered me. I'm serious. Remember 'Blue in Blue'?"

Paul tried stretching his memory back far enough. Something seemed familiar. Then he had a flash of recognition. "'Blue in Blue.' That was you?"

The officer nodded.

"The cop married to a cop."

Another nod.

"Spousal abuse?"

One more nod, slower.

"She beat you up with her nightstick."

The officer looked around as if he were a fugitive. He reached his right hand through the open window, and Paul grasped it.

"Peter Baumgartner, patrolman, LAPD."

"Well, it's nice to meet you," said Paul. "I can't believe the coincidence. Out of the thousands of cops in this city, out of all the people who've written to me, you should walk up and shine a flashlight in my eyes."

"To tell you the truth, at first I thought I was going to find some kind of weirdo sitting in the car."

"What makes you think you didn't?"

"Oh, I doubt that. May I see some ID though?"

Paul wondered what he had done to warrant showing proof of his identity. But he complied, retrieving his driver's license from his wallet and handing it to Patrolman Baumgartner, who turned on his flashlight again, studied the bad photo of Paul, and read the name aloud: "Paul J. Malouf."

"Do I need to step out of the car?"

"No. In fact, I'll step in and have a seat, if that's okay. Maybe talk a little."

The officer helped himself to the passenger seat, took off his cap, and sighed, looking straight ahead to the blackness that was the bay.

"You know, it took a lot for me to write that letter. I didn't know who you were, other than some guy named Paul who wrote a column. Up until now, it wasn't even a real guy named

Paul. Could've been a what-do-you-call-it, a fake name,"

"Pseudonym."

"Yeah, whatever. But I had to tell someone, and I figured that way, with no name other than 'Blue in Blue,' I was safe. Didn't even say what city I was a cop in. Can you imagine what it would be like at the station house if anybody found out my wife beat me up?"

He made a whistling sound as he shook his head. "They wouldn't give a damn that I *let* her work me over. I mean, I may be a lot of things, but I don't beat up on women. So I let her hit away. Lost a front tooth for the trouble."

He tapped what must have been a replacement tooth with his finger. "Eleven hundred bucks for that."

"What was it again that made her attack you?" Paul asked.

"Some street punk, an informant, actually, got pissed at me and sent her a letter saying I was screwing around with a hooker up on Sunset. Said I made her go down on me in the squad car a couple of times. Like I was some kind of—I can't think of his name, that English actor guy. It wasn't true, so help me God. I've never cheated on my wife."

He fell silent for a moment. Then, "Remember what you told me to do?"

Paul shrugged, indicating he did not.

"You said I had to confront her—that was the word you used, *confront*—which is what we do to perps, and tell her she prejudged me and that she had to make a decision of who she trusted: me or some street creep she never met."

"And?"

"Well, I guess she decided on the street creep. She left me. Broke my goddamn heart is what she did." He fell silent, shaking his head. Then his chest began to heave as he fought to keep his sobs inside. He finally let go, ashamedly, in tears.

Paul felt himself sink under the weight of what he had just heard. *Great advice you give*, he said to himself. Finally, he found words. "I'm sorry, really sorry."

"Well, it's not your fault. I decided to write you. And you gave it your best shot. No sense feeling guilty about it."

"You're right. There's no sense in it. But I feel totally guilty. You listened to me and ended up paying the price for it."

There was a long silence in the car until the officer said, "Maybe it's time for closure. Isn't that what the shrinks call it? Closure? Like a door. On the whole thing."

Paul saw, out of the corner of his eye, the officer pull his revolver from its holster and turn to him.

"What are you going to do?" Paul asked weakly, wondering if he was going to be the object of the closure.

"Maybe it's time to just get it all over with."

Paul could imagine the headlines in the *Times*: Cop shoots columnist over bad advice. "If you feel that way, I suppose I could say I have it coming,"

"*You* have it coming? What are you talking about?" said the puzzled officer. "Wait. You think I'm gonna shoot you?" He shook his head. "I'm talking about me, for God's sake."

"No, don't!" Paul blurted out. "You can't do that!"

"Why not?"

"Put that thing back in that thing."

"The gun?"

Paul nodded, speechless.

"In the holster?"

He nodded again.

With a tremor in his voice that he could not conceal, Paul said, "You can't just go shoot yourself in the head because your marriage went bad. Or because some fool gave you the wrong advice. Things could change. She might come back to you. Or you might find life better without her. You can't do something so final."

"Why not?"

Yeah, why not? How are you going to answer that, you subway-jumping, pier-diving, artery-clogging hypocrite?

"In all honesty, I can't give you the answer. But please, trust me. That's not something you want to do. If nothing else, think of the disgrace you'd bring on your uniform. What about your family? Think what it would do to them."

"I don't have a family."

"Oh. Well think about your friends."

"I lost them when they heard what my wife accused me of."

Paul was running out of reasons. Who is there, after family and friends? "Do you have a girlfriend?" he asked.

"Nope."

"Someone you've been thinking would make a nice girlfriend?

He shook his head.

"Well, *somebody* will feel the loss," Paul said.

"Like who?"

No answer.

"Here," he said, offering the gun to Paul, who could do no more than stare at it.

"What do you want me to do?"

"Do it for me."

"Put that thing away. It could be loaded."

The officer stared at him curiously. Then he slid the gun back into its holster while Paul watched apprehensively. Finally, the officer broke into a smile, which turned into a laugh.

"What's funny?" asked Paul, not sure he wanted to know.

The laugh got larger, louder. "'It could be loaded'? My service revolver? That's very funny."

"You mean that thing *is* loaded?"

"Paul, I'm a cop."

"Yeah, well, I don't have a lot of experience with those things. I actually don't have *any* experience."

"The sad truth is, most people don't. They get the experience quickly, on the way out," replied the officer.

Then he paused for a moment and asked reflectively, "Do you have any idea what it's like to realize there's no reason to keep living?"

"Yes, I do. I really do," answered Paul.

"Would you ever do it, to yourself?"

"I don't think so."

"Why not?"

"Do you have any idea how polluted that water is out there?" he said, pointing to the bay.

Puzzled, the officer replied, "Water?"

"Think about it," said Paul.

"I'm trying."

Whether or not he chose to think about it, the officer fell silent, opened the door, and stepped out of the car, waving over his shoulder as he walked to his own vehicle. Paul could see the man's face lighted by the green lights of the instrument panel as he drove past. He was laughing and shaking his head and seemed to be talking to himself as he turned his police cruiser around and headed toward the highway.

Paul waited a few minutes before starting his car. He thought about the strange encounter with the troubled police officer. Could he have done anything to relieve the poor man's anxiety? Had he been too perfunctory in his response to the plea for help with a troubled marriage? More to the point, was the affair further proof that Paul had absolutely no business advising men on the problems they faced? How many others had he driven to such extreme measures as trying to blow their brains out? Having an answer to none of these questions, he drove out of the parking lot, onto PCH, and headed north toward Malibu.

He chose a long, circuitous route home, hoping he would arrive back late enough to find Sam asleep, saving himself from another confrontation and the embarrassment certain to accompany it. He drove to Topanga Canyon Road, which, like Sunset Boulevard, ended at the bay. The steep, winding road crests at the top of the Santa Monica Mountains and Mulholland Drive, the dividing line between the San Fernando Valley and everything in Los Angeles referred to as the west side. It is far more than a physical division. The valley, viewed derisively by smug westsiders as the world's largest and dullest suburb, is an endless string of neat, safe, and boring communities populated by two million families named Cleaver. The Cleavers claim, with equal derision, that the other side of the mountain, from Hollywood to Venice Beach, is the largest neo-Gomorrah on earth, where decadence, drugs, lust, and materialism reign, for which its denizens never apologize but, rather, revel in. A radio-talk-show host once summed up the difference between the west and east sides with the following diatribe: "If you want to snooze your life away in the safety of lily-white suburbia with nothing more exciting than a mall to titillate you, settle in the valley. If you prefer the nonstop unpredictable hedonism, the daily freak show, the music, the culture, the beach, go west and stay there. You know the movie *To Live and Die in L.A.*? The west side is where you do the living. The valley is where you die. Ever notice all the cemeteries there, for God's sake?" The talk-show host was reportedly burned in effigy at several impromptu valley bonfires, one of which ignited a brush fire that worked its way to the top of the dividing ridge and started its way down the west side. This prompted the host, whose ratings were soaring over the dispute, to accuse valley dwellers of trying to start the nation's first suburban riots, in which they were willing to burn down their own clean communities to show their frustration with all the boredom. It surprised no one in that unique megalopolis when the San Fernando Valley tried to secede from Los Angeles. And, of course, the radio personality took credit for starting the movement and supported it enthusiastically. The issue eventually went to the voters and lost by a wide margin, to no one's surprise, perhaps because Angelenos would fear the normalcy of only a single personality.

By the time he reached home, Paul had logged seventy-eight miles and four hours. He saw to his relief that the lights were off in the apartment. He took care to enter very quietly and tiptoe past the sofa. *Let sleeping ex-wives lie*, he told himself, and headed straight to the bedroom without so much as a stop in the kitchen for a late-night dose of cholesterol and saturated fat.

As he groped for the switch to a bedside lamp, he was startled by a hand grabbing his wrist. He recoiled, knowing full well whose hand it was.

"What the hell are you doing?" he asked Sam, who reached over and turned on the lamp on the other side of the bed.

"Waiting for you. I couldn't sleep in there," she said, sitting up.

Now he saw not just the grin on her face, but the lack of anything on her upper body as well. The bedcovers were not doing much of a job of covering, gathered up as they were just below her waist and revealing breasts that had not lost their fullness or firmness in the years since he had last seen or held them.

"Okay, then I'll sleep in there," he said. "And cover yourself up, will you please?"

"Am I making you uncomfortable?" she cooed.

"No, you're making me thoroughly pissed off at your antics."

"You think all I want to do is get you into bed with me, pull your face down to my breasts where you can caress and suck them, while I reach down and open those pants you're wearing and take you in my hand, before I slip down and let my mouth finish the job. Is that it, baby?"

He stared down at her, fighting the memory he had of her favorite trick for defusing his anger over something she had done to him, like the series of affairs he had caught her in. It had worked, more times than he liked to admit, until he finally decided to end the torture—and the most pleasurable sex he had ever experienced. But it was not going to work tonight.

"I don't seem to recall enjoying that sort of thing," he said.

"You're denying it happened?"

"No, it happened. But as I said, I don't recall enjoying it."

"Could've fooled this girl, with all that moaning."

"Just the sound of the regrets I saw coming."

She pulled the covers off the rest of her body and, smiling up at him, swung her legs around to sit on the edge of the bed. Then she reached out her hand, trying to take hold of his belt. He stepped back to avoid the grasp and turned to leave the room.

"You don't know what you're missing, sailor," she said as he walked out into the darkness and closed the door forcefully behind him.

In a sudden rush of anger, she shouted at the door, "Go blow yourself! I'm sure your new girlfriend doesn't do it for you!"

He smiled and thought of Helen, trying to picture her doing what Sam was offering to do, but it was something he could not imagine. He approached his desk and the computer perched atop it, its blue light glowing in the darkened room. He hit the Enter key and then clicked on his current column file. His fingers then began their high-speed dance on the keyboard:

> *Dear Paul:*
>
> *My former wife, from whom I've been divorced for four years, arrived, unannounced, on my doorstep today. She looked as beautiful and appealing as I've always remembered her. But she also served as a painful reminder of why our marriage ended. God gave her a barely average intellect, a substandard sense of humanity, and a basement-level morality—but a heavenly body and the knowledge of how to use it to her advantage.*

Which is what she tried to do to me, once more. She apparently was forced out of her own home by the cretin with whom she had been having an affair during our marriage. He's younger than her and, if possible, even more intellectually and morally challenged. It came as no surprise that he eventually tired of my former wife, took up with another woman, and, to make room for her, forced my ex out of her own home. Which is why she appeared on my doorstep with her luggage.

She pleaded with me to let her stay in my apartment. She also dangled the only thing she knows how to use to get her way: her sexuality. She tried to seduce me in my own home, twice, in fact, in one evening. When I left in search of some fresh air, she planted herself, naked, in my bed, moving off the sofa I had assigned to her. On my return, she tried every trick she knows—and believe me, she knows many—to get me into bed with her. I confess that she has not lost her appeal, physically speaking, nor has she gained any new appeal, morally speaking.

Difficult as it was, I resisted her seduction, left her in my own bedroom, and sat down to write this letter to you, out of utter frustration and in a quandary.

The quandary? I have met another woman,

someone with whom I feel a rapport while at the same time I feel trepidation. She and I might be particularly well suited for one another, largely because we seem to share what I would call an unorthodox view of life and the options available for dealing with its disappointments. The trepidation? I have my doubts about our ability to seek and sustain a commitment any deeper than agreeing to take an occasional walk together. We share an aversion to the future, given our disappointments of the past. Still, I am drawn to this woman, with whom I have shared nothing more intimate than conversation that is more circular than linear.

The last thing I need in my life right now is a former wife encamped in my home, naked and seductive. But I'm not sure how to dislodge her. Call me cowardly, but I simply can't bring myself to remove her forcibly, which is the only way she will leave until she is good and ready to go on her own.

If you have any suggestions for solving the problem that has descended on me, I'd be grateful for them.

Hoisted On My Own Petard

He paused, looking at the words on the screen, and then began typing again:

Dear Hoisted,

I've always wondered what a petard is, so I looked it up in the dictionary. It's a metal cone filled with explosives and used in ancient warfare, a kind of firecracker that was hung on a fortress gate and exploded to force an opening. When someone is "hoisted on his own petard," I think it means his own little bomb has backfired on him, which could be embarrassing if there's anyone around, or, worse, it could put out your eye.

It sounds as though your petard has backfired on you twice: once when you married a woman whose claim to relationship fame was her sexuality and again now that you let her back in your home, either out of some sense of duty or an erection for old time's sake.

My advice: Lose the duty thing and the hard-on. Both will block your ability to reason; neither will get you anywhere but into serious trouble.

Then, take whatever steps you feel are necessary to rid yourself of this woman who has staged a home invasion. Tell her there's another woman in your life, a strangely wonderful woman who won't eat in public, who talks in circles that oddly make profound sense to you, and whose hair can stand up in back on command, it seems.

Put up a petard, one that won't backfire on you again. Let it blow a hole in your bedroom wall and send her packing in fear of what might come next.

Let her know you're serious about getting her out of your life, that you're capable of action she never dreamed you could countenance or commit.

Tell her stories you've heard about men who were pushed beyond their human limits to unpredictable levels of passion and anger.

Regale her with tales of unthinkable acts of violence by ordinarily passive men. Talk of guns, knives and clubs.

And light up the petard.

But just be sure you stand back.

Paul

As he looked back on what he had written, he felt a sense of catharsis. His eight-hundred-word laxative loosened the pressure in his head enough to let the backed-up anger flow out of him.

Mission thus accomplished, he popped an Ambien into his mouth and his body down on the sofa for some badly needed sleep.

The sleeping pill did its job. He remembered little of a dream he had been having when something awakened him from a deep sleep. The dream included a voice that kept repeating the words *You bastard*. Propping himself up on one elbow, stiff from a night on the soft sofa, he saw that someone was sitting at his computer, saying, "You bastard" as she read what was on the screen. The someone was Sam, of course, wearing a white chenille robe. Paul's robe, for which he had been billed a hundred and twenty-five dollars by the Ritz after packing everything in sight during a frenzied rush to make an airplane home from London.

"I don't recall inviting you to read what's on my computer, or to do it in my bathrobe," said a groggy Paul.

"'Substandard humanity'? 'Basement-level morality'? That's what you think of me?"

"You never did like my writing much, did you?"

"I don't have a problem with your writing. Just what you say in it."

"I'm sorry, but aren't they one and the same?"

She turned to look at him, puzzled.

"What are you saying, that I type nicely but you don't like what I type? It's like that Mel Brooks joke, when he says Shakespeare was a terrible writer. He would make a *p* that looked like a *t*, an *f* you couldn't tell from an *s*. Terrible penmanship."

"Very funny. If you want me to leave, you don't have to sit up all night writing insults about me—to yourself, for God's sake. You could just ask me to go."

"I thought I did."

"I suppose you're going to print this column," she said, ignoring his response.

He only shrugged.

"Well, if you do, you'll hear from my lawyer so fast your head will spin like Damien's."

"Is it clockwise or counterclockwise in this hemisphere?" asked Paul

"You have to turn everything serious into a bad comedy routine."

"Someone else said that recently."

"Who, your new girlfriend who doesn't know what a mouth is for?"

"Actually, she tends to use it for something you haven't yet discovered: intelligent discourse."

"That's right, I barely have an intellect, as you say in this drivel."

"No. I said you have one. But it's barely average. There's a difference."

"Stop splitting hairs."

"If you'll stop using clichés."

She stood, pushing the desk chair back so hard it sailed across the room and hit the sofa then tipped over onto the floor. She faced him down, hands on hips, her face flush with anger. "You never got over my affair, did you?"

No answer, just a study of the fallen chair.

"You couldn't let it go, even after all this time, could you?"

Still no response.

"And now, when I need a little help, you have to keep on punishing me, don't you?"

"I guess it's a failing of mine—an inability to overlook the fact that you were on a mission to bed down every male under the age of thirty in Los Angeles with a double-digit IQ."

"But I married you, didn't I? Maybe it was because yours is four digits—your IQ. Too bad everything else isn't oversized."

"That's very good, Sam. You should think about writing. I imagine you type nicely."

"Yes, I do. And I also delete well," she said with a dramatic flourish, and bent over the computer mouse, dragging it downward, highlighting the entire document, then ceremoniously hitting the Delete key with the long, red nail on the end of her index finger, sending into cyberspace the entire letter to Paul from Paul.

"See, nothing to worry about. It's gone. Simple as that," said Paul. But the way she looked at him suspiciously told him she had a feeling he was being too calm, that he had probably saved the letter onto a CD or knew how to retrieve it somehow. "You'll never know, will you?"

"Know what?"

"The answer to the question that's running through your head. Guess you'll just have to read the paper and find out."

He stood and started for the bedroom. "I'm going to shave and shower. I have an appointment downtown. I'll also be gone tonight. I assume you will be too."

"Of course, Paul. Even with my barely average intellect,

I can tell when I'm not welcome."

He smiled gratuitously and bent over to pick up the fallen desk chair, which he rolled back to its place. "Nice to see you again, Sam," he said.

Chapter 13

Paul was grateful he had things to do that would keep him away from home for the rest of the day until it was time to pick up Helen for their dance date. There was a meeting with Milton and the program director of the radio station where his show would be launched, followed by his weekly visit with his mother. The meeting would be, according to Milton, "a couple hours of brainstorming about how the show should go." Paul hated that word *brainstorming*, which he had made clear to Milton by launching a discourse on brains raining down and pummeling everyone in the meeting. Lunch with the survivors of the storm would follow at a downtown Japanese restaurant for some de rigueur sushi. The visit with his mother would only serve to sadden him, he knew, because her condition was one whose only change could be for the worse. The latest troubling news he had received from his mother's caregivers was that she had entered a dangerous wandering stage. She had become obsessed with leaving what she thought was a prison she claimed she had been unjustly committed to for crimes she had not committed. Paul was shocked during his last visit to see a device locked around his mother's ankle. He was told it was a monitoring anklet that would sound an alarm if she tried to leave her floor. The decision to monitor her electronically was reached after she followed a visitor out a locked hallway door all the way to the parking lot, where she was seen with her foot up on a fire hydrant, exposing a good deal of leg and holding her thumb out to passing cars.

The funny thing was, though, that his mother proudly showed him her new ankle bracelet, claiming it had been given to her by Yassou, the twenty-fifth suitor on her fictional list. "A Greek," she had said admiringly. "You know how they are."

Following the visit with his mother, he had scheduled a haircut—not, of course, at Helen of Troy, but at one of the few remaining barbershops in Los Angeles. The shop was simply called Pete's, even though Pete had died years earlier and a man named Hank had been the owner ever since. A classic red-and-white barber pole rotated on the sidewalk in front of Pete's, located in the Silver Lake district, a treed enclave that clung tenaciously to its neighborhood character in spite of its proximity to the seedier extremes of northern Hollywood. Paul was a week early for his usual once-a-month cut, but he had felt a need for a trim on the day of his next date with Helen. He wondered, though, if she might notice the fresh cut and ask why, unlike Milton, he took his hair business elsewhere. He had an answer prepared: he didn't have the heart to abandon Hank after years of a standing appointment every four weeks. The truth: he would be too humiliated to face the din, the curious stares, and Harvey's high theatrics at Helen's salon. Besides, he did not want his hair styled, but simply cut. Which made him a walking anachronism in L.A. But he preferred it that way.

His final stop of the day would be at a small florist shop in the Fairfax district, where he planned to buy a fresh gardenia, which seemed appropriate to give to Helen for the evening. He chose the pungent flower in part because he detected the fragrance on Helen the night he tried to rescue her from the fish impaled on her heel. He also chose a gardenia because of memories he had of his junior and senior high school proms, at which no girl appeared without one of the flowers on her wrist or her organza dress.

At five-fifteen he had been to his meeting and his visit, had his hair cut, picked up the gardenia, and was on his way home. His hopeful vision was of an empty apartment with nothing slashed or shattered in angry retribution, where he could shower, shave, and dress for his evening with Helen.

But oh how quickly a vision can be dashed, he warned himself as he turned the key in the door. He paused long enough to imagine a scene of battlefield chaos: dishes smashed, drawers emptied, pillows sliced open, even toilet paper—yes, toilet paper—wrapped around everything in the apartment: proof that Sam had never outgrown her adolescence. He took a deep breath and braced himself for the worst.

To his cautious relief, though, nothing seemed out of order when he entered. Doctor Kevorkian still scowled down at him from the wall, unslashed. Every pillow seemed intact and in place. Even his computer seemed untouched. In the bedroom, the bed was neatly made, prompting him to wonder if Sam actually had grown up.

His breathing returned to normal as he stepped into the shower. Still, he could not help conjuring up the well-defined shadow of a raised hand holding a long knife on the other side of the curtain. He laughed at himself, looked away, closed his eyes, and covered his face with lathered soap, thanking whatever power had removed his former wife from his apartment.

But then, without warning, he was nearly knocked off his pale feet by the sound of shower-curtain rings screeching across metal like a braking subway train. He opened his eyes, wincing from the sting of soap, and tried to focus on the shape before him.

There was no psychotic man or woman leering at him, no knife poised in the air. Instead, it was the smirking face of Sam, confronting him eyeball to stinging eyeball.

"Hope I haven't frightened you," she purred.

"You always have, Sam."

She looked down at his groin area and raised one eyebrow. "Looking good," she chortled.

"I wish I could say the same for you."

"Aren't you going to invite me in? Remember that time in *our* shower?"

"When you tried to strangle me with the soap-on-a-rope?" he asked.

"No, silly, the other time."

"Would you mind telling me why you're still here?"

"I hope you noticed I cleaned the place up."

"Mostly I noticed you didn't tear it apart, for which I suppose I should be grateful."

He pulled the shower curtain back across the rod and addressed her lingering shadow. "Excuse me, but I'd like to finish showering, if you don't mind. We can continue the conversation, if we really have to, some other time."

Sam apparently got the message and retreated to the living room while Paul readied himself for the evening. She managed to make her presence felt in the bathroom, though, where Paul inflicted a deep razor nick on the underside of his nose. The styptic pencil he applied did nothing to stop the bleeding, but only stung the sensitive area enough to send him into a fit of sneezing. *You're going to show up at Helen's house with a flourish of bloody sneezes. That's attractive*, he told himself.

Eventually, he managed to stop the bleeding and get dressed in a sports shirt, slacks, and sports coat in his favorite palette: black and black and black. The only color he wore was the dark-red clotting that had formed on his nose, which he hoped would not break open at some inopportune time.

"You've got something on your nose," said Sam, sitting on the sofa and looking up from a magazine.

"Yes, I know," he said, avoiding looking at her while he searched for the ring of keys that was not in its usual place atop his desk.

"Looking for these?" she said, holding up and shaking the keys.

He turned and approached her. "Yes. What are you doing with them?"

"I had a copy made of the door key while you were gone so I won't get locked out."

"Weren't you going to leave tonight?"

"I still haven't found a place to stay."

"There are places designed for people who need a place to stay. They're called hotels, and they're catching on," he said, taking the keys from her hand.

"The truth is, I can't afford a hotel."

"Did he take your money and credit cards too?"

She could only shrug an admission.

"This guy's a genius at obfuscation. And that's not something that's done in bed."

"Just one more night and I'll be gone. Promise," she said.

He stopped at the door, turned to her, and let out a long sigh. "Okay. One more night. On the sofa, not in my bed. And don't worry about returning the key. I'm going to have the locks changed. I hear there's a ring of former wives working the area. Good night."

"Thank you," she said.

"Don't mention it. And I mean it, please don't mention it," he answered, and closed the door firmly enough to add a loud punctuation mark.

———

It was precisely seven thirty, not a minute earlier or later, when Paul rang the doorbell at Helen's house. He had, in fact, arrived at seven-twenty-three on a first pass and, as a result, took a seven-minute detour rather than risk the embarrassment of premature arrival. The door opened so quickly it seemed as though Helen had been standing in wait behind it.

"Stay," she said over her shoulder as Paul drank in the image of her. This time she wore a red satin blouse and black skirt cut well above the knees, revealing perfectly shaped legs in dark hose accentuated by stiletto-heeled shoes. On anyone else, he would have found her outfit borderline tacky. On her, he found it drop-dead beautiful.

Basic instinct urged him to pull her body to his and suggest staying home to dance in the dark. His superego kept him standing his ground. "Nice to see you," he said.

She stepped onto the porch and pulled the door shut behind her. He wondered why she had not invited him inside. The roar of her giant dog on the other side of the door answered his question.

He brought forward the hand he had been keeping behind his back and offered her the gardenia in its clear acetate box.

She smiled down at it. "For me?"

He returned the smile and nodded.

She seemed as awkward as he felt, standing on her front porch and being offered a corsage.

"Should I wear it?" she asked.

"I was hoping you would."

She opened the box and inhaled deeply to enjoy the fragrance of its contents. "I'm very fond of gardenias," she said. She removed the large single flower and held it against her right upper chest, then on the left side. "I'm not quite sure where to put it."

Paul took her hand and guided it to the center of her blouse, at the top button.

She looked down at herself and nodded. She then held the flower out to him. "Would you like to do it?"

Would I like *to?* He asked himself. *I'd die for the chance.* "Okay, if you'd like," he said aloud with false indifference.

He withdrew the long hatpin from the flower's stem and held the gardenia at the intersection of red satin and ivory flesh. He looked up into her eyes as if waiting for permission to proceed.

"Have you ever performed the procedure?" she asked.

"Not without anesthesia," he answered, touching her bare chest with two of his knuckles. A surge of delight rushed through his body.

"Ouch!" he gasped in response to the stab of pain in his left thumb as the pin missed the buttonhole he had aimed for. "Glad it wasn't your … " He stopped short of the word.

"Chest," she offered.

"Yes. Let's give it another try," he said, holding his stuck thumb out like a hitchhiker to avoid bloodying her blouse.

He finally succeeded in securing the flower with no further injury to either party.

"Lovely," she said, looking down at herself.

"Yes, you are."

He didn't care how adolescently foolish he sounded. She apparently didn't either.

"Where is it we're going to be dancing?" she asked as he drove westbound along Olympic Boulevard.

"In Venice."

She seemed puzzled. "What sort of a place?"

"The beach."

Further puzzlement.

"It's outdoors, actually."

"Not on a pier, I would hope."

"No. Do you know Muscle Beach?"

She turned to study him. "Yes. But I haven't heard of dancing there."

"It's something that takes place once a month, during the summer. Next to Muscle Beach. On the esplanade."

"Ballroom dancing?"

"Not quite. It's a form of folk dancing."

"Oh. Irish?"

He shook his head. "Jewish. It's a wonderful tradition."

"It's funny, I didn't think of you as religious."

"I'm not," he said.

"But you're Jewish."

"No. Presbyterian."

"I don't understand. You're not Jewish, but you're drawn to the traditions. Why?"

"The sadness."

"Oh, I see," she said, tugging her short skirt downward.

The conversation was of things small and insignificant as they continued along Venice Boulevard until reaching its terminus at what is called The Boardwalk, which is a misnomer, since there are no boards along its way, only concrete and macadam. Stepping out of the car, they could hear the sounds of amplified music.

"Klezmer," Paul said.

"Beg your pardon?"

"The traditional music. Ever been to a Jewish wedding?"

"Yes. A few, in fact."

"Are you Jewish?"

"No. I was Catholic."

"But you're not now?"

She shook her head as they came closer to the esplanade and the music.

"After all, it's a religion that takes a strong position on people like us. We go straight to hell," he said.

She turned to him as if to respond, but chose not to.

"Welcome, dear friends, welcome!" a deep, strong voice boomed over a loudspeaker, above the music. "Tonight, we dance!"

They reached the edge of a sizeable group of men and women gathered before a portable stage on which a bearded man, dressed in a black frock coat, an open-collared white shirt, and a wide-brimmed black hat, stood before a microphone.

"It's a mitzvah, so many people joining us in the dancing that has been our tradition throughout our history."

An elderly man with a long white beard approached Paul. He held in his hand several blue-and-gold metal cylinders suspended on thin chains. He held them out and nodded to Paul.

"Mezuzah?" asked the man, with a thick accent.

"No, I'm not, actually. A gentile."

"Dese, dey are mezuzahs," the old man sighed, shaking his head. "To hang on the door. Or your neck. Ten dollars. For *der kindella*."

Paul shrugged, confused.

"Little children. Charity. *Fishtei*?"

"Oh, a contribution. For one of those. Sure," said Paul. He reached into his pocket and pulled out a ten-dollar bill, which he gave the man, and then slid one chain and mezuzah off his outstretched arm.

"Thanks, mister. It'll bring good luck. Even to a gentile," said the man, suddenly losing his accent. Paul placed the chain around his neck and dropped the mezuzah down the front of his shirt.

"One for der lady?" the man suggested, regaining his accent.

"Thanks, but we only have one door," said Paul.

"You got two necks," the vendor said, moving on through the crowd.

Some of the people who had gathered in front of the stage were dressed in traditional Chassidic garb, others were not. The bearded members of the klezmer band, sitting behind the man at the microphone, wore billowing peasant blouses over blue jeans in a generational compromise and, of course, black hats. They held at the ready their instruments, which included violins, trumpets, and what appeared to be wind pipes and a miniature accordion.

"Let's rock, baby!" shouted a man at the rear of the crowd, a bearded African American with a broad grin and glazed eyes.

"Yes, yes, we shall do that," said the man at the microphone. "We shall indeed rock, as you say. But first, we must roll. I would like to roll through an introduction of our musicians who honor us tonight with their presence and their talent."

He turned and bowed to the men and signaled them to stand. Then he recited their names: "Izaak, Jacob, Avrom, Saul, Shmuel, Levi, and Sean."

The last name brought laughter from the crowd.

"It's true, his name is really Sean. Sean Lifschitz. Go figure."

"Are you ready to dance?" asked the master of ceremonies.

Shouts of "Yes," "All right," and even a "*Vuh den*?" came back along with applause.

Paul leaned close to speak into Helen's ear, picking up the scent of gardenia. "What do you think so far?"

"We're not wearing hats. Is that all right?" She had to shout above the crowd noise.

A hand came forward from behind her and placed a bandanna on her head. Startled, she turned to see a smiling woman in a peasant dress that touched the ground. The woman nodded.

Helen looked at Paul, not knowing what to do next. He took the ends of the kerchief and tied it under her chin. "I think it's called a babushka," he said in her ear.

She smiled weakly.

A man standing next to the woman behind them now put his hand out, holding a black skullcap. He made a motion with his hand, prompting Paul to take it, which he did, and placed it atop his head. He turned back and said, "Thank you."

"What do they call that?" Helen asked Paul.

"A *yah-mool-ka*," was his butchered answer.

"*Kepa*," corrected a man next to him, with a suffering sigh.

"Whatever," said Paul.

"No, not a whatever, a *kepa*," repeated the man. And Helen gave Paul a reproachful nudge of the elbow.

"Please," boomed the host, "form a circle for the dance. Yes, yes, everybody, join us. No time to be bashful."

The band began playing as the crowd responded, arranging themselves in a ring, holding hands.

"Ah-ah, no hand-holding. Custom does not allow," said the enthusiastic host.

Some people simply let go of one another's hands. Others, though, seemed to know what to do. Men pulled handkerchiefs from their pockets; women pulled scarves from around their necks, and they used them as buffers between their hands and their partners'.

"For those of you unfamiliar with our ways, men and women are not to touch one another in public. So we use a piece of cloth to join us. You may find it old-fashioned, perhaps even foolish, but there is a simple reason we do these things: Tradition!" he shouted.

It was a cue for the band to play the familiar refrain from *Fiddler on the Roof* while the host beamed and clapped his hands to the slowly building melody. The crowd joined in, swaying and clapping. Paul glanced toward Helen, who seemed enthralled by what she was seeing and hearing.

The host stepped to the microphone. "Arms outstretched, everybody, but remember, no touching," he cautioned like a kindergarten teacher.

"These folks have an interesting idea," Paul said. "Keep men and women at hankie length. Just think of the problems that could be avoided."

Helen didn't respond, perhaps because she was concentrating on the music and bouncing from one foot to the other with a smooth swinging of her shoulders, something else for Paul to admire in her.

Paul pulled a neatly pressed white handkerchief from his pocket, unfolded it, and offered it to Helen. She grasped one corner.

"Please," said a man next to her, holding out a brightly patterned silk scarf, which she cordially accepted.

A heavyset woman in traditional dress with a determined, almost angry, expression on her face handed the end of a kerchief to Paul without looking at him.

He leaned close to Helen's ear and said, "I think she likes me."

The circle of about sixty people began moving slowly, in time with the music. Paul and Helen both found it easy to pick up the purposeful sideways step, one leg crossing over the other. The tempo of the music gradually increased, leading the dancers to do the same until they eventually were jumping more than stepping. Paul's breath became more labored. He looked at Helen and saw the same in her. But then he looked to the stern-faced woman to his right, who showed no signs whatsoever of exertion.

"You must work out," he shouted to her, between breaths.

She glanced at him sideways like he was an alien.

By the time the first dance ended, both Helen and Paul's faces were glossed with perspiration. He offered her his handkerchief to mop her brow, then took it to blot his own face, which sent a thrill through him. He told himself it was their first exchange of bodily fluids, albeit an indirect one.

"Now, we have a surprise!" the host exclaimed. "We are honored tonight with the presence of a man and a woman who took their wedding vows at sunset in the Shul by the Sea, on Venice Boulevard. They have come to celebrate their holy union with us. Is that not a gift for all of us?"

The crowd answered with an enthusiastic round of applause, sprinkled by several shouts of "Mazel tov!" The host reached out his hand toward the back of the circle of people, which parted to allow a smiling young couple to enter. The groom, in his twenties and looking very earnest, was dressed in a traditional black suit, white shirt, and black hat from which black curls flowed. The fringes of a prayer shawl hung down from the suit coat. The bride, dressed in an embroidered white gown, showed only a hint of a modest smile, her eyelids lowering as she seemed to float forward, connected to her new husband by a length of white satin they both held.

Two men appeared in the circle, each holding a simple wooden chair. They placed the chairs on the ground and stood back while the groom sat in one and the bride took her place in the other, both holding on to the connecting length of satin. The men then faced the circle and held out their arms, signaling with their hands for other men to join in. Six stepped forward, seeming to know exactly what to do: three each bent over and grasped the bottom of a chair leg, and the two men who had beckoned them each took hold of the fourth leg. A nod of heads cued the eight men to hoist the chairs as high into the air as they could reach while the bride and groom looked toward one another with understated bliss and without apprehension. The music began again and the chair holders started to dance. The chairs tilted to and fro with the motion, but neither the bride nor the groom worried. She, in fact, simply looked happily at peace with the world; he looked confidently pleased, yet shy.

The circle began to move again in a clockwise path. Every face in it bore a smile; even the stolid woman to Paul's right broke into a reluctant grin. The pace gradually increased again with the lively, yet sad strains of the twangy music. One of the dancers made a move toward the swaying bride and groom, his hands held high, and everyone in the circle followed suit, meeting the couple in a tighter circle and then retreating back again. The movement was repeated several times, with increasing speed to keep up with the music. Eventually, the circular dancing reached frenetic, dizzying proportions.

Helen focused on the couple in the chairs, the man looking adoringly upon his new wife, she gazing straight into his eyes with a look that seemed to foretell, in all innocence, the mysterious joys she would soon discover for the first time.

The vertigo she felt from trying to focus on the dizzying scene turned Helen's vision blurry. Through the haze, though, she could see the groom's face and the anticipatory smile upon it. But the face was no longer that of an eager twenty-something groom. It was now Paul's, topped by a black hat and ringed by long prayer curls floating on the wind. The smile became overly confident, self-congratulatory.

Helen turned her attention to the bride and, as she feared, it was now her own face she saw, wearing a look that bordered on the fearful as she struggled to keep from falling out of the chair onto the concrete below. The faster the music became, the more she tilted, until she finally flew from the chair and catapulted, in a long arc, out and over the ocean.

At that point, Helen felt herself hit a hard surface, not a body of water. It was the concrete promenade floor on which she sat, legs askew, her head spinning, her vision darkening.

The music continued while Paul bent over her. The dancers did not stop; some, in fact, laughed as they passed her.

"Are you all right?" Paul shouted.

"No," she answered, shaking her head.

"She's hurt," Paul bellowed to anyone who would listen.

"No, I'm not. I'm just not all right."

The host saw Helen on the ground and seemed to have heard Paul's outcry. He waved an arm at the musicians behind him, and their playing came to an uneven halt, the accordion remaining a lone trailing chord behind.

"We have a mishap," said the host, with sincere concern. "Please, someone help her."

The dancers surrounded her in a cacophonous expression of concern and willingness to help.

"Get her water."

"No, a blanket."

"Call a doctor."

"I *am* a doctor."

The young man claiming to be a doctor approached Helen, but she waved her arms in the air as though trying to brush away a mosquito. "No, I'm all right. I don't need a doctor."

Undaunted, the man leaned over her and moved an index finger back and forth across her line of vision.

"Why are you doing that?" Helen asked him.

"Checking your eye movement is all," the doctor answered. "It's fine."

"So is your finger movement. But it's making me dizzy."

The doctor turned to the crowd confidently, as if he had actually done something to help. "She's okay," he proclaimed.

"Thank God."

"You sure?"

"Should we call 911?"

Several cell phones appeared from pockets.

Helen held out a hand to Paul, who took it and helped her to her feet, steadying her with his other arm around her waist. She wobbled uncertainly as he led her through the circle. A hand holding a bottle of water reached between two concerned dancers. Helen waved it off and walked in the direction of the beach, seeming more humiliated than injured. Paul watched her attentively as she retrieved a brown paper bag from her purse and began breathing into it. Between breaths, she looked at him, wide-eyed, even a bit suspiciously.

"You'd better sit down," Paul said.

"No. I need to go," she said, removing the bag from her mouth.

"Where?"

"I don't know."

"Were you about to faint? Is that why you fell down?"

She shook her head and took another breath from the bag.

"Did the dancing make you too dizzy?"

She shook her head and then took two more breaths before removing the bag and putting it back in her purse.

"Okay now?" he asked.

Yet another head shake.

"Then will you please tell me what happened?"

"I saw something."

"Where?"

"There. Where we were dancing."

"What was it?"

"You." She stopped. "And me."

"I have no idea what you're saying. You and I were dancing, having what I thought was an enjoyable time. You saw something: the two of us. And you fell down. What am I missing?"

She started to say something but stopped. He noticed the fork of hair was up again. She threw up her hands, turned, and walked onto the sand. That she didn't remove her stiletto-heeled shoes added a touch of comedy when each step made one leg shorter than the other. He followed her toward the water's edge.

"Don't forget, that water's very dirty," he called to her.

"Thank you for reminding me," she called back.

No more than twenty yards from the surf line, she stopped and turned to face him, hands on hips. "You were wearing one of those big black hats." She emphasized the size of the brim by holding her hands out from her head. "And you had curls coming down from it. A beard too."

"That was the groom."

"Not what I was seeing. And I was wearing a white gown."

"You were fantasizing. An interesting fantasy, I'd say,"

he said with a smile.

She ignored him. "We were in those chairs, holding onto a white cloth. Then everything started to spin, and that's when I fell down."

He approached her. "That's quite a transference. You, the bride; me, the groom."

"It's *I* the groom," she said.

"No, you're the bride."

"And you think you're being funny again."

"And you take everything too grammatically."

"I can't help it. It's my nature."

"Why are you so upset?" he asked.

"I'm not upset. I'm—" Her mouth stood open, but the word did not come out.

He waited.

Then she closed her mouth, took a deep breath, and puffed up her cheeks before letting the air rush out. "Confused," she finally said.

"I agree with that. You see a bride and groom on chairs, and then you see you and me—or is it you and I you see? No, you can't see I, you see me."

She glared at him.

"Sorry. Okay, you see the two of us in the chairs, and you fall down over it. Yes, I can see why you're confused. Why do you think you saw us there?"

"You seem to have so many answers. Why do *you* think I saw us?"

"The answer might be very simple."

She waited.

"Wishful thinking,"

"Ha!"

"Ha? That's your response?"

"Now you *are* being funny. You think that's what I wish for? To be a bride, on a chair, with a man in a big hat and a beard and curls? Ha!"

"That would be so terrible? To commit to someone?"

"You can't possibly be serious," she said.

"And why not? In case you haven't noticed, I'm, well, drawn to you. Let me rephrase that. I was drawn to you when I first saw you on the subway platform. More so when I watched you prance around the pier with a fish on your foot. And I was drawn closer and closer at Farmers' Market, the tar pits, and the Santa Monica steps. I found everything you did absolutely adorable, in a quirky way."

She stood motionless, her eyes wide, her lips slightly parted, as if waiting for a punch line. He delivered one.

"And now, I find that I'm more than drawn to you. I'm, well, I'm at a loss for anything but the most ordinary words to describe the extraordinary way I feel about you. So I'll say them. I think I'm falling—"

"No, don't say it!" she blurted out, putting her hands over her ears. "You can't."

"Yes, I can," he said softly.

She turned, her hands still over her ears, and faced the surf. Then she began walking in a circle around Paul, looking at the sand, shaking her head. Her high heels sank deep with each step, making her walk like a high-stepping drum major-ette, until, exasperated, she kicked off the shoes without so much as missing a step and continued bare-stockinged.

"I don't believe this," she finally said to the sand. "He kisses me a few times, and then wants to make whoopee with me."

He burst out laughing. "*Whoopee?*"

"If you think I'm going to use that word, you have another thing coming," she said, resuming her roundabout walk.

"What do you have against the word *love*?"

She stopped again.

"I asked you not to say that."

"And why not?"

"I'm surprised you even have to ask." Back to the walking.

He fell in behind her, knowing full well how ridiculous the two of them must look. "Will you stop walking in circles, for God's sake? You're going to erode the beach, which is against the law."

"What do you suggest I do?" she asked.

He reached out to her and took hold of both her shoulders, stopping her. She turned to face him. He said nothing, but pulled her close to him. She neither resisted nor complied, which left her folded toward him at the waist, the rest of her still planted in place. He kissed her and, still, there was neither resistance nor compliance. He dropped his hands, but she remained hinged at the waist. And he kissed her again.

This time, she straightened and allowed him, beckoned him, it seemed, to come closer, which he did, then put his arms around her waist, gently pulling her to him. The soft warmth of her body thrilled him more than he had imagined it would.

"Something has begun," he whispered in her ear. "And I don't want it to end."

She pulled back. "Do you hear yourself?"

"The music's a little loud, but, yes, I can hear myself."

"How can you possibly talk about not wanting an end. That's all you think about. Subways, piers, icebergs … "

"Icebergs?"

"The thing you told me Eskimos do. And consuming cholesterol, climbing those steps—I'm sorry, but I find it hard to believe you're interested in beginnings. You're an ender."

"Forgive the cliché, but it takes one to know one."

She started off again, but he stopped her in her circular tracks. He put his hands on her shoulder and pulled her to him again. "Maybe I am an ender. We both seem to be. We have that in common. It's what brought us together. An affinity."

"It's not a book club," she said.

"We can help each other."

"How? With a push off a cliff? Holding each other's heads underwater? It's insane."

"Maybe it is. But I just want to be with you."

She stood silent, assessing him. He kissed her again. She made no effort to stop him. In fact, she pressed into him, her hands moving up to the back of his neck, holding him tightly. Her breath came more rapidly, along with a soft moan. They paused, only briefly, and then kissed again. Her knees buckled, and they slid down to the sand together, facing one another on their knees, still locked in an embrace.

Finally, she pulled her head back and searched his eyes. "What is this we're doing?" she said.

"Maybe you're reluctant to call it what it is. It doesn't mean we shouldn't enjoy it. Does it feel pleasurable to you?"

A nod.

"Does something inside push you forward?"

Another nod.

"I feel the same way."

This time, she led the kiss, leaning into it so strongly he fell backward onto the sand with her landing on top of him. He felt every inch of her body against his and reveled in it all—her breasts against his chest, her belly on his, their hips together, as well as their thighs and pelvises. The kisses grew deeper, more urgent, as their bodies pressed against one another, as if trying to become one.

"Wait, please," Helen suddenly cried out, coming up for air. She rolled off his body and sat upright, her legs splayed in front of her.

"What's wrong?"

"Now where are we going?" she exclaimed —more of a demand than a question.

"I was hoping it was obvious," he said.

"I imagine it is. But, I'm sorry, I'm just not prepared."

"I am." He grinned and reached into a side pocket. Out came a foil package.

She stared at what he held up. And then she nodded, looking off. "Well, I see you had plans."

"Shouldn't I have?"

"Don't you think it a bit presumptuous?"

"No, I don't think it has anything to do with presumption. It's protection, as simple as that. Unless my memory fails me, you keep a nice little supply on hand yourself."

"That's completely different."

"I don't think it is."

"You are entitled to think whatever you wish."

"Come on, Helen, this isn't about condoms. It's something else that's bothering you. We were getting along just fine and, out of the blue—or the sand—you jump up and put a stop to everything."

She got up on her knees again, but he didn't join her. He remained on the sand, propped up on one elbow, too self-conscious to get up on his knees, what with the protrusion in his trousers that would point directly at her—yet another sign of presumptuousness.

"I'm sorry. I'm sure you find me unfair. Or unreasonable," she said.

"Or unfathomable."

"Think what you will, but I can't have sex with you in the sand."

"What if I had brought a blanket?"

"That's not what I meant. I realize, all too well, that I

have been, like you, shall we say … Actually, I don't know what we should say."

"Aroused?"

Shrug.

"Impassioned?"

Shrug two. "You may think I have encouraged you. And you would be right. Sometimes the body gets ahead of the brain."

"We men call it the little head taking over for the big head."

She thought about that for a moment or two. Then, flustered, she replied, "Yes. Well, we women don't have little heads. I was thinking more of the heart."

"So you're saying we're not destined to ever have sex."

"I wouldn't say ever, necessarily. But there *is* a problem with that word, at least as it relates to us. For normal people, ever is infinite. We're finite."

"It's not like we're going to put plastic bags over our heads tomorrow morning. Is that what's holding you back?

"Actually, it's something I never thought of," she said.

"Holding back?"

"No, plastic bags. Do they actually work?"

"I think they do," he said.

"Oh." She stared at the sand.

"In any event, the way this conversation is going, and where it's going, I'm getting the feeling that a consummation is probably out of the question tonight."

"I'm afraid it is."

He opened the foil package he still held in his hand. She watched attentively as he took out the rolled-up condom and examined it, then held it up.

"Every one of these has a story," he said. Then he unrolled it, placed it to his lips, and blew into it until it inflated to the size of a party balloon. He tied a knot at the bottom, held it up, and slapped it away. The offshore breeze picked up the inflated condom and carried it to the water's edge and out over the bay, into the darkness.

"I should have thought to put a message in it," he said. "'Stranded on the beach with a woman who won't let me use this, or the word I feel for her.'"

No response.

"Home?"

She nodded and pulled herself up, brushing sand from her skirt. "Thank you," she said.

"For what?"

"For understanding."

"But I don't."

———

The drive back to Helen's house was uncomfortably quiet. In one of two attempts at conversation, Paul asked, "Would you like to stop for something?"

To which she replied, "I can't think of anything I need to stop for, thank you."

The second and final try was "Would you like to make

one more attempt?"

Her response: "At what?"

He chose not to answer.

When he parked the car at her house, he opened the door for her and reached in with his handkerchief. She looked at it. He shook it at her. She reluctantly took the end. They walked to the front door looking perfectly ridiculous, holding a hankie between them as if playing some parlor game.

"I'm sorry if the evening didn't turn out the way it should have," said Paul.

"I am too. But I think you and I have different notions of how it should have turned out," she said.

"I suppose you're right. Well, good night."

He moved closer to her and dropped his end of the hankie. He put his hands on her shoulders, but felt in her a reluctance to move toward him. So he dropped his hands and kissed her politely on the forehead instead. If he had had a daughter, it was how he would have kissed her good-bye as she left for school.

"Good night. And thank you again, for everything," she said, turning her back to him to unlock the door. She went inside without another word. The door closed firmly enough to send a message he had not wanted to receive.

Chapter 14

Sleep was barely attainable to Paul throughout the long night. Even though he had his own bed back, thanks to Sam, who had moved to the living room and the sofa there, Paul tossed, changed pillows, took an Ambien, read a dull magazine article on the Mediterranean fruit fly and its threat to California crops, and, in desperation, watched a string of infomercials on the bedside TV. Still, nothing tired him sufficiently. He even thought of phoning an 800 number to order a gadget with flashing red lights that promised restful sleep by stimulating blood flow.

His interest was peaked further with the warning that flashed on the screen: Caution: As with Any Electrical Device, Use in Water Can Cause Electrocution. He thought better of the idea, but wondered if his electric toothbrush might achieve the same results in the bathtub. Probably not, since it was only battery powered. Besides, if it did work, his insurance company could hardly call it an accident when a man brushed his teeth underwater.

Shortly after four A.M., Paul knew that any further attempt at sleep would be in vain. He dressed in a sweat suit and running shoes and tiptoed through the living room toward the front door.

"Where are you going?" was the sleepy question that came from the sofa.

Shit, he said to himself. *Now I'll have to talk to her.* "For a run."

"In the middle of the night? That could be dangerous, especially dressed in black," said Sam.

"I can always hope," he said as he opened the front door.

"What did you say?" she asked as the door shut behind him.

———

While Paul ran through his darkened neighborhood, Helen paced the floor of her living room. At four-fifteen, she had not yet fallen asleep. She, too, had tried television, then a book of Sylvia Plath's poetry. While pacing the perimeter of the room, she noticed a smudge of dirt on top of the white baseboard, which convinced her a thorough cleaning was needed, and it would keep her occupied for a while. Until ten past five, she worked her way around the baseboards of both the living and dining rooms on her knees with a Q-Tip sprayed with Endust. She then sat down on the sofa to review, for at least the tenth time, the confusing events of the evening.

She engaged herself in a conversation, one from which

the only thing missing was the sound of her voice, since the prevailing view is that people who talk to themselves are generally unbalanced. She moved her lips, along with her hands, and, occasionally, shook her head or nodded it. But she uttered not a sound, for the sake of balance.

He caught me completely off guard with that odd dancing. He could have at least warned me that people would be holding hankies and riding on chairs! It might have been nice to be prepared. Something a tad more conservative than the short skirt and tall heels might have been in order. Okay, so you weren't prepared. Cut the man some slack. He wanted to surprise you with something he thought you'd find interesting. All of a sudden, I see myself up on one of the chairs, and he's in the other, and I'm in a Jewish wedding, holding hankies with him. And what was that scene on the beach all about? It was all about sex, that's what. I swore I'd never get married again. But I don't recall a vow to never have sex. You think he wanted to have sex with you as a prelude to marriage? I don't know. But I do know he had plans. And he brings out one little condom and you get weird. You've got a shoe box full of them, remember? It's just so easy to get tangled up in the whole business of sex. And you start walking in circles like a wind-up toy. Then you let him kiss you and you fall on top of him, and bingo, you go off the edge when he shows you he cares about you. So what do you want me to be? Reasonable. Cut the man some slack. He claims he's falling in love with you. He wants to be with you. Sure, on the edge of a cliff or inside a plastic bag. How can he be serious? I can just see the ceremony. Do you take this woman to be your wife, to love and cherish, until a dive off a tall building do you part? Maybe the two of you could work something out. Like what? You might change your mind, you know, about checking out early. Forget it. Okay, okay, but you at least can hear him out. You like him well enough, don't you? Don't you? (A nod of the head.) You find him attractive, right? (Another nod.) He makes you, well, you know what he makes you, down there. Enough! I get the point. Then do something about it. What? Do you have his address? It's on the card he gave me. Then you know what to do. Surprise him. Show up at his door. Bring coffee. Go crazy, maybe even some Danish too. Tell him you were just confused. I was. I am. You asked me, and I told you. Okay, okay. Coffee ... Danish. And some truth. Jeez. Truth.

By eight-thirty, Helen had dressed, changed, and dressed again six times, until finally she looked in the mirror and settled on a formfitting white linen blouse and black silk pants, also formfitting, an outfit she logically would wear to the salon. Doing her hair required almost as many changes as choosing the outfit, moving from wet, pasted-down to spiked, every-which-way, and back, finally, to the style she had worn each time she had been with Paul. The finishing touch was a liberal spray of gardenia on the throat and behind the ears, followed by a last wistful look in the mirror at a reflection she did not, of course, find attractive at all. But it was too late, and she was too anxious, to start over again. It would all have to do. The challenge had been to appear as though she happened to be in the neighborhood on the way to work and, on impulse, decided to drop by Paul's apartment and clear up any misunderstanding about the previous night. Her appearance would serve as contrition without admission.

Recalling the dialogue with herself, she took her own advice, stopped at a Starbucks, and ordered one black coffee and one currant scone. She also asked the server if he could possibly put some plain water in a coffee cup, which he was happy to do, at no charge.

Thus she would be able to stand at his front door, holding two coffee cups and a paper bag (which she might need if a breathing problem occurred), and offer her "happened to be in the neighborhood" explanation for the visit.

Checking again the address on the card he gave her, she parked the car across the street from Paul's building and stole a quick glimpse of herself in the rearview mirror. Nothing on the front teeth. The hair fork had risen again, but she reminded herself that he found it oddly attractive. She turned away from the mirror toward the front door of his apartment and felt a shock wave as the door opened. Was he leaving? Or just picking up the newspaper that lay on the lawn?

But Paul didn't emerge. A woman did. A blond woman. An attractive, young blond woman. Carrying a suitcase. For a nanomoment of hope, Helen thought she might be looking at the wrong door. But the number atop it confirmed her fear. It was his address. A quick scan of possibilities included a cleaning woman, a sister, or an Avon lady with the wrong address, but they were all summarily dismissed with the emergence of a man in striped pajamas. A tall man, in need of a shave and a comb, looking down at the young, blond woman, the very same man on whom she had lain, whose tongue she had welcomed, whose advances she had found hard to resist just twelve hours earlier on the sands of Venice, California.

She froze in place and her jaw fell down to its limit as she watched the blond woman throw her arms around Paul and kiss him on the lips. She stepped back and wiped a red smudge from his mouth with her hand and laughed. He stood staring after her as she waved and happily stepped along the walkway, hailing a yellow taxi that appeared and pulled to the curb. Helen slid down in the seat, holding her breath as if it might be heard by the woman or by Paul, even through the closed car window. She waited until she heard the sound of the departing taxi before slowly inching herself up just enough to peer over the sill of the passenger-side window to see Paul staring off after the departing cab. She panicked when she saw him walk toward the street, but he stopped halfway, bent over, and picked up the plastic-bagged *Los Angeles Times*, then turned, went back to the door, and disappeared inside, seeming not to have noticed Helen's car. *Notice?* she screamed at herself. *He wouldn't have noticed a seven-forty-seven taxiing up the street after the night he must have just had with that young, blond, attractive woman who left her red lipstick all over his face!*

Convinced Paul was no longer near the front door, she turned on the ignition, put the car into drive with one hand, and emptied the paper bag beside her with the other hand. As she slowly drove down the street, away from the scene that would surely be burned into her memory for the rest of her life, she sucked a deep breath from the paper bag, which sent a large crumb of scone flying down her throat, forcing her to choke and cough uncontrollably. She barely managed to avoid driving into a garbage truck parked in her path, as well as into the frightened trash collector who, seeing her car careen toward him, dropped a barrel and its contents in the street and ran for cover behind a palm tree. After she brought the choking and the car under control, she managed to navigate the streets of L.A. all the way back to her house, her fingers gripping the steering wheel so tightly that her hands grew numb and her tearless eyes focused straight ahead with such intensity that they seemed capable of setting on fire whatever they might fall upon.

Turning into her driveway, she pressed the garage door opener on the visor above her head, as she had done a thousand times before. She drove into the garage, pulling forward until the yellow tennis ball tethered from the ceiling gently bounced off the windshield, placed the shift lever into Park, turned off the ignition, and pressed the remote control again to lower the garage door behind her.

But that was where the familiar routine ended. She did not, as habit always dictated, check the rear seat for any packages or detritus that would disturb the perfect order of the car. Instead, she pulled down the sun visor and viewed herself in the vanity mirror. She smoothed down the hair fork, but it immediately sprang back up. She checked her lipstick and saw that she had worn some of it away by grimacing so forcefully on the trip home, so she applied a fresh coat. She also noticed a thin thread a few millimeters long coming out of the top buttonhole of her blouse, and she fished a small pair of scissors from her purse to make a quick snip of things. One more glance in the mirror told her everything was in order.

Next she turned the ignition back on, starting the motor, but did not reopen the garage door. She did, however, open all four windows of her car with the power switches to her left. She then folded her hands in her lap, leaned back against the headrest, and closed her eyes.

It both troubled and reassured her when she saw behind her closed lids the scene in front of Paul's apartment. It played itself repeatedly, opening with the appearance of the suitcase-carrying blond, followed by Paul in his pajamas, and ending with the kiss. It was like the worst nightmare on continuous replay, a brief tragedy in one awful act.

She lost track of time as she waited. She also lost interest in the tragic movie, and soon it faded out, leaving a more comforting blank screen in its place. She sensed a slight drowsiness and wondered how long it would take for what would come next. Would it be as simple as drifting off to sleep? She thought how unusual it was to not leave a note behind, but it seemed a logical choice, since she did not know what to say other than that she did not want to go on nearly killing trash collectors while spying on a man who lied that he was falling in love with her while sleeping with someone else. She could have written something to Harvey, but why not spare him the added pain and just go quietly into the morning?

There were no tears, no fears, no wishes to turn back. There was, though, a feeling that something had changed. At first, she could not place a finger on what was different, but something clearly was. She slowly opened just one eye and saw no change. The tennis ball still rested on the windshield. The garage door was still closed. And then it dawned on her: noise. Actually, lack of noise. She opened her other eye and realized that the steady hum of the car engine had stopped. She put her hands on the steering wheel and felt no vibration. She grasped the ignition key, which was still in the On position. Then she saw the problem: the fuel-gauge needle was resting, almost in mockery, at the very bottom of its arc, below the red *E*. How ignoble it was to realize that she, of all obsessive people, had forgotten to do something as routine and mundane as filling the tank with gas.

"Shit!" she blurted out uncharacteristically. "Shit!" she repeated. And then she accompanied herself by slamming her fists against the steering wheel powerfully with each successive "Shit!" until a sudden explosion filled the car. In one instant, a white balloonlike shape flew into her face, throwing her back against the seat and then releasing her as it deflated. As only her luck of late would have it, she had managed to activate the car's air bag and, in the process, it took its toll on her in the form of a painful bruise to her right eye.

She sat there for several minutes, fearful of moving lest some other force be unleashed on her. The acrid smell of the explosive charge that had triggered the air bag hung on the air along with the lingering fumes of the now-dead engine.

When she finally felt secure enough to get out of the car and go into the house, she pulled down the visor to glance in the mirror again. She was alarmed to see the vivid purple welt ringing her eye, which would undoubtedly mark her as a victim of some terrible abuse at hands other than her own.

Is there anything else—anything—at which you could possibly fail? she asked herself, struggling past the white, spent air bag, which looked like a large balloon that had been punctured, a metaphor for her entire life, she concluded.

Entering the kitchen, she was greeted by the sight of the huge dog, Tabby, and the sound of the phone ringing. She started to pick up the receiver, then stopped. She wanted to talk to no one. But then it occurred to her that it might be Harvey wondering why she had not shown up at the salon for her first appointment. She let it ring two more times until the answering machine picked up. The voice was not Harvey's, but instead the last voice she wanted to hear for the rest of her brief life on earth.

"Hello, Helen. This is Paul."

She felt the blood rush from her hands and feet in the classic fight-or-flight fashion. But for her, it was not a choice of one or the other. She wanted to both fight *and* flee.

"The strangest thing just happened. I thought I might have seen your car parked across from my place a little while ago, when I was getting the paper. But I can't imagine it would have been you. There was no one in the car. Then when I checked again, it was gone. Just a coincidence, I guess. In any event, I'd like to talk to you. Last night shouldn't have ended the way it did. Please give me a call back."

She stared down at the answering machine as if Paul were somehow inside it. "A call back? I suggest you not hold your breath. On second thought, I wish you would hold your breath, for longer than your body can withstand. You don't like the way the night ended? Ha! You could have fooled me!"

When she noticed the answering machine winking its red light at her, she took it personally and tore its cord from the wall then went to the kitchen. She looked at the single banana placed perfectly on the counter, picked it up, glared at it, peeled it, then ate it aggressively. Truth was, she only liked the look of bananas, not their taste.

———

"My God, where have you been?" exclaimed Harvey when Helen finally entered the salon two hours late. Then he noticed her black eye. "And what hit you? *Who* hit you?"

"I walked into something."

"Bullshit. You've never walked into anything. You're too careful. It was him, wasn't it?"

No response.

"That son of a bitch. I knew it would come to this." His voice was raised enough to stop two clients who had been arguing over whom Helen should take care of first. They both turned to see the black eye, which Helen could not conceal with the hand she held over it.

"Don't worry, a good layer of pancake will hide it,"

offered one of the women.

"She doesn't need pancake, for God's sake. She needs a cop. A lawyer," said Harvey, reaching for the phone.

"No," insisted Helen. "Please. Don't call anyone. I'm fine."

"Good," said the other waiting client. "Take your mind off it and get started on me."

"Out!" said Harvey. "Both of you."

They looked at one another in shock, then at Helen, and finally at Harvey, who stared them down until they turned and meekly retreated out of the reception area.

"If he shows his face around here," said Harvey, "I'm going to do a makeover on it he won't forget. What kind of creep hits a woman in the eye?"

"Harvey," said Helen quietly, "calm down."

"How can I calm down? Look what he did to you."

"He didn't. I did it to myself. It was an accident."

"You expect me to believe you ran into something?"

"Not exactly. Something ran into me."

"What, for God's sake, could run into you and smack you in the eye?"

"An air bag."

"A *what*?"

"In my car."

Harvey stopped long enough to think about what she had said. Then, "You had an accident? Where?"

"In my garage. The air bag went off, accidentally. It just exploded in my face."

"By itself?" He wasn't buying the story.

"Not exactly. It was a freak thing."

"Oh, then you ran into the front of the garage, and that made it go off. I get it."

"No. It wasn't that. I didn't run into anything."

His eyes darted about as he seemed to wrestle with the improbability of it all. Then something struck him. His eyes widened, and he studied Helen's face, looking for an answer to a question he didn't ask. "Helen," he said, almost in a whisper, "I need to know something."

"No you don't," she answered.

"Please, tell me you didn't—" He cut himself short. "You weren't trying to ... my God, no."

The two clients reappeared in the doorway. "You were only kidding, about us getting out, weren't you, Harvey?" said the first one, meekly.

"We know you're stressed, but you really wouldn't want us to just leave, would you?" said the second client, with uncharacteristic humility.

"No, I wasn't kidding. And yes, I really want you to leave. I'll do you free next time. Anything. Helen isn't going to be doing any hair today."

"Why can't you do us then?"

"I'm booked," said Harvey.

"And you're screwed, right out of my business," said client number one.

"Mine as well," echoed number two.

"Out!" hissed Harvey, his eyes narrowing threateningly,

and both women scurried off in fear.

When Harvey saw how pale Helen had become and heard how rapidly her breaths were coming, he reached over the reception counter and picked up a brown paper bag from a pile that was always kept there. He handed it to Helen, but she shook her head.

"It's all right, Harvey. I can breathe, unfortunately."

"What's gotten into you?"

"Paul. Figuratively. He opened me up and got inside, to a place I swore no one would ever enter again," she said.

And the tears finally came, spilling down her cheeks. Harvey pulled her close to him and she buried her face in his Armani shirt.

"It's my own fault. He said things to me I refused to believe. But he repeated them enough, and I began to let my guard down further and further. Everything happened so quickly. One minute we were dancing, and the next we were being held up in chairs for a wedding dance."

"Oh my God! You got married!"

"No."

"He's Jewish."

"No."

"Then what's with the chairs?"

"He took me dancing. It was religious. The men with black hats and long curls. Then *he* was in a chair and *he* had the black hat and curls."

"You're losing me here, baby. He's grown long curls already?"

"And then, next thing I knew, we were on the sand."

"I thought you went dancing. How did you wind up on the beach?"

"That's where the dancing was. In Venice. Then I was on top of him."

"At least you got that part right. Go, girl."

"Then we were arguing. Over a stupid condom again."

"He didn't have one?"

"No. I mean yes, he had one. And that somehow set me off."

"You don't want to get pregnant, do you?"

She shook her head emphatically.

"Or a disease?"

The next head shake was even more emphatic.

"Then what was the problem?"

"I wasn't ready for that. I thought I was when we kissed, when I was on top of him, when I got tingles that were definitely off the Richter scale. But something held me back. And he kept trying to go forward. Then we both got angry, and he took me home."

"And the air bag that gave you a black eye?"

"It happened this morning. I spent the night convincing myself that I had been a fool to fight it, that I'd been unfair with him. I finally believed what he said to me and decided to admit I was wrong. I went to his house."

"And you told him?"

"No, I saw him."

"Okay," said Harvey, trying to be patient through the

confusion. "And?"

"He was on the front porch. In pajamas."

Harvey nodded slowly.

"And so was this woman, a blond. A very pretty blond. With a suitcase. And she was kissing him good-bye."

"Ohhhhh." It seemed the word would never end.

"He told me last night he wanted to be with me forever," she said, between sobs.

"He just forgot to tell you that someone else would be joining you. Hell of a guy. What did you say to him?"

"*Say* to him? Nothing. I drove home as fast as I could."

"And that's when you ran into nothing in your garage and got a black eye."

She nodded and moved her face to a dry part of his silk shirt. "I don't know what I'm going to do. It's all so black."

"No, honey, that's just my shirt." He grasped her face in both hands, gently pushing her away. "Take a look around. The sun came up this morning. The world's still here. Maybe a little screwed up. But it's here for you."

"I don't want it," she sobbed.

"You have to." And he kissed her gently and briefly on the lips.

She looked up at him, searching for the right words. Then, "Do we have any plastic bags? Thick ones?"

The phone on the reception desk rang and Harvey picked it up. "Helen of Troy," he said.

"Who's calling, please? Is it about an appointment? I see. Do you want to make an appointment? This is Harvey. I don't do men, contrary to what you've heard."

He put the phone on hold and frowned, dangling the receiver on its cord. "It's him. Mister Nice Guy. Hitler in prayer curls. He wants to speak to you."

"I'm not here."

"She's not here," Harvey said into the phone. Then, with a long sigh, he put it on hold again. "He wants to know when you'll be here."

"For him, never."

"Never," said Harvey into the phone. "Because she just told me. That's right. I said she wasn't here, because she's not here for you, if you know what I'm saying. Call me crazy, but I think she has a problem with your sleeping habits." A pause. "I'll pass the message on." And he hung up.

"He says there's been a misunderstanding. He's sure it was your car he saw at his place, but he didn't see you. Were you hiding?"

She nodded.

"He wants to explain."

"Ha! Explain, indeed. He can tell it to the navy."

"Actually, I think it's the marines. But no matter. You sure you don't want to hear him out? Maybe it was his sister."

"Kissing him on the mouth?"

"Well, it *is* L.A."

Chapter 15

Paul stared at the phone he had just hung up. He picked it up again and dialed Helen's home number so that he could at least leave a message for her. Not only was there no answer, but there was also no answering machine. After a dozen rings, his hopes rose when he heard the receiver pick up. Actually, though, it wasn't really a picking up, but more of a dropping down, onto the floor. And then a bark. A deep bark, as from a very large dog. The animal had somehow knocked the phone off the receiver and was barking at it. Next came a munching sound.

"Hello, is anyone there? The dog's eating the phone."

He realized how incredibly stupid he must sound, especially when the dog responded with a long, plaintive howl. *Is this the pathetic state my life has descended to, having a phone conversation with a dog?*

"Just tell her I called."

Paul's day did not improve much from there. He convinced himself that not only had Helen been parked in front of his apartment, she had seen Sam leave, only after planting an unwelcome kiss on him. That had to be it. Why else would she refuse to take his calls, other than his general undesirability?

He had managed to work himself into a state of hopeless despair when the phone finally rang. But, of course, it wasn't Helen calling. It was Milton.

"Ready for your test?"

"What test?"

"Well, obviously not for sexually transmitted diseases, the way your life is going. The radio show. Remember?"

"Oh, that," said Paul.

"Yes, oh that," Milton mocked. "Just the biggest step in your career. The regular evening guy quit without notice, and they don't have anyone to go on tonight. So the P.D. had this idea to spring you on the audience and see how the idea goes over."

"What's a P.D.?"

"Program director. Be there at seven. You're on at eight. Just for an hour. They want to see if you can generate calls without a lot of advance hype. They'll do as much as they can today, with on-air promos in every break."

"You really think I can just walk into a studio and do a radio show?"

"I don't know how else you can do one."

"What about preparation?"

"Hey, you've got all day. You can start by reading from the column. The real one, not that weird crap you've been playing with, telling people to go jump off a bridge or something."

"You call it crap?"

"Okay. Not the *experimental* stuff."

"You really think people are going to call in?" asked Paul.

"That's what the station wants to find out. I told them you'll light up the switchboard."

"And how am I supposed to do that?"

"You can start with a simple question: anyone out there having relationship problems? Right off the bat, that's got to be about ninety percent of the population in L.A. The other ten percent are in nursing homes."

"That's what I like about you, Milton, your rose-colored glasses."

"It's life."

"It's depressing."

"That's what I said. See you at seven."

———

"And now," boomed the baritone voice of someone on tape, "it's time for Man to Man ... the nationally syndicated column with the answers to your relationship problems. And here's Paul."

Next came a musical flourish that sounded too self-important to Paul.

A bearded man on the other side of a glass window raised his hand in the air then brought it down, pointing directly at Paul, who was wearing cumbersome earphones and sitting in front of a microphone suspended from an erector-set sort of contraption on the desk in front of him.

"This is Paul," he said, shocked at his own voice, which sounded like the weak whimper of a man who had been asked if he had anything to say before a judge passed sentence on him for killing fourteen nursing-home residents.

"Louder, and closer to the microphone" were the words that came through the earphones.

"This is Paul," he repeated, louder, but still in a voice constricted by a tight, dry throat. "And we're going to talk about relationships … about things that might not be working out as well as they should. If you've been having problems of the heart, if you're feeling unfulfilled, give us a call, and we'll talk about it."

He paused, wondering what to say next, when the voice came through his headset again. "Give the phone number! It's on that big sign right in front of you!"

Paul looked up and read from the banner that stretched across the wall above the window to the control room. He read, "Just call three-one-o-L-A-TALKS. That's three-one-o, five-two-eight-two-five-five-seven. I just wonder how many people in this city are feeling alone, troubled by the way their relationships are going."

As he spoke, he saw out of the corner of his eye a line of green lights flashing. The lights were on the large telephone console to his right, just below a computer screen. All fifteen phone lines were blinking, and a list of names and areas were being rapidly typed onto the computer screen.

"Bingo!" boomed the voice into his ears again. "Every line is filled. Amazing. Never seen a response that fast."

"What did I do?" asked Paul.

"Your mike's open!" boomed the voice. Paul looked up through the window and saw it was the engineer who had been talking to him.

"Oh, Christ," said Paul.

"You did it again," came the voice. "Don't say anything you don't want going out to twenty thousand people!"

A shaky start, obviously. But Paul began to gain control over such issues as an open microphone and how to bring up a phone caller without cutting the person off, which he did several times before getting that process down. All the while, Milton sat in the corner of the small studio saying nothing, at least aloud, but saying a great deal with his shaking head, grimaces, and, occasionally, a broad smile when Paul managed to get something right.

Paul was surprised how quickly the hour went by once he stopped cutting off callers and blurting out things not meant to be broadcast (including one series of "Can you hear me?" directed at the engineer but sent out on the air). The calls were generally predictable: men with relationship problems who were not too timid to talk about them on the air, helped by the anonymity of radio.

Two calls had to be cut short, both of them because the callers were obviously under the influence of alcohol, or perhaps something worse. Their speech was slurred and mostly incoherent.

Example: "Hey, don't get me wrong … I don't got nothin' against people who … I forgot what it was I don't got nothin' against … but you write that thing in the paper, and now you're doin' it on radio, and, well, hell, how about that. Know what I'm sayin'?"

"I have absolutely no idea," said Paul and thanked the caller before pressing the button that disconnected him.

With only five mutes to go to the end of the hour, a call came in that was very close to home for Paul:

"Hey, man, how ya doin'?" asked a man who at least sounded sober.

"I'm doing fine," lied Paul.

"Really? Hey, I caught the *Oh, Christ* thing. That was funny. But anyway, I'm having this problem with my girlfriend."

"Tell me about it," said Paul, who noticed Milton nodding his approval.

"She won't talk to me about something that happened. And she doesn't want to hear from me or see me, ever. I called her at least ten times today, and she won't answer the phone."

"That happens," said Paul, seeing an image of the dog chewing on the phone and Helen in the background with her hands on her hips.

"I finally left her a message and told her to turn on your show tonight when I heard you were gonna be on. Hi, baby," he said. "So, if you're listening, baby, you got it all wrong. You think I was cheatin' on you. There's no way I would. You should know that. Okay, so you say you saw me with somebody at the Rail—that's a neighborhood place we hang out at, the Brass Rail," he explained.

"So you weren't with somebody else?" Paul interjected.

"Well, yeah, I was. But that's what she doesn't know. Okay, baby, I'm tellin' you, on my mother's grave, there's nobody besides you. Nobody."

Paul picked up the pause. "That sounds earnest to me, invoking your mother's grave."

"Invoke it? I'm standin' on it … at the cemetery, talking on my cell phone."

"Why?"

"Because there's no regular phone out here."

"I meant why are you in the cemetery?" said Paul, seeing Milton double over with quiet laughter.

"Because that's where I'm gonna be, right next to her, if you don't listen to me, baby. I mean it. I don't want to live without you. That woman you saw me talking to, the one who kissed me? That was Sylvia, from work. She just found out her husband cut off his hand on a power saw in the scenery shop where he works, at Paramount. I was just tryin' to give her a little comfort, tellin' her how lots of people get along okay with only one hand. They make mechanical ones now that can do just about anything, like those ones in the arcade machines that pick up stuffed animals? Anyway, she appreciated what I had to say, so she kissed me. That's all there was to it."

"This is a classic case of things not being what they seem," said Paul. "Your girlfriend saw something, there's no doubt about that. But she jumped to the wrong conclusion. Now you're ready to make the wrong jump."

"You mean like off a bridge? No, I wouldn't do that. I got a gun."

"Now the first thing you have to do is get rid of that gun. Now," said Paul.

"No way. I paid ninety bucks for it."

"Fine. Keep it then. Get rid of the bullets. Throw them as far as you can."

"Jeez, I don't know. What good's a gun without bullets?"

"Very good," said Paul. "Please, don't even think about using it. What's your girlfriend's name?"

"Liz."

"Okay. Liz, if you're listening, please, you've got to understand. Things have gotten completely out of control here, just because of an honest mistake. This man meant nothing more than to help someone who was hurting. Now he's hurting so badly, he doesn't even want to go on. The two of you have to talk. Right now."

"But she doesn't want to hear what I've got to say. And like I said, I don't want to live without her. Okay, maybe not with the gun. Too messy. Maybe I should just go and find a bridge somewhere."

"We don't have any," said Paul. "There has to be a better solution. Do you smoke?"

"No."

"You could think about starting."

Paul could see Milton bolt forward in his chair with panic in his eyes, drawing his hand across his throat.

"Just kidding," said Paul into the microphone.

"You think this is funny?" asked the agitated caller.

"Maybe it is, in a slightly bizarre way. Think about it, you're in a cemetery, on a cell phone, getting ready to move in next to your mother. You don't see the humor?"

Only the sound of wind came through the man's phone. Then, "Well, when you put it that way, I guess it is kind of wacky. And the bridge business, that's kind of nuts, too, seein' as how there aren't any—high enough, anyway. Takin' up smokin'. You're a funny guy."

"Take my advice. Go to your girlfriend and stay there until she hears you out. Do you know where she is?"

"Yeah. That's a problem. She's at her mother's."

"Why is that a problem?"

"She hates me, her mother. She'd love to shoot a hole in my head."

"See, throwing away the bullets is a good thing. Give her your empty gun and she can just keep clicking it until she works out her anger," said Paul.

Another pause. "You're kiddin' me again, aren't you?"

"Yes, I guess I am. Look. This is something you can work out. Trust me. Go to her mother's house and ask her to listen to you, if she hasn't already, here on the air. And then you both can get on with your lives. No guns, no bridges, no smoking, okay?"

"Yeah, I guess."

"And stay away from the cemetery, unless it's to bring your mother flowers."

"Yeah, well, I didn't think to stop on the way. But hey, thanks, Paul. You're okay in my book. And you know what? You got me thinkin'. This whole idea of knockin' yourself off, it's so stupid, the way you put it."

"Thank you."

"Yeah, thank you. I like what you're doin' there on the radio, even if you got a weird sense of humor."

Paul saw the engineer waving his arm and pointing to the clock, which was just seconds away from the end of the hour.

"That's all we have time for tonight. This is Paul. Thank you for listening, and for calling. Good night."

He took off the headphones, which left his ears red with warmth, stood, and stretched.

Milton stared at him for a few moments, then shook his head and looked down at the floor.

"What did you think?" Paul asked.

Milton got out of his chair, put his hands in his pockets, and said, "The bad news is, you got into that suicide crap again."

"I didn't. The caller did."

"Yeah, right. But the good news is, I think you may have talked the poor schnook out of it. Of course, the Psychiatry Association is probably going to demand to know where you got your training."

"Nice going, Paul" came the echoed voice of the engineer

on the other side of the window. "You broke a record."

"For what?" asked Milton.

"Calls in one hour. We lost count at two hundred and fifty attempts, and then the lines got blocked solid from the load."

Milton turned to Paul and a sardonic smile appeared on his face. Paul merely shrugged.

"Congratulations," said Milton. "Buy you a drink?"

"Thanks, but I have to go somewhere."

"Got a date?"

"Not quite. I need to see a woman who didn't see what she thought she saw."

"The woman who wouldn't listen to that poor schnook? Are you crazy?"

"Probably."

"You can't do that," said Milton as Paul opened the studio door and left. Milton called after him. "What the hell's wrong with you? Those are crazy people. You want to get killed, for God's sake?"

Paul smiled to himself and stepped into the waiting elevator.

Chapter 16

There was a single light coming from Helen's house, through the living room window. Paul sat in his car for a while trying to convince himself that he had done the right thing, going to her house unannounced, uninvited, and, of course, unwelcome. But he agreed with himself that it wasn't a case of doing the right thing. Seeing Helen was the *only* thing his overburdened heart would settle for.

He walked to the front door, his pulse thumping in his temples at the rate of two beats per step, and stopped, pausing to listen for any sign of life beyond the door. Nothing. Not even a bark or a growl. He pressed the doorbell and still heard nothing. He reached into his pocket for a note he had written on a yellow Post-it in case Helen had not been home: "Stopped by to talk. Please call. P." He rang the bell one more time and, hearing nothing, tried to wedge the small piece of sticky-backed paper into the crack between the door and the frame. But, as his continuing luck would have it, the seal was too tight to accept it. He bent down on one knee to try and wedge it under the door, when, with no warning, it opened. Before he could straighten up, Paul found himself eyeball to eyeball with the giant dog guarding the doorway.

Paul couldn't resist the opportunity: "Hi, is Helen home?" he asked the expressionless dog.

"No, I'm not" came the answer from somewhere beyond.

Paul stood and saw, at the far end of the living room, Helen sitting on the sofa.

"How does he do that?" he asked.

"What?"

"Open the door."

"What is it you want?" she said.

"You."

"Ha! I have the feeling I'm not the first person who's heard that from you today."

"May I come in?"

"I'd rather you didn't."

"Then how about you come out?"

"For what purpose?"

"I need to talk to you. To explain. Please."

He could hear her long sigh from across the room. Then he saw her stand and walk toward the door. When she came into the light, he saw no anger in her face. But he did see a sadness that he had not seen before. The corners of her mouth were ever-so-slightly turned downward, and her lower lip seemed to be quivering slightly. And he saw the purple bruise around her eye, which he thought better of asking about. His instinct was to put his arms around her, but his better judgment told him to do no such thing. Even the dog seemed to be warning him against any false moves.

She stepped past the dog and onto the small porch, saying nothing.

"Shall we sit?" asked Paul, gesturing toward the brick steps.

She said nothing, but sat down on the top step, folded her arms, and looked down at her feet. He sat on the same step, put his hands in his lap, and looked straight ahead into the darkness.

He finally broke the silence. "Why did you come to my place this morning?"

"It was a mistake."

"You mean you accidentally found yourself in front of my apartment?"

"Stop trying to be funny. It was a foolish thing to do."

"But something changed your mind. You never got out of the car. What was it?"

"Now you're trying to be coy. I almost liked funny better."

"Okay. I know what happened. You saw Sam come out the door," he said.

"No, I saw a woman."

"Sam. My wife."

"Ha! I knew it. You're married."

"No, I'm not. Sam's my *former* wife."

"I see. So, you were having a reunion."

"She was homeless."

"And you just happen to run a shelter. How altruistic.

I know of a couple of men who live in the alley behind the salon. Might I send them over?"

"Her husband threw her out of her house. My house, actually. And she showed up at my place."

"And in your bed. I admire your sense of humanity."

"You actually think I slept with her?"

"I know it's such a silly conclusion, especially given the kissing."

"Okay. She kissed me on the porch."

"No, on the mouth."

"This is pointless. She's a troubled woman. I felt sorry enough for her to let her stay two nights. She's gone. I hope for the last time."

"It doesn't matter," said Helen, still staring at her feet.

"Yes it does. And I'll tell you why. Just as I told you last night, I'm falling … "

"Don't," she said.

"Why do you have such an aversion for the word?"

"You don't know?"

He shook his head.

"When did you start taking an interest in the future?"

"When I saw you in it."

She stood up, paced back and forth across the porch, stopped, and looked away. "What do you want from me?"

"Money."

The voice didn't sound like Paul's. Because it wasn't. Helen's jaw dropped, while, at the same time, Paul stared at a scruffy young man, wide-eyed and very agitated.

"I want your money. And don't give me any shit," said the excited man, waving a small silver pistol.

"Oh my God!" said Helen.

"No," said Paul. "Helen, get into the house and close the door, now."

She was transfixed.

"You didn't hear me? You don't see this gun?" said the man, his voice wavering.

Paul remained calm. "I heard you. I saw it. And I still say no, no money."

With that, Paul stood, blocking Helen from the robber's view.

"You crazy or something? You're saying 'no' to a bad guy with a gun pointed at you? Don't you know what happens with that? This is L.A."

"Sorry, no money," said Paul.

The shaggy man looked around as if hoping to find another victim in the darkness. "I don't believe this," he said.

Paul took a step closer to the robber, who took a step back. Then he reached into his shirt pocket and pulled out the yellow sticky-note he had tried to slide under the door. As the robber's jaw dropped, he pressed the note on his forehead, positioning himself between the gunman and Helen to block her as best he could.

"You want to shoot somebody? Here, I'll make it easy for you." He pointed to the sticky note, stuck absurdly on his brow. "Put one right there. Bull's-eye. Bingo."

Helen remained frozen, her mouth open as if ready to

scream. The robber took another step backward.

"You're crazy, man. No shit, this is the story of my life. Out of the whole goddamn city, I get the one whack job who wants to play hero."

The gunman took still another backward step, but this time he backed into a round shrub and lost his balance. As he started to fall, he waved both his arms and, in the process, the silver revolver went off with a cracking sound.

Paul grabbed his chest, turned slowly to face Helen with a strange smile on his face, then fell to the ground, his eyes closing. The stifled scream finally came rushing from Helen's mouth, while the robber got up from the ground on his knees and started to tremble. He threw the gun down.

"Jesus Christ, he's been hit. Oh, no. Mister, say something. Don't die," said the terrified man. He looked up at Helen. "Do something. Call nine-one-one."

Helen stepped off the porch and bent over Paul, tears streaming down her cheeks. She nodded, stood, and raced into the house. She dialed the three numbers and waited. Then she spoke into the phone, her voice tight and hoarse. "A shooting. There's been a shooting. Hurry, send an ambulance. I don't know. His eyes are closed. Please, just send somebody."

——

Milton had just turned on the local television news before watching a DVD of *Moulin Rouge* for fifth time when he heard something that stunned him:

"This just in," intoned a news anchor. "Popular men's advice columnist Paul Malouf was shot this evening in a West Los Angeles neighborhood in an attempted robbery. There's no report from Holy Family Hospital, where he was rushed by paramedics. This is strange, but we're told the alleged lone gunman went to the hospital with Malouf, at his own request. We'll update this story as soon as we learn more."

Milton's hands began to tremble. He fell into the leather recliner in front of the wide-screen television monitor and uttered, "Jesus Christ almighty." He put his head in his hands and shuddered. Then he jumped up, grabbed his car keys, and hurried out of his townhome into the garage, where he climbed into his Mercedes-Benz and sped down Century Boulevard toward the nearby hospital in Beverly Hills.

Helen sat, her body crumpled in on itself, on a blue vinyl sofa in the ER waiting room. The air was heavy with antiseptic hospital smells, and the fluorescent light cast a blue-green hue over the area and Helen. The shaggy gunman had been taken into custody by two Los Angeles police officers who had not arrived at her home before the ambulance left, but caught up with the man as he waited outside the ER entrance. The gunman, who repeated over and over how sorry he was, had pleaded with the officers to allow him to stay outside the entrance until Paul's condition was known. The officers finally agreed, and one of them went to the cafeteria for coffee and donuts.

The automatic entrance door whooshed open and a

concerned Harvey, whom Helen had phoned, rushed through it and sat next to her. He took her in his arms.

"Any word?"

She shook her head.

"Are you all right?"

She shook her head again. "He was protecting me. He told the man to shoot him."

The door whooshed open again, and an ashen Milton rushed through it. He saw Helen and Harvey.

"How is he?" said Milton.

"I don't know," said Helen. "They took him in there a while ago." She pointed to a closed door with a sign declaring No Admittance.

A woman in green scrubs with a surgical mask pulled down around her neck came through the door and went to a desk, where she found a clipboard and made a notation on it.

Harvey approached the woman. "Excuse me, nurse."

"Doctor," said the woman, still writing.

"Sorry. Can you tell me anything about the man in there?"

She looked up from the clipboard and studied Harvey. "Are you a relative?"

"No. An acquaintance."

"I'm sorry," she said, shaking her head. "You'll have to get any information from admissions."

"Where's that?" he said, looking around.

"Down the hall, to the right," she said, pointing with the clipboard. "But there's no one there until morning."

"So I'm supposed to wait all night to find out the man's condition?"

"I'm sorry," said the doctor. "I'm merely trying to follow protocol."

She finally put down the clipboard. "The truth is, a ninety-two-year-old man simply can't withstand that kind of trauma."

Harvey was stunned. He walked back to Helen. "How old is he?"

"I don't know," she said. "Why?"

"She says he's ninety-two," Harvey said, nodding toward the doctor.

Milton jumped up. "What the hell is she talking about?" he roared.

The doctor turned and said in a loud whisper, "Please, sir, this is a hospital!"

"Where the hell do you get ninety-two?" he bellowed.

The doctor quickly approached him, clipboard in hand. "Right here," she said, pointing to a data sheet. "Date of birth: March 10, 1912."

"Who the hell is Hiram Oberholtzer?" said Milton.

"My patient. The man who was found in his bathtub."

"What about Paul Malouf?" he asked.

"I don't have a patient by that name." She reflected for a moment, shaking her head. Then, "Wait, you must mean the gunshot victim."

Milton nodded, smiling facetiously. Helen looked up, fearful of what she might hear next.

"You'll have to speak with Doctor Rossi, who's still with him. Are you a relative?"

"Yes, we all are," said Milton. "I'm his brother, she's his sister," he said, pointing to Helen. And nodding toward Harvey, "And he's his—" He had to think. "Other brother. We're a large family."

The sliding glass door opened again, and through it came the holdup man, his eyes revealing his fear, or concern, or both. On either side of him was a police officer. One was finishing a donut.

"How is he?" asked the gunman.

The doctor peered at the man over her glasses and asked Milton, "Another brother?"

"No, I'm the one who shot him."

Before anyone could react, the wooden door through which the doctor had appeared opened again. A man, also in scrubs but wearing a hat that was covered with brightly colored picture of animals, emerged, holding a steel tray.

Everyone looked expectantly at the man.

"I'm Doctor Rossi. And I'm assuming you are Helen," he said to her in a monotone revealing nothing.

Helen nodded and stood. The doctor looked down in the pan he held and shook his head. Everyone waited for what might come next.

"It's the damnedest thing I've ever seen."

"How is he?" asked Helen, her voice weak.

"He took a bullet in the chest. Over the heart."

"How *is* he?" echoed Milton.

"Amazing," said the doctor. "This is what saved him."

"He's alive?" asked Harvey.

"Oh, yes, definitely. Thanks to this." He picked up a mass of twisted blue-and-gold metal from which a torn scroll of paper protruded. "He was wearing it. I think it's called a mezuzah, sort of a Jewish version of a crucifix, which usually gets hung in a doorway, not around the neck. Good thing for him he didn't know that. I suppose you could call it divine intervention, if you believe in that sort of thing."

The gunman crossed himself, and one of the officers followed suit.

"It gave him one hell of a bruise," the doctor continued. "He's got a perfect imprint of some Hebrew letter on his chest, which is probably going to be permanent, like a tattoo."

"Anything broken?" Milton asked.

"Just this thing," he said, examining the mezuzah's remains. "Anyway," he said to Helen, "he's been asking for you repeatedly, wanting to know if you're all right. You can go back and see him. Second cubicle on the left," he said, holding the door open for her.

Doctor Rossi studied the shaggy man being held by the arms between the two officers and asked one of them, "What do we have here?"

"He shot the guy in there," said one officer.

"You brought him in to be IDed?"

"No, he came here on his own. Wanted to be sure the guy was okay. Praying like a demon out there."

"He shoots a man in a robbery," said Doctor Rossi.

"The man gets saved by a brass thingamajig around his neck that's supposed to be on a doorway, then the shooter comes in and prays for the guy." He stopped and looked off, thinking. Then, "How does the old guy they fished out of the bathtub fit into all this?"

"That's a completely different movie," offered the woman doctor, still writing on the clipboard.

Helen pulled back enough of the white curtain that enclosed cubicle number two to see Paul lying in bed, staring at the ceiling. She noticed the large mound rising beneath the white bedsheet over his chest. She tiptoed in, even though he was not sleeping.

"Are you all right?" she asked.

His head shot up from the pillow, and he winced in pain. "Except when I move," he said, smiling. "Are *you* all right?"

She took a step closer to the bed. "I am now. But I had a terrible feeling that you were … that you might have … "

"Bought the farm?"

She was puzzled.

"Checked out? You know … " He made the familiar gesture with his fingers doing a dive, a gesture Helen had grown to truly dislike. And he paid the price of his tired humor, which revealed itself in another painful wince.

"Thank you," she said.

"For what?"

"For saving my life. You were very brave, the way you stood between that awful man and me."

He shrugged, with yet another wince. He tried to sit up,

but couldn't.

"I wasn't any hero. The guy just really pissed me off. I hate guns. I'd never do it that way. It's a matter of principle."

"Like dirty water," she said.

He smiled. "I guess."

She took still another step closer and reached out to touch the edge of the bed, with some hesitation at first. He noticed, and slid his hand over hers.

"I'm so thankful," she said.

"For what?"

"You're alive."

"Foiled again," he said, glancing down at the mound on his chest. "By a religious symbol, worn by a nonbeliever. There's no end to the irony."

He looked into her eyes, which glistened in the bright light. "You're beautiful," he said.

She gasped and started to withdraw her hand, but he tightened his grip on it.

"Why do you react that way when I tell you how you look?"

"I suppose I'm not accustomed to that sort of thing."

"But you're deserving of it."

"Have they given you something?" she asked.

He glanced at the clear plastic tubing leading from a hanging bottle down to a needle in his arm. "Just for the pain. No hallucinogens."

He noticed the crimson hue that had overtaken her face. "I love the way you blush." And the crimson deepened even further while she made a funny little sound of rushing air through her lips and looked away.

"I also love the way that fork of hair stands up sometimes. It's flat now, though."

She reached up with her free hand to feel the spot where the fork normally rose and let a smile come forth.

"I love your smile, even when it's goofy, the way it is now."

The smile disappeared.

"Nice goofy. Charming goofy," he said, squeezing her hand.

"You make me sound like a Disney character."

"Not at all. There's a wonderful innocence about you, a humility that makes you uncomfortable. I love it."

She looked down at their hands.

"There, it's that look, right now. I love the way your hand feels under mine. I especially love the way your body felt on top of mine. I love the way you smell, even when I'm nowhere near you. I love the way you think, I love your strength of character, I love your sense of self, even when it deprecates. I love your lips, the way they feel on mine, the way they taste. I love the way you walk, with a rhythm you don't even know you possess. I love your legs, your arms, your neck. It's a beautiful neck. A proud neck. Sensuous too."

The smile returned, albeit self-consciously, and she touched her neck, deep in thought. "I don't know what to say," she said.

"How do you feel?"

"Tingling."

"Good. So do I. Men tingle too, you know. It's not androgynous."

"I suppose it's only fair … that you can tingle."

"I also want you, more than I've ever wanted anything. Or anyone. Right now, this instant," he said.

She looked around the small space. "That's not possible, is it?"

"Anything's possible," he said, drawing her hand closer until it touched his side.

"But maybe not permissible?"

"It wasn't mentioned on the rules form I signed. Just smoking, drinking, outside food, and loud radios."

He reached up with his free arm and gently placed his hand behind her head. He urged her downward to him until her lips reached his. They kissed, lightly at first.

She pulled back. "Is it painful?"

"It will be if you stop," he said, and pulled her back for a kiss that had the intensity and honesty of the kisses they had shared on the beach.

"Everything all right in here?"

It was a voice that intruded from the curtain at the foot of the bed, pulling Helen away and upright as she turned to see a nurse in scrubs peering in curiously.

"Everything is perfect, actually," said Paul.

"No pain?" asked the nurse, smiling knowingly.

"Only when we're interrupted."

"Sorry," said the nurse, who ducked back out through

the narrow curtain opening.

Paul urged Helen back to him, and they kissed again, with even more eagerness, if that were possible.

"I can't believe what we're doing," said Helen through heavy breaths. "Where we're doing it."

She pulled away again. "Wait," she said. "Do you have any, you know?"

He shook his head.

"I don't either."

"Do you think they might have some? It *is* a hospital," he said.

She looked up at the crucifix. "Not that kind of hospital."

"Do we really care?" he asked.

"Shouldn't we?"

"A question answering a question."

"Is it?" she asked as she eased herself, carefully, onto the edge of the bed while he reached under the sheet and pulled away a foam rubber pillow that had formed the mound on his chest, tossing it on the floor.

"You *will* be gentle with me, won't you?" he said before he pulled her to him and began sliding her blouse upward while she sighed and laughed softly into his mouth, mumbling something he could not quite understand, although one word in particular was of interest. It sounded something like "lumpfoo."

He came up for air and said, "You shouldn't try to talk with your mouth full."

Chapter 17

California can be kind to plans for outdoor events, and it was true to form on this Sunday afternoon, offering brilliantly clear blue skies that only lost their luster at horizon level to the west, where ocean met sky.

"Welcome aboard the *EcstaSea*," said the beaming captain, who was, in fact, Malcolm, the multitasking, visually challenged pilot who had taken Helen and Paul on their nighttime helicopter adventure. He squinted through his thick glasses at the gathered group waiting to board the gleaming white motor yacht tied to a berth in the Marina del Rey boat harbor.

Paul, dressed in a black suit, black shirt, and black tie, all of which blended together in one monochrome, offered his hand to the captain, who didn't seem to see it.

"Remember us?" asked Paul.

"Sure. I never forget faces. I took you and the kids on a helicopter tour of Knott's Berry Farm, right?"

"Something like that," said Paul, turning to Helen, who wore a low-cut, formfitting black satin dress and matching pillbox hat. She clutched a generous bouquet of flowers, all gardenias, tied with a white ribbon, with two words embossed in gold: To Life.

"Are you sure he can do this?" she whispered.

"Take us out in the bay? Sure. He's got radar," said Paul, pointing to the turning white arm atop the boat's cabin.

"I mean, he can perform weddings?"

"He tells me that as a licensed captain, he's empowered to do them."

Paul turned back to view the group. Standing at the railing behind him was his mother, wearing a flowered silk dress, a broad-brimmed Queen Mother–type hat, and white high-top basketball sneakers, her footwear of choice for all occasions. Next in line were Milton and Harvey. Milton looked as though he had stopped at Brooks Brothers on the way to the marina to be outfitted in a blue business suit. Harvey was dressed, well, like Harvey: pistachio gabardine pants, black silk sports shirt, and pale yellow linen sports coat. Next came the complete klezmer band; Paul had persuaded its members to play for this unorthodox wedding, reminding them that they were, after all, stakeholders. And finally, there stood some thirty young, exuberant employees of Helen's salon, laughing and chattering, forming a bright rainbow of L.A. hipness.

Malcolm held a battery-powered bullhorn to his mouth to address the waiting group, although no amplification was really necessary. "Your attention, please," he said.

No one stopped talking.

He continued: "This is your captain."

Milton shot Harvey a give-me-a-break look.

"We will now begin the boarding process for the wedding cruise. First, the bride and groom will board. Where are they?"

The fact that they were standing directly in front of Malcolm did not seem to register. "Bride and groom?" he repeated.

"Right here," said Paul.

"I knew that," said Malcolm, putting down the bullhorn. "Just kidding."

Paul reached for his mother's arm with one hand and took Helen's hand with the other.

"Bridesmaid?" asked Malcolm, squinting.

"Groom's mother," said Paul.

"Okay, I have an idea. Why don't the three of you board together," said Malcolm, a bit late, as they were already well along the gangway.

Once they were on board, Malcolm used his bullhorn again to direct the remainder of the guests and the band, but no one listened to him. They all just ambled up the gangway past him, where they were greeted by white-jacketed servers.

Once everyone was on board, the vessel, an old motor yacht converted to a party boat, pulled away from the dock with three short blasts of the horn and edged out into the main channel. Crepe streamers and black and white balloons fluttered and bobbed in the wind, and well-wishers on shore waved at the wedding party. Someone in a small sailboat going the other way shouted, "You'll be sorry!"

As the boat steamed along the rock jetty that protected

the harbor from the sea, a strong smell of ammonia wafted across the open deck. People looked at one another with wrinkled noses.

"Pelicans," said one of the crew, pointing to the hordes of large birds poised on the white-stained rocks.

"Smells like pee to me," said Paul's mother.

"It is," said Paul.

As soon as the boat passed the end of the jetty and turned into the swells of the bay, Paul reached into a plastic bag he had been carrying and retrieved a long length of blue nylon belting. He unraveled it and went to his mother. "Here, Mom, we need to put this on you, for safety."

She stared at him. "Have we met?"

Paul nodded and wrapped one end of what looked like a leash around her waist and fastened the clip on itself.

"What's that?" asked his mother.

"It's a safety lead," said Paul. "Sailors use it to keep from going overboard in rough weather."

He took the other end and clicked a large silver fitting onto the boat's railing. "Just a precaution."

"What am I, a poodle?" she asked, looking down at the lead. Then she bared her teeth and growled at her son, followed by a bark.

Paul brought over a deck chair. "Please, Mom, have a seat. I'm sorry about the lead, but it's for your safety."

She sat in the chair, cocked her head, and asked, "Why do you keep calling me Mom?"

He leaned over and looked into her eyes, but saw no

recognition. "Because that's what you are. A wonderful mom. And we're happy you're with us today. I love you." And he kissed her cheek, fighting back tears at the sight of this once vital woman who now had to be tethered like a child. She turned and stared off at the sea with a beatific smile.

The boat cruised in a northerly direction for fifteen minutes until it lay a few hundred yards off the end of the Santa Monica Pier. As prearranged with Paul, the captain slowed the vessel's speed, reversed its engines, then drew it to an idling stop.

Malcolm came out of the wheelhouse and looked toward shore with a pair of powerful binoculars. He took them from his eyes and adjusted the focus. Then he looked again. Paul could not only see the pier, but he could make out the fishermen standing at its rail.

"It's over there," said Paul, pointing.

"I'll take your word for it," said Malcolm. "These things must be out of adjustment." And he let the binoculars fall to his chest. "This where you want to do it?"

"Yes. It's fine," said Paul.

"Okay, let's rock and roll."

Malcolm stepped back into the wheelhouse and spoke into the P.A. system: "Well, folks, we've arrived at the wedding site, just off the Santa Monica Pier, where the happy couple spent their first evening together. Fishing, I think. Even though you can't see the pier from here, it's off the starboard side."

Of course everyone turned, and *could* see the pier, which

sent up a curious chattering among them.

Malcolm came back out of the wheelhouse and acted as though he truly were in charge, directing Paul and Helen to stand in front of a wooden podium that was ringed with white flowers. "Okay, who's the best man?"

Milton stepped forward, holding up a hand as though he had been called on in class.

Malcolm squinted, looking around, and said, "Good, you get over here, next to the groom."

Milton took his position and whispered to Paul, "The guy's blind as a friggin' bat, and he's driving the boat."

"You should see him fly a helicopter," said Paul.

"And next, we need the maid of honor," said Captain Malcolm.

All the guests looked around. Finally, Harvey stepped forward and said, "That would be me" with a small wave of the hand. He sauntered up to Helen.

The group from the salon applauded. Some whistled. One shouted, "You go, Harvey."

Malcolm moved close to Harvey and cocked his head, then nodded, suspiciously.

"He's my best friend," said Helen. "My *man* of honor."

"Do we have any parents?" asked Malcolm.

"My mother," said Paul. He turned to the chair, but it was empty, save for the long blue nylon lead.

"She's gone!" Paul exclaimed. "Anyone seen my mother? The older woman with the big hat and the basketball shoes?"

People turned to each other, shrugging, shaking their heads. Paul ran to the rail and looked down at the water. Seeing nothing, he ran to the opposite rail. Still, no sign of his mother.

"Sound an alarm!" Paul shouted to Malcolm.

"What alarm?"

"Man overboard. Woman overboard, for God's sake!"

Malcolm looked puzzled. "I don't think we have either one."

"This damn elevator's stuck!"

All eyes shot toward the wheelhouse, to see the broad-brimmed hat. Paul's mother had locked herself inside and was banging on the door.

Paul raced to open the door, and his mother stepped out. "You pay all this money for a ticket on the *Queen Mary*, and the damn elevator doesn't even work."

"Mom, it's okay You're fine now. Come on, the wedding's about to start."

"Whose wedding?"

"Mine. Remember? Helen and I are getting married."

"Helen? And who are you? Wait." She moved closer. "Randolph? Is that what it's all about? You're running off with that tramp, Helen?"

"Come on, Mom, you stand next to me, okay?"

She shrugged and let him guide her to where the rest of the party waited. He nodded at Malcolm, who didn't see him. "Captain," he said, "we can begin now."

And so, the ceremony began, against a perfectly stunning backdrop. The sun was beginning its descent to the horizon, sending brilliant hues of orange and magenta up to the layer of billowing clouds above. The balloons and streamers, fluttering in the breeze, picked up the warm tones, as did the boat and the faces of the passengers. Captain Malcolm opened the black book he held in his hands, with the gold leaf inscription on its cover: Wedding Ceremonies, Large-Type Edition. And the klezmer band began a soft, almost mournful tune as Malcolm spoke.

"Dear friends, we are gathered at sea to join in matrimony this woman and this man, Helen and Paul. The state of California has vested in me, as captain of this vessel, the power to perform the ceremony of marriage. And," he said, lifting a white card from the book, "Helen and Paul have chosen to write their own vows, which they will now read."

Paul took the card and read first: "Marriage vows are only as enduring as the love between the two parties who utter them. Ours is as deep as the sea beneath us, as broad and limitless as the sky above us, as rock solid as the bonds we hold with the loved ones around us. I pledge to Helen that love, which will endure for as long as we are able to draw our breaths, until, as the traditional vow dictates, death do us part."

He handed the card to Helen, who dabbed at a tear at the edge of her eye and read: "Love is sometimes difficult to recognize or to accept, until circumstance leads us to acknowledge it through the impact it has, not just on the two of us, but on the entire world in which we are blessed to find ourselves together. It is the grandest of discoveries, the most joyous of feelings. It changes us forever, and, if nurtured to the extent it deserves, it lasts for all the days of our lives, which will be measured not in number, but in the depth of the joy they bring us."

Paul turned to Milton, who fished a gold band from his pocket and placed it in Paul's hand. At the same time, Harvey handed an identical band to Helen, kissing her on the cheek.

Paul placed the ring on Helen's finger and said, "I, Paul, take you, Helen, to be my wife, so that we can stand together, accepting all joy, overcoming all travail, until that time may come when death will us part."

Helen then placed the other ring on Paul's finger, saying "And I, Helen, take you, Paul, to be my husband, so that we may step away from cares of the past and walk into the happiness of the future, for as long as it lasts, until death does us part."

"And I have the distinct pleasure of now pronouncing you husband and wife," said Malcolm, beaming.

With that cue, the band changed from its slow, soft melody to a burst of something that resembled a lively wedding recessional.

Everyone applauded as Paul took Helen in his arms and as they kissed one another with an earnestness that left no doubt whatsoever as to the depth of their proclaimed love.

Paul's mother tapped Helen on the shoulder. "Excuse me, sweetheart, but I want to kiss my son." Which astonished

Paul. He grabbed his mother, knocking her big hat off her head, and embraced her, rocking back and forth. "She knows me," he said over her shoulder to Helen. "She knows me."

Helen reached her arms around both Paul and his mother. Which seemed to spark a contagion. Harvey stepped in, opening his arms to embrace all three of them. Milton followed suit, but, of course, could not embrace the entire group, so he settled happily for Harvey, who shot him a nervous glance. Then the guests came forth, forming a tight circle around the nucleus of the wedding party. They swayed to the music while Malcolm stood back, quite satisfied with himself, also swaying to the beat.

A server appeared from the main salon and announced, "Ladies and gentlemen, kindly proceed to the salon for our champagne toast and reception. Thank you."

The band led the way, continuing to play, stepping to the music, swinging their instruments from side to side. The entire party followed, and each guest was handed a glass of champagne. The first toast was from Harvey, the second from Milton.

At the end of his toast, Milton leaned close to Harvey and said, "I've got tickets to *Moulin Rouge* Friday night. Interested?"

Harvey replied, "Gosh, I'm sorry, I'm going to the Lakers game. But we need to talk."

Paul's mother raised a glass, but instead of offering a toast, she said, "It's so nice to be back in Palm Beach again with all my friends." She kissed a surprised Malcolm and said to him, "Especially Raoul, who traveled all the way from Rio to be with me."

At some point during a long, rambling toast by one of the stylists from the salon, someone interrupted and said, "Where's the wedding couple?"

People looked around, shrugging, shaking their heads. Paul's mother was there, as were Milton and Harvey, and, of course, Raoul, née Malcolm. But Helen and Paul were not.

"There they are!" exclaimed one of the young men, pointing. "On the back."

"The stern," corrected Malcolm.

All eyes turned to see Paul and Helen at the railing, facing the sea. The music stopped, and the only sound was the hum of engines as the boat passed close by the end of the Santa Monica Pier.

"What the hell are they doing?" asked Milton, watching Paul climb up on the lowest white rail, then the second, balancing himself on a stanchion, and finally up to the highly polished mahogany top rail.

"Is this some part of the ritual?" Harvey wondered aloud.

The wedding couple seemed oblivious of the guests watching their every move. Paul turned to Helen and kissed her.

"I love you, Helen, like no man has ever loved any woman."

"I love you, Paul, because you showed me how I *could* love after all."

"'Til death do us part," he said.

"'Til death do us part," she repeated.

Paul turned to face the guests. "Come on back here. This is important," he called out.

Milton and Harvey led the way. Paul's mother followed on the arm of Malcolm. Then came the guests and the band.

"Are you ready?" Paul asked Helen. She nodded and turned back toward the bay again, as did Paul.

Helen bent at the knees for leverage, straightened them quickly, and flung her gardenia bouquet over her head, toward the gathered guests.

A cheer went up, and everyone watched as the bouquet was picked up by a sudden gust of wind and sailed above the heads of everyone, over the starboard side of the *EcstaSea*, coming to rest on the water's surface. Some of the guests voiced disappointment; some applauded. All watched the flowers bob on the surface of the water, floating toward shore.

"For a second there, it looked like they were going to take a swan dive," said Milton as Paul and Helen climbed back down from the rail.

"Don't be so melodramatic," said Harvey.

"Let's dance!" shouted one of the band members.

On cue, the musicians began a lively tune, and Malcolm, back in the wheelhouse, tugged on a white braided cord, setting off a resounding blast of the boat's foghorn.

"Will you dance with me?" Paul asked Helen, offering his arm.

"In chairs?"

Paul shook his head. Helen smiled, relieved, and accompanied him to the small parquet dance floor, to the warm applause of the guests who awaited them.

———

As the boat moved north, toward Malibu, a man and a woman in their thirties stood at the rail on the side of the pier, close to the end, looking down at the water below.

"No one would even see us," said the man.

"You're probably right," said the woman. She glanced at the group of fishermen on the end of the pier. "Those people are engrossed in what they're doing."

"Probably wouldn't hear the splash from up here."

"The water is so filthy, though," said the woman.

"Like that would make a difference?"

No response.

"You might not sink. Ever think of that? What would happen if you just floated?"

They fell silent and peered down at the black water.

A short distance away, a man said, laughing, "Hey, look what he caught," pointing over the rail toward the water and watching an unhappy Asian man reel in the line on his long fishing rod, which was bent over by the weight of his catch.

The fisherman stopped reeling and swung his rod sharply over his back. A dripping bunch of white gardenias, tied with a satin ribbon, flew off the end of the line, landing with a splat at the feet of the man and woman.

They looked down, curiously, at the soggy ribbon's message: To Life.

"Where did that come from?" asked the man.

"Obviously from down there," said the woman.

"How?"

She shrugged.

"What did you say your name was?" he asked.

"I didn't."

He thought for a while, then said, "Would you like to get a cup of coffee?"

"I don't drink coffee."

"A glass of water?"

Acknowledgments

My sincere thanks go out to the good people who guided me in bringing this book to life, particularly the entire Fulcrum family, everyone from the front desk to the back offices.

Publisher Sam Scinta and chairman Bob Baron are both valued friends and sources of continuing support.

I am especially fortunate to have worked with an outstanding editor, Faith Marcovecchio, whose skill and insights added immeasurably to the effort and gave me a better book as a result.

A special thanks to my good friend author Sandra Dallas for her encouragement and support, without which I might still be staring at a blank computer screen, and to my loyal and patient pal author and former governor Dick Lamm for bringing this book to Fulcrum's attention in the first place.

Finally, my appreciation goes out to that unique American metropolis, Los Angeles, where life is so often played out on a bigger-than-life screen as a continuing human comedy.

About the Author

Arnold Grossman held some real jobs before becoming an author. They included magazine journalist, television producer, and media consultant to political candidates who became governors, senators, representatives, and mayors. His previous books were two novels: *1988: A Novel of Politics* and *A California Conspiracy*, and a piece of nonfiction in the Speaker's Corner series: *One Nation Under Guns, An Essay on an American Epidemic*. When asked why he has turned to writing comedy, Grossman cited his mother, who once said,

"If you think you're so funny, go write funnybooks." He also feels his years living in Los Angeles, where he survived riots, earthquakes, wildfires, and floods (but no locusts), together with working in politics, helped him find a sense of humor, albeit a dark one.

He currently lives in Denver, where there has not been an earthquake or other serious calamity in some time, but he thinks he has seen a locust or two, plus a number of political candidates.